SUDDEN DEATH

A Dan Shields Mystery

The detective who breaks all the rules

MARK L. DRESSLER

© 2025 Mark L. Dressler – all rights reserved.
Published by Satincrest Press, USA
ISBN: 978-0-9990623-5-7

Chapter 1

Being in the wrong place at the wrong time can be a deadly destiny, but when you have been targeted, there is no escaping that frightful fate.

▲

Twenty-four-year-old Emilio Sandovar's green Subaru Forester idled outside a local hotel on this April evening, waiting for his passenger to get in. She did and the car proceeded toward Bradley International Airport.

As the vehicle approached the airport, the female fare sitting in the back seat looked up as darkness was settling in while a low-flying 737 passed overhead. With its engines roaring and landing gear down, the airliner descended on runway E5.

Vehicles lined the drop-off area and the Forester came to rest at the curb. Ariel Adams, an attractive, blue-eyed, blonde flight attendant stepped out of the car. She wore her signature Delta uniform, a red skirt, matching jacket and white blouse. Ariel, as she usually did, opened her purse and handed the driver a ten-dollar tip while he slipped her his cell number. As the good-looking flight attendant walked away from him, he shouted, "Call me when you get back in town."

▲

The next evening at nine-fifteen, Emilio Sandovar's Forester was on its way to the airport again. Neither he nor the middle-aged couple inside were aware of anything out of the ordinary.

A black Volkswagen Jetta shadowed the Subaru, staying approximately three car lengths behind its target. Barkley Malone knew what he was doing.

Emilio stopped his car at the Delta terminal and exited as did his passengers. Emilio assisted the male and female with their luggage, accepted a gratuity and hopped into his car.

Malone's Jetta idled at the curb and as the Subaru pulled away from the terminal Emilio glanced to his left. He attempted to merge into traffic when the sound of screeching tires made him slam the brakes. The middle finger of a silver sedan's driver accompanied by a honking horn made Emilio mutter. Asshole. He waited until the harried man had driven away before the Uber driver continued his journey home.

Emilio checked his rear-view mirror and thought nothing about Malone's dented black Jetta lurking behind his car. The husky, tall, previously arrested burglar munched on a Snickers while keeping his prey in sight.

As both vehicles traveled I-91 South, Sandovar noticed his vehicle's fuel gauge was nearing the empty mark. He exited the highway and a few blocks from home, pulled into an Exxon station and fueled the thirsty car. After placing his credit card in the pump's payment slot, he snatched the card and receipt and resumed his trek without noticing the Jetta that had trailed him.

Yawning as he entered Vassar Village, Sandovar swerved his car into the dimly lit driveway of his condo, grabbed the garage door opener and clicked it. While the door began rising, the menacing Jetta came to rest a few inches from the Forester's rear bumper.

Startled by the unexpected intruder, Emilio got out of his car and

Malone, wearing a dark hoodie, slammed the unsuspecting victim's back against the Forester. The deep-voiced thug, oblivious to the fact that Uber drivers rarely carried much cash, demanded Emilio's wallet and pocket money.

The trapped Uber driver attempted to fight off his assailant by foolishly trying to land a crushing blow to the attacker's neck. The infuriated Malone blocked Emilio's fist and then a bang echoed through the neighborhood. Emilio's bullet-stricken body, gushing blood, fell to the pavement.

The brazen Malone shoved his warm gun into his waistband and helped himself to the Uber driver's wallet before hustling into the idling Jetta, backing out of the driveway and speeding away.

The front porch light of the unit across the way went on, and fifty-five-year-old Ruth Gaddy spotted her neighbor's fallen body. She screamed as she watched the Jetta disappear and hurriedly called 911 as nearby front porch lights lit up. Several startled neighbors joined her as they neared the lifeless victim.

Within minutes an ambulance and three police units arrived. The horrified crowd gathered near Sandovar's driveway. Ruth Gaddy was shaking, with tears streaming down her face. She was barely able to tell police what she had seen while being tended to by paramedics. Her only recollections were the gunshot and a dent in the getaway vehicle's driver's side door.

Malone now had a murder on his hands as well as a robbery that netted him twenty-five dollars and a couple of credit cards.

Chapter 2

One week after assaulting Emilio Sandovar, Barkley Malone downed the last drop of whiskey from a bottle and set out to purchase a full one.

It was nearing noon. He grabbed his recently acquired billfold and drove toward a package store. Two blocks from his destination, the traffic light at an intersection was red and he ignored the stop signal.

Patrolman Gary Branch clicked on his car's siren and flashing lights and took off after the offender. Malone stepped on the gas and Branch radioed for assistance.

The chase ended suddenly when Malone tried to avoid an oncoming car. His Jetta swerved, crossed a sidewalk, and crashed sideways into the brick wall of a barbershop.

Malone stumbled as he escaped from the car and tried to bolt from the scene, racing into a nearby alleyway. Branch ran after him and shouted, "Stop, or you'll get tasered."

Malone kept running and Branch held the taser, finally pulling the trigger and sending two dart-like electrodes into the back of the escapee's shirt. Malone fell to the pavement, writhing in discomfort. "Get 'em out!"

Backup arrived and two officers dashed toward them. Branch knelt by Malone. "Hold tight. An ambulance is on the way. They'll extract the prongs. It's your own fault."

Another set of flashing lights came into view and an ambulance came to a stop before a paramedic got out to extract the taser barbs. "Be still," she said as she began to remove the probes.

Malone's back stung and he flinched, yelling, "Fuck, fuck!"

The paramedic held up the extracted barbs. "Relax, they're out."

Branch pulled Malone's arms behind the lawbreaker's back and handcuffed him. As Branch raised him off the pavement, Malone whined, "You're hurting me."

Branch adjusted the cuffs as witnesses talked amongst themselves. "What's your name?"

"Pac-Man."

A whiff of alcohol accompanied his smart answer. "You're under arrest, Pac-Man."

Malone was Mirandized and shoved into the back seat of Officer James Batterson's squad car. Pedestrians, including a man still wearing a barber's apron, watched.

Branch made his way to the wrecked Jetta and saw a handgun on the floor of the passenger side. The officer retrieved it and placed it inside his own car. Scanning the area, Branch addressed the crowd. "Anyone hurt?"

His query was answered with a chorus of bystanders shouting no. Branch dismissed the ambulance and headed to the police station.

▲

The police station was familiar to Malone. He had been arrested twice before. Once for petty theft. The other incident involved a firearm robbery of a convenience store that resulted in a two-year jail term he completed six months ago. The uncooperative arrestee's identity surfaced as he was being booked. Then a wallet that had dangled from his back pocket fell to the floor. Branch picked it up and rifled through it, finding a driver's license, two credit cards and a small amount of cash. The license and credit cards displayed the name of Emilio Sandovar. Branch held the wallet to Malone's face. "Where did you get this?"

"Never saw it before."

"You're sure."

"Let me see it. Nope, not mine."

"And the gun?"

"What gun?"

Branch sneered. "The one I found on the backseat of your car."

Smugly, Malone retorted, "Like I said. What gun?"

The officer backed away. "Have it your way, but you know this is no Burger King."

The smart-assed Malone wriggled his nose. "Yeah, more like Chuck E. Cheese."

Fingerprinting and a new mug shot were next, and then down to the jungle and into a cell, but not before Malone made his one phone call to defense attorney Hancock Sasser, the slick lawyer who had previously defended him.

The wallet and gun recovered from Malone's car were logged into evidence and turned over to the forensic experts. Subsequently, the bullet extracted from Sandovar's body matched the firearm seized from Malone's Jetta.

Chapter 3

Malone, accused killer of Emilio Sandovar, exercised his sixth amendment rights to request a speedy trial. Sixty-one days later it began at Hartford's Superior Court.

Among the small gathering of courtroom observers on this warm June day were law students as well as Emilio Sandovar's parents, Alejandro and Merriel Sandovar, and their younger son, Elijah.

Seven men and five women comprised the jury. When they filed into their seats, Elijah Sandovar rose and left the courtroom. Ten minutes later he texted his mother. Went for a smoke. Going home. Can't bear being there.

At the table nearest the jurors sat dapperly clad Attorney Hancock Sasser. His briefcase and a couple of manila file folders were set on top, inches away from two glasses and a pitcher of water. His client, Barkley Malone, was dressed in street clothes and sat quietly.

At the prosecutor's table were the state's attorneys, sixteen-year veteran Evan Lincoln and his assistant Sarah Waverly, working her second murder trial. She set paperwork in front of the lead attorney.

At 10 a.m., Judge Janis J. Merino entered the courtroom and sat in a high-back chair, all five-two of her. The retirement-aged woman resembled television's Judge Judy.

Attorney Lincoln's mission was to convince the jury to come to a unanimous guilty verdict. He attempted to do so by coaxing the arresting officer, Gary Branch, policeman, James Batterson, who aided in Malone's arrest, as well as chief forensic examiner, Michelle Lee to respond to questions with incriminating answers.

Conversely, Attorney Hancock Sasser set out to deflect the trial from murder and point it in the direction of police misconduct, specifically by Branch. He threw out questions to those same witnesses, pointing to possible evidence tampering. He focused on Branch's fingerprints, which were found on the wallet and gun in question. Sasser also introduced the possibility of sloppy forensic analysis into the mix, as well as Batterson not witnessing Branch's seizure of the firearm.

While Branch testified, Sasser resorted to a dark tactic and stood close to him. "Officer Branch, please tell us about the case of The State versus DeAngelo Barlow."

Lincoln stood and objected. "Relevance, Your Honor."

Merino motioned the attorneys to approach the bench. Lincoln argued, "Your Honor, this line of questioning has nothing to do with this case. I fail to see the relevance."

Sasser, standing beside Lincoln, firmly stated, "Your Honor, this has everything to do with Barkley Malone. The two officers involved in that case compromised evidence and were fired for doing so. Barlow went free. Planting evidence is relevant."

Lincoln protested, "Your Honor, Officer Branch is not on trial here."

Sasser asserted, "Your Honor, the truth is on trial."

"I agree. Go ahead, Mister Sasser."

The contented attorney received the answer he sought and stood in front of Branch.

"Again Officer, please tell us about the planting of evidence in the DeAngelo Barlow case."

Branch looked to the judge. "Answer the question," she ordered.

He had no choice and provided the answer Hancock fished for. "Yes, it had occurred."

With that admission, the sly attorney had planted a seed of police interference in the jurors' minds that they should consider regarding the Barkley Malone arrest.

When testimony was completed and after each attorney presented their closing argument to the jury, the panel was sent to the deliberation room to decide the verdict.

After several hours, the jury returned to the courtroom.

Attorneys Sasser, Lincoln, and Waverly took their designated seats as did Barkley Malone. The murder victim's father, Alejandro Sandovar, wore an angry grimace on his wrinkled face. Emilio's mother, Merriel, was in tears and clutched her husband's hands.

Judge Merino glanced at Barkley Malone, who wore the expression of a cold-blooded killer.

Jury foreperson Elliot McIntire, a middle-school teacher wearing a buttoned cardigan sweater, stood. Mr. Rogers he was not, but he bore a close likeness to the man.

Merino scanned the sitting panel and observed their body language. Juror number seven's red hair surrounded her face, her hands trembled, and her stylized eyeglasses didn't hide her glance at Malone. The judge shifted her eyes to the foreperson. Malone and Sasser stood, as did Lincoln and Waverly.

When the verdict was read, a loud, if it can be loud, hush came over the courtroom. Judge Merino took off her reading glasses before sitting back, taking a deep breath and then leaning forward. The inability of the jury to reach a unanimous verdict stunned the crowd. Judge Merino pronounced the proceeding a mistrial, hung jury.

The victim's father, a postal employee for the past two decades, rose to his feet and flung one foot over the pew-like railing, attempting to charge at Malone while shouting, "Killer! Rot in hell, you motherfucking bastard!" Two courtroom guards intervened, grabbing the angry father and ripping his shirt open in the scuffle before removing him from the courtroom.

Evan Lincoln and Sarah Waverly glared at each other, disappointed, while Sasser advised Malone that the decision did not mean he was free to go. Evan Lincoln approached the bench and requested Judge Merino to poll the jury.

She scanned the panel and then commanded the jurors to stand and addressed them, one at a time. "Juror number one, please state your decision."

"Guilty," the foreperson, Elliot McIntire, answered.

The same response was voiced by jurors number two, three, four, five, and six. Then came the dissenting verdict from juror seven. "Not guilty," she stated.

Jurors eight, nine, ten, eleven, and twelve all replied by answering "guilty."

The final tally was eleven guilty votes and one not guilty vote.

As soon as the polling was over, a dark-haired woman who had been sitting in the courtroom's back row and was wearing a green dress smiled as she left the premises. Her loud footsteps caught the ear of Waverly who turned around. "What's she so happy about?" she said to Lincoln.

He viewed the woman. "There's always one deranged person in the crowd."

CHAPTER 4

Labor Day gave Detective Dan Shields a short break from the police station, then he was back at work. He sat inside his cubicle at Hartford's police headquarters. The gray walled, second-floor squad room had eight identical workstations spread along the walls. Five were occupied. His sometime-partners Joe Scott, known as Scotty, and Bev Dancinger, the squad's only female detective, were nearest him. Luke Hanson, a tall, lanky, blond-haired sleuth, and his partner Mal Jones, who had played one year for the football Giants before suffering a career-ending injury, were also nearby.

Captain Harold Syms occupied the office located at the end of a short corridor that housed two bathrooms, a meeting room, and an interrogation room.

Dan began his day by seeking a cup of coffee and toted his Yankees mug to the table in the corner of the squad room. He hated the Keurig, specifically the pods, but managed to fill his cup with hot liquid caffeine anyway. Scotty nudged him. "You finally got the hang of this thing?"

"What the hell is this pod crap? I wouldn't have a Keurig or anything like it in my house. I barely got used to the old one that was here." He pointed to Bev. "Now there's this thing, thanks to her."

The slightly perturbed detective growled, "I heard you. And do not forget to drop your coffee fund contribution in the brown box on my desk. I don't know why I babysit you guys, but I do all the shopping and never get a thanks. And none of you are as sweet as the sugar in the bowl next to the machine you despise."

"Bitter, are we?" Dan commented. "I like it black anyway."

"Is that how you talk to your wife?"

Dan took a sip. "Sorry, Bev. We do owe you, and no, Phyllis would have me sleeping in the garage next to the garbage cans." He reached into his wallet and led the way as the other law officers followed suit.

Bev was satisfied. "Now that's what I call teamwork."

Wearing his dress uniform, Syms tore into the squad room after returning from Sergeant Carlos Cabrera's funeral. The slain officer was gunned down ten days ago as he sat in his squad car outside a church near midnight. The captain muttered, "None of us are safe anymore." He headed directly to his office.

Dan didn't ignore the bothersome comment and followed the captain down the hall. Syms slouched into his office chair as Dan barged in. "Are you okay?"

"What do you want?" the boss barked.

Peering at Syms with his hands on his hips, Dan pleaded, "Calm down."

Syms spun around with his back to Dan and unsnapped the top button before he took hold of his trusty squirt gun and misted the bonsai trees that rested on the credenza underneath the rear window. Rotating back to Dan, he grimaced. "You do know where I was right? Sometimes, I wonder why I took this job. Chief Hardison is as unnerved as I am."

Dan set his hands on his boss's desk. "We all do, but you don't see any of us throwing temper tantrums and running around like chickens with our heads cut off."

The captain grabbed the large aspirin bottle that occupied a permanent spot on his desk. "I have you to thank for these. What the hell did I just say? I mean *blame you* for these damn things."

Seeing Syms's scrunched nose, Dan asked, "Why don't you go home and rue the day you came here?"

There was silence as Syms brushed his hand across his face and loosened a few more buttons, while opening the aspirin bottle and plopping two pills in his hand. "Damn you!" he shouted. "We're all gonna get killed. We're outmanned and outgunned."

Dan threw his hands in the air. "Is that it? Are you afraid now to be identified as a servant of the law? None of us want to be dead, but we have to protect each other as well as all the innocent people we serve. I'm sick of the pile of homicides on my desk!"

The captain took a deep breath. "I don't want my wife to be a widow. And in case you haven't noticed, the hair on top of your head is thinning and turning white."

Dan curled his lip. "We all have to leave sometime, so chances are she will be one someday. Meantime, I'm sure she would like to see the tough guy she married doing his job."

Syms sought a cup of water from the fountain outside the restrooms, downed the aspirin, and returned before chiding. "Damn you, get the hell out of here."

Dan shrugged and gave his boss a mock smile. "That's more like it."

The captain's rant sent a chill throughout the detective's body and it reminded him of the dangers of his job.

Luke entered Dan's cubicle. "He's off the wall, isn't he?"

"He'll settle down and be back to normal. He watered his trees."

"Yeah, he treats them better than us," Luke mused as he chugged his coffee. "We have our hands full trying to track down Cabrera's assassins."

Joining the discussion, Mal agreed. "His killing was execution-like. We have to get those bastards."

Dan realized Scotty and Bev were not around. "Where are Scotty and Bev?"

Mal answered, "A call came in and they went to investigate a house fire where a woman was killed."

"Fire. What will come next?"

The detective's answer was a few seconds away. Dan winced as Syms walked steadfastly toward him. The captain's voice was in command mode and he shouted at Dan, "You're up." He dispatched him to the scene of a dead body.

Dan rushed toward the exit. *Here I go again.* The veteran sleuth was on his way to investigate another death. He thought he'd seen it all and thought nothing would rattle him, but he was only a few minutes away from the most bizarre scene he'd ever witnessed, one that would curdle his blood.

Chapter 5

Red, blue, and white strobing lights came into view ahead of his Accord as Dan neared Jewel Street, a mere mile from the police station.

Bushnell Park was swarming with police. Dan observed a crowd of a dozen or so curious bystanders who were watching from behind the cordoned-off area surrounding the apparent crime. The detective spotted a gray-bearded male who wore a tattered raincoat and was holding a liquor bottle in one hand as the staggering guy headed toward a park bench. The man seemed oblivious to what was taking place and the lit cigarette in his other hand fell to the ground as he sprawled himself on the wooden bed.

The detective neared one of the city's favorite destinations, the colorful, normally joyful carousel that came to Hartford in 1974 when it was relocated from Ohio.

Dan walked toward an ambulance when his EpiPen began dangling from his pocket and he shoved it back inside. He then sidled up to muscular officer, Lionel Jackson, known as Train and said, "I haven't seen you at a crime scene in a while. What have we got here?"

The policeman warned him, "This one is a real ballbuster, and it stinks in there."

"What happened?"

"A call came in at eight-thirty from the lady who opens up. Her name is Gracie Allen. She's in the back room and an officer as well as paramedics are with her."

Dan quipped, "I suppose his name is George Burns."

Train broke into a wry grin. "You're getting old. Let's go." He and Dan proceeded inside, but not before Train yelled for one of the uniforms to stand in for him. Dan scrunched his nose as they entered. "I warned you," the officer said.

Dan momentarily stopped. "Holy mother," he said as he stared at the naked torso of a woman who was slumped atop a wooden carousel horse. He stepped back as he tried to avoid the urine and excrement that had run down the mount's navy-colored saddle onto the floor.

A female with long blonde hair straddled the saturated palomino replica. Flashes from a camera blurred the detective's vision, and after his eyes refocused, he shook his head in disbelief. "Who the hell did this?"

"Some sicko," Train replied.

"Any witnesses?"

"You're kidding, right?"

Observing the carousel's interior, Dan mused, "My kids have been here a few times, they always loved this place." He pointed to another wooden horse. "That was Mike's favorite and the one next to it, Kate and Josh used to fight over."

Dan stepped aside as Gina Fernandez, the newest addition to Max Arnstein's medical examiner staff entered. "That was fast," the detective said. "Syms must have called you. I haven't had a chance to study the body yet."

"Follow me."

The unavoidable wretched odors were stronger as Dan got closer to the diminutive technician who wore a mask, a white gown, and had gloves on each hand as she examined the corpse. She pivoted away from it and stated the obvious. "For one thing, her bladder gave way."

Dan grimaced. "Very observant. Urine is one thing but this damn feces is another." Carefully avoiding the bodily waste, he used his phone to snap a few pictures of the victim.

Train donned a mask and Gina spoke. "I may be new, but I never dreamed of anything like this."

"Welcome to my world," Dan said. He observed a pair of red-framed eyeglasses drenched in urine on the floor before noticing the dastardly inscription inked on the dead woman's back. *WHORE*. "That's not a tattoo. It was done with a pen, most likely a marker of some kind. Maybe a Sharpie."

Train noted, "Not a trace of clothing around, and thus far we haven't found a shred of evidence."

The heavy stench flared Dan's nostrils as he inspected the corpse, whose torso had a bluish hue and revealed no unusual marks, no bullet holes, and no blood. He tried not to breathe too deeply and swatted a few flies away. "I thought I'd seen it all until now."

A red-spoked iron half-railing surrounded the carousel. The two policemen stepped aside to allow forensics examiner Alex Sarkisian inside. "I thought you retired," Dan said.

Sarkisian grinned. "I should have." Avoiding a puddle of waste material, he stepped over it. "This kind of mess makes me want to stay home. A shooting, stabbing, run-of-the-mill crime this isn't."

Dan took one more whiff of the strong odors. "I need a mask."

Gina handed him one and he covered his face and said, "Her body is stiff, and you can see the color of her torso. It tells me she died more than eight hours ago."

"Raped?" Dan asked.

"You would assume so, but where the hell would it have occurred? I've heard of strange places and positions. No clothes, not a bra, panties. Nothing. A real Lady Godiva. We'll let you know when we get results from the rape test."

Dan studied the victim and commented, "The 'whore' inscription on her back is either one of lust or disgust."

Gina brought in a body bag and the corpse was placed into it before it was transported to the Farmington morgue.

Dan bristled as he said to the officer by his side, "And there is nothing to indicate she was beaten, shot or anything else. "How the hell did this happen?"

Train wore a frown and said to Dan, "She sure looks familiar, but I can't place her."

Dan smirked. "You are talking about her face, right?" He pointed to the open door to the back room. "Tell me about Gracie Allen. What's her story?"

"She's still with the paramedics."

Dan muttered to himself. *This is crazy. A carousel right in Bushnell Park. And no clothing.* He walked around the children's joyride and stood beside the sobbing Gracie and the uniformed officer who was with her. Gracie lifted her head when Dan attempted to console her. "I'm sorry you had to see this. May I ask you a few questions?"

The paramedic still with her backed away. "She'll be okay."

Gracie, fifty-one, had a blanket wrapped around her shoulders and used a corner of it to wipe away tears that streamed down her face. At first speechless, she nodded and then began spouting a bit of her past. The story she told was one of memories. Gracie had visited this building many times as a child and throughout her later years. Even though she never married and did not have children, the carousel fascinated her. There were forty-eight wooden horses to choose from, and as a child she always sat on the mount named Freedom. The one that today supported a dead, naked woman.

Dan touched Gracie's hand as her eyes met his. Snapping back to the present she swiveled her head and viewed her surroundings. The detective asked, "When you arrived this morning, did you unlock the door?"

"No. It looked like it had been forced open and was slightly ajar."

Dan summoned Sarkisian to join them. "Did you inspect the door? She said it looked like it had been tampered with."

"It was, but there are more finger smudges on both sides of the door than on a set of playground monkey bars."

"I hear you."

Dan turned back to Gracie. "After you saw the body, what did you do?"

Gracie, shaking, answered softly, "I screamed and felt like I was going to faint. I was barely able to dial 911 and the next thing I remembered was the ambulance and being helped over here by paramedics. They examined me and gave me something and I'm a little better."

"What about the victim? Have you ever seen her before?"

"No."

"Is there anything else you can tell me?"

"I don't think so."

Unexpectedly, a fiftyish man clad in jeans rushed toward Gracie, ignoring the police officer and the detective. "Are you okay?" he asked Gracie, taking her hand.

"I want to go home."

Dan asked the intruding man. "Are you her husband?"

"No, I work here too."

"May I ask your name?"

"Wally Forin."

An empty chair was next to Gracie. "Why don't you have a seat?" Dan suggested. "Which one of you was last to leave here yesterday?"

Forin sat. "I was."

"Did you lock the door when you left?"

"Yes."

"What time did you leave?"

"A little after dark. This smell is getting to me."

"You're not alone. The cleaning crew should have been here by now. Did you see or hear anything suspicious while you were here?"

"There is nothing suspicious about kids enjoying the carousel."

Forin coughed and Gracie meekly said, "I need to go home."

"I'll take her home if it's alright with you," her baritone voiced coworker said to Dan. "She lives in Rocky Hill and I'm about two miles from her."

Dan moved away. "Go ahead."

Forin escorted Gracie out of the building and the detective walked slowly around the room taking more pictures with his phone. After doing so, he said to Train, "Do me a favor. There are trash receptacles around this park. Have your guys check them out. She sure wasn't here alone. Maybe her clothes are in one."

They both went outside and disposed of their masks, throwing them into a nearby trash receptacle. The uniformed officer rounded up three nearby policemen and ordered them to begin the search.

Dan noticed the crowd size had increased. "It's time to break them up."

"Yup. We'll disperse them now."

Fifteen minutes later, results of the trash exploration exercise were known. "We didn't find anything unusual," a two-striped officer reported.

Dan was ready to be on his way. "I'm wrapping it up here. I'll get your report in the morning. By the way, who is closing the carousel?"

Train held a keyholder in his hand. "I have Gracie's key, but the carousel will be out of operation for a few days. We need to get someone over here to fix the door."

Dan turned toward his car. "See you back at the station."

Chapter 6

Dan couldn't shake the image of the naked corpse he'd just seen. He was sure Lady Godiva was murdered and he wanted to call it a homicide but had no evidence to support his belief. *How the hell does a naked woman die atop a wooden horse? I know she didn't kick the door in with her bare feet and write "whore" on her own back before deciding to somehow kill herself.*

Syms remained inside his office and the door was shut.

Scotty and Bev entered the squad room, with Bev mumbling, "Arson. What a savage way to be killed."

Dan asked, "What happened?"

"We met with the fire captain, Stanislawski," Scotty replied. "A woman identified as Tamara Ashford died in a fire that destroyed her home. The suspected cause of the blaze was arson started by butane. According to neighbors she was single, around thirty-five, and lived alone."

"Kids?"

"We don't know. Neighbors said little except for the fact she had been beaten in the past by her boyfriend, a guy named Kendal Westley."

Bev sat at her computer and keyed "Kendal Westley" into the criminal database and came up with a hit. "Hey, guys. We have a definite suspect. He's served time for a domestic on Tamara

Ashford. She pressed charges and he served three years before being released less than a year ago."

"He's a start," Scotty said as Bev printed out a rap sheet.

Dan furrowed his brow.

"You look frazzled," Scotty said.

"Christ, you think fire is something. I just saw a dead Lady Godiva." Dan took a seat and brought his comrades up to date. "We have no idea who she is. I hope we get a name soon. Train was the first one there and he thought he recognized her but couldn't remember where he may have seen her. Have a look at my camera photos." Dan held his phone out to show them the shots he'd taken as Scotty and Bev viewed the naked victim.

"Pretty disgusting," said Bev. "I never saw anything like it."

"Neither have I," said Dan. "I intend to squash the bastard who killed her. You better get after Westley." Dan peered over at the captain's office. "And that stubborn ass down the hall isn't helping any. If I thought trying to get his head out of his ass would do any good, I'd bust in there. I'm getting out of here."

▲

Dan often tried to separate his job from his home life, but the gun strapped to his holster didn't make it easy to do. He loved his wife and the thought of losing her made him drift back in time. He remembered when he met Phyllis at the University of North Carolina and didn't have any idea what she was about. Ironically, she later revealed she had vowed to never wed a policeman. The memory of her father, a decorated police captain who had been shot and killed when she was a teenager, cemented her self-promise to never get married to anyone in law enforcement. Or so she thought.

It was no wonder, every time Dan went to work, Phyllis worried he might never come home. Her realistic fear nearly manifested several years ago when Dan was shot. After spending a week with a bandaged chest in Woodland hospital, he went home, but the scar on his chest constantly reminded him of his mortality.

He neared the Suffield colonial he and his wife purchased twenty years ago that was undergoing a transition with a new roof having been installed and now phase two with exterior painting underway. The van in his driveway with a ladder hanging on its side was a not-so-subtle reminder of the money he was spending. The painters were finished with their work for the day and Dan liked the transformation from yellow shingles to Federal Blue.

He opened the freshly coated white front door and performed his daily chore of locking his handgun inside the nearby closet's specially built metal box before advancing toward his wife as she prepared dinner. "Hi, hon. I have to go upstairs to change."

Phyllis's nose twitched. "What is it I smell? Did you pee in your pants?"

"No, but I may have gotten some urine on myself. It's a hell of a story."

"Do tell."

"Not now. I'll be right down."

"Wait. Remove those pants and throw them into the washer."

"Okay."

"And take a shower."

Dan did as ordered and returned to the kitchen sporting jeans and a Yankees sweatshirt.

Phyllis asked, "Care to tell me about this one?"

"You know I don't like to talk about this stuff."

She sighed in exasperation. "Oh, really? We've been down this road before and it always helps to say what's on your mind."

He sat on a chair and shared his Lady Godiva story.

"Oh, my God."

"And we don't even know her name." Hearing the sound of a

bouncing ball, Dan remarked, "Josh is playing basketball. How long has he been out there?"

"Ever since I got home. Kate is with him."

The proud father joined his kids in time to hear the clang of the backboard as the ball hit it and soared through the net. "Nice shot," he mocked as the basketball bounced on the ground. "Hey, you keep it up and you'll be better than Mike."

The older son was a baseball standout at Arizona State. Josh shook his head. "I am better. He plays baseball, remember?"

Dan retrieved the ball and threw it at the hoop. The kids laughed when the ball flew over the basket without hitting anything and landed against the backyard fence. "Nice try, Dad." Josh said.

The outdoor activity came to a halt when Phyllis let them know dinner was ready. During the course of supper, Dan asked his wife, "Have you heard from Connie?"

Connie Costanza was the former owner of Connie's Place, a popular diner near headquarters that was a police hangout. The eatery had been forced to close when the city claimed the building via eminent domain to clear the way for renovations. Dan and Phyllis then hired her as a part-time nanny when their kids were younger. A recent visit to see her brother and sister-in-law at the Villages in Florida had Connie considering leaving Connecticut. Phyllis replied, "Yes. She loves the Villages and she's going to sell her house here." Phyllis paused. "It would be great if we took a summer vacation in Orlando."

Dinner was soon over and Dan said to Josh, "Hey, keep practicing. You are good."

"Come on Kate." The budding teenager and his sister sprinted toward the back door.

Dan smiled. "Kids. It won't be long before they go off to college."

"Please, let them get through high school. Mike growing up so fast is one thing. I can't imagine Josh and Kate in college."

"And we shall someday be empty nesters."

"Good, my laundry load will be a lot less, as well as the food bill. Go watch TV."

Chapter 7

Dan's head spun as he tossed and turned all night. Lady Godiva had left an indelible, beleaguering impression in his mind. Again and again, he struggled with the vision of that unnamed naked woman who was straddling a wooden horse. *What the hell happened and where are her clothes? Who wrote whore on her back? Was this some kind of ritualistic or symbolic slaying?*

In the morning, he groggily grabbed a corn muffin from the bread box on the kitchen counter before retrieving his weapon and wishing his wife a nice day as he kissed her goodbye.

▲

The clock perched above the façade of the police station read: 6:59 a.m. and the temperature was 68 degrees. Dan nestled his Accord beside Luke Hanson's Ford truck.

Proceeding to the station's metal rear door, he swiped his badge under the identification scanner and heard a buzz as the door clicked and unlocked. Once he made it into the squad room, he gazed down the hallway at an unsmiling Syms.

Strolling into the captain's quarters, he asked, "You still stewing?"

Syms simply responded, "What's up?"

"I'm really bothered, I have never seen anything like it. Who the hell is Lady Godiva and what the fuck took place there?”

“What the hell happens anywhere? You don’t expect the answers to come easy, do you?”

“Nope. I’m heading down to the carousel. How about getting up and coming with me?”

“I like it fine here.”

Dan sneered at Syms. “Do you want to sit there like a couch potato? You still have a job to do you know. Get up and let’s go!”

Syms jumped to his feet. “Whoa, are you telling me what to do?”

Dan pounded the desk. “Apparently someone has to.”

Syms rose and fired a warning at Dan. “I’m still in charge here and don’t you forget it.”

“Then act like it!”

“You have some nerve,” the captain grumbled as he grabbed his gun. “Let’s go.”

“I want Alex Sarkisian to meet us there,” Dan said. “Hand me the phone.” He then called the forensics examiner who agreed to meet them at the carousel.”

▲

The crime scene was still taped off and a patrolwoman stood outside. Her last name, Zeto, was inscribed on a patch above the pocket of her uniform. “How long have you been here?” Dan asked.

“Too long. The door is fixed and I have a key. Train thought you would be back.”

“Open up.”

Once inside, Dan flipped on a light switch and browsed the room. Except for the lingering odor of bleach, the carousel appeared ordinary.

Sarkisian made his way into the house of fun. “Captain, been a long time since we’ve seen each other.”

"Not long enough."

Dan aimed to inspect the facility again. "You know there are a lot of prints all over this carousel and plenty of smudges, but whoever put her on that horse must have used gloves. We found no evidence but it's obvious to me that someone put her there. There's always the possibility we missed something."

Even though the entire inside of the building had been cleaned and disinfected, the three men scoured every inch of the place. Dan moved to the concession stand where he spotted an item on the floor next to the popcorn machine and caught the attention of his boss as well as the forensics expert. "Take a look at this."

Sarkisian and Syms came to him. "What do you make of this?" The detective asked as he knelt.

"I don't remember that being there," Sarkisian said.

Dan didn't touch the black Sharpie. "It may have rolled out from underneath. Do you have a bag?"

"I have gloves, too. Let me bag it. If we're lucky, this may be what was used to write the word 'whore' on her back. I'll check for prints."

They completed their inspection and were about to leave. Dan took the baggie from its holder. "After I log it in, I'll get it to you."

Syms smiled at his detective. "You do know about the chain of evidence after all."

They went outside and Sarkisian said, "I'll be waiting for it."

▲

As soon as Dan returned to his cubicle, the desk phone signaled an incoming call, and he hurried to answer it. "Hi, what's up?"

Dixon said, "You better get down here now. Train has something interesting to tell you."

"I'll be right there." Dan put the receiver back onto its base and walked past Scotty and Bev. "I'm going to Dixon's office. We may have something."

He rushed downstairs and once inside the office, he noticed an award of appreciation on the back wall and acknowledged it by saying, "Twenty-five years of service. Now I know you are old."

"Deserving, not old." Dixon pointed to the framed photo of his son that rested next to his in-basket. "Brian recently entered the academy."

"And you didn't talk him out of it?"

"He's always lived on the edge. Now he'll see exactly what the edge is."

Train, who was already seated lamented, "He's crazy like you."

Anxious to know what the sitting officer remembered, Dan asked, "What can you tell me?"

"I had breakfast with Batterson this morning and we were discussing Lady Godiva as well as Barkley Malone. I was at the trial when it began but was called back here and never went back to the courtroom. Batterson testified and maybe he wasn't supposed to do it, but he snapped a few pictures and showed them to me. One was of the jury when they were being polled. Remember, I thought Lady Godiva seemed familiar? It finally dawned on me. I'm almost sure it's her. The damned blonde hair threw me off, but I knew I'd seen those glasses somewhere. You have some photos from the carousel. I want Batterson to see them. He may be able to second my opinion."

"Let me get him in here. Sit tight." Dixon left the room momentarily.

A few minutes later, he and the patrolman came into the office and Dixon said to Batterson, "Dan wants to ask you a question." The detective proceeded. "I understand that you testified at the Barkley Malone trial."

"It ended with a hung jury."

Dan held his phone and allowed the policeman to browse the

pictures from the carousel crime scene. "Damn. Bare assed? What the fuck?" Batterson said.

Dan directed him to concentrate on her face. Batterson studied the photos, wrinkled his nose, and scratched his head. "Man, those glasses."

Train chimed in. "What about them?"

As if a light went off in his head, Batterson remembered, "Holy shit … she has blonde hair now, but she's the one, the juror who voted not guilty. Number seven. It's because of her it was declared a mistrial. She was a redhead then, but I'm sure it's her."

"Do you know her name?" Dixon asked.

"No, juror number seven is all I remember. A poll was conducted, but names were never given."

"Who were the prosecutors?" Dan asked.

"There were two. Evan Lincoln and Sarah Waverly."

"Lincoln, I'm familiar with him, but not Sarah Waverly. Thanks."

"And fucking Sasser must have gotten to her and convinced her that us cops are no good. That bastard drilled Branch and me real hard trying to convince the jury to acquit Malone because of theoretical bad behavior and evidence analysis. It must have worked because she must have been convinced."

"Maybe so, and someone wanted her dead," Dan said. "Thanks. We'll take it from here."

Dixon handed Dan the police report. "Anyone reported her missing?"

"Not yet."

"I'm going back upstairs."

The informed detective rejoined Scotty and Bev. "We have an identification, but not a name. The Barkley Malone trial. Officer Batterson had testified and I showed him the photos I took at the crime scene. He recognized her as juror number seven, who had cast the lone dissenting vote that kept Malone from being convicted. I need to talk with the prosecutors."

Bev reminded Dan, "You mean the state's attorneys."

He sneered. "State's attorneys, prosecutors … same thing. "Evan Lincoln and Sarah Waverly, they should have helpful information. And Sasser, he was Malone's lawyer. That smart-assed guy tried to hijack the jury into believing the trial was about police misconduct. I can't wait to burst in on him again."

Dan retrieved the phone number for the state's attorney's office and called it. After his brief conversation with Lincoln, he tore off the piece of paper he'd written juror number seven's personal information on and waved it at Scotty and Bev. "I have a name. Lady Godiva was Nicole Brezinski."

Bev queried the criminal database and found nothing. Then she opened Facebook and got a hit. "Holy Jesus. It's her and you have to see this post."

Dan perused it. "Are you serious?"

The post with a purple background read: *I did it. Trial is over.*

Bev observed, "She was a flight attendant for Delta. Her profile says so."

"Lincoln told me. It's an interesting post. If it means what I believe it does, then she intended to acquit Malone from the get-go. But why? I need to see Evan Lincoln."

Dan walked toward Sym's office, where the captain seemed to be staring at his inbox. The detective barged in. "We have an identification of Lady Godiva. Her name was Nicole Brezinski and she was the lone dissenting juror at the Barkley Malone trial. I have to see Evan Lincoln. Wanna come?"

"Hell no. My in-basket is full. See the paper on top? It's the requisition I put in for hiring more hard-asses like you. Rejected twice."

"Will you get off it?"

"Have a good time with Lincoln."

Chapter 8

Dan had obtained Nicole Brezinski's address from Evan Lincoln and knew she resided at 120 Biscayne Drive, East Granby, but he did not know whether she lived alone or whether she had a spouse, lover or a roommate. Before he decided to go there, the detective exercised his subpar computer skills and his search of the town's property records revealed the address was a condo owned by a woman named Alicia Greenstein. Nowhere did the name Nicole Brezinski appear.

Dan ran with that information. It was early afternoon when he arrived at Greenstein's residence where he observed a silver Elantra occupying the driveway, so his Accord rested at the curb. Eyeing his surroundings as he made his way to the single-level home, he encountered a jogger passing by, as well as a man walking with a large, leashed dog.

The detective marched up two front porch steps and rang the bell. When the door opened, he was met by a woman he assumed to be Alicia Greenstein. "May I help you?" she asked.

Dan displayed his credentials. "Are you Alicia Greenstein?"

"I am. What is wrong? Why are you here?" The pretty woman appeared to be in her mid-twenties and was dressed in black sweatpants. Her hair was tied back, and her t-shirt bearing a picture of the Dixie Chicks was obviously missing a bra underneath it.

"Does Nicole Brezinski live here?"

"She does. Why?"

"May I come in?"

Alicia stepped aside and directed Dan to a beige living room couch. "Have a seat. I'll be with you in a minute. I'm almost finished ironing my uniform." She lowered the music and went into the kitchen as the detective wondered, *Is she a flight attendant too?*

She reentered the room and sat on a comfortable looking cream-colored chair. Crossing her legs, she asked, "What's going on?"

She doesn't know. I hate doing this. Dan gritted his teeth and delivered the devastating news. "May I call you Alicia?"

"Yes."

"Alicia, Nicole is dead."

The stunned woman screamed. "What? She can't be. What are you saying?" Tears flowed and the woman began shaking. She clutched a tissue she retrieved from the coffee table beside her.

Dan waited until she was ready to listen. "Why haven't you noticed her absence?"

Wiping her eyes, she said, "I was away and got home last night. What happened?"

Her eyes widened as Dan shared the unsettling news. Alicia's body shook and she screamed expletives unbecoming of anyone. Dan attempted to calm her. "Breathe slowly."

He waited until she, with teary red eyes and a long face, was ready to resume. She sniffled and her hands were unsteady. Dan grimaced. "This is extremely unsettling and quite unusual. Nicole was found naked, sprawled on top of a wooden horse inside the Bushnell Park Carousel."

Alicia, wiping her eyes with another tissue was horrified and her jaw dropped. She angrily demanded, "What did you say? I don't understand."

"Neither do we. I have to show you a picture." The detective placed his phone in front of her to show her a photo of her nude roommate and the word "whore" written on Nicole's back.

Alicia gasped. "Oh, my God. Oh no, she was no whore. Who did this?"

Dan digested her comment. "We don't know and at this point we can't say she was raped. We do know she was a jurist in the Barkley Malone trial and she was the lone juror who had cast a not guilty verdict."

Alicia sighed. "She was. I still don't understand. Was she shot or stabbed?"

"Neither. There were no detectable wounds on her. And there is no explanation for the absence of her clothes, which were nowhere to be found. It gave the impression that she walked in or was escorted in there. I'm quite sure she wasn't naked then."

"Oh, my God. I don't understand at all." Tears flowed again.

"Frankly, neither do I. Can you think of anyone who may have wanted to harm her?"

"No."

"Anyone on Facebook?"

"We're both on it. Why are you asking?"

"Because she posted about the trial saying she 'did it,' meaning she was the reason the Barkley Malone trial ended with a hung jury."

Alicia was silent and utilized another Kleenex.

Dan watched her blow her nose. "By the way, you told me you were not home."

"It's our schedules. We don't always have the same days off. I got in yesterday from Atlanta. She was not here. I did try to call her and thought she worked the red-eye and was in San Diego."

"How is it she got time off to be a jurist on the Barkley Malone trial?"

Nicole's roommate was quiet and began trembling. "I don't know." Alicia rose. "I'm not sure if I shut off the iron."

Dan detected nervousness in Alicia and watched her walk to the kitchen. The detective did not like her sudden bolt from him. *She didn't answer my question nor did she like my comment about Facebook. I suspect the iron had not been left on, and my last question struck a deep nerve.*

He watched her as she supposedly unplugged the iron. *What kind of story is she up to, and why?"*

The flight attendant put her uniform on a hanger and hung it over a closet door. Dan spotted a wings pin attached to the dress pocket. She couldn't avoid Dan any longer and sat again, crossed her legs and appeared to regain her composure. He knew when someone was hiding a truth. He let her be for a minute and redness adorned her cheeks. The veteran detective pressed her, seeking more information. "Alicia. You know something, don't you?"

She didn't speak, but her lips twitched and she cowered. Sheepishly, she uttered, "I can't lie to you." She sat back and began to cry again while wiping her eyes. "It was the trial; Nicole was hell-bent upon becoming a jurist. The oddest thing is that she got a summons for jury duty several weeks before and they chose her."

"Why? What motivated her? And what made her vote not guilty?"

Her face drawn tight, Alicia harshly blurted out, "Because she was raped after coming home from a flight." She paused. "By that Uber driver, Emilio Sandovar. He picked her up at the airport around ten at night and gave her a ride home where he brutalized her, forcing her to have anal. She was traumatized afterward."

Dan brushed his forehead, stunned by this revelation. *So, there it is. She wouldn't let Malone be convicted because she was thanking him for killing her rapist.* "Did she report it?"

"No."

"Why didn't she report it?"

"She was scared and didn't want to say anything because she

was scheduled to fly to Honolulu the next evening and didn't want to lose her trip. She knew people would say it was her fault or not believe her. And it would be her word against his and it would be in the papers. Publicity is the last thing she wanted."

"But you knew?"

"Not then. I was in Orlando. She told me a week after she was molested."

Dan knew that more than half of committed rapes never get reported.

"Does Jeff know?" Alicia asked.

"Who is Jeff?"

"He's a pilot she'd been seeing."

"His last name?"

"Karas."

"How long were they dating?"

"I'm not really sure. It was on and off."

"Do you know where he is?"

"Not right now. He flies a lot." The distraught young woman uncrossed her legs, stood. and angrily shouted, "Who the hell would have stripped her and propped her on a wooden horse?" She sighed. "Does Stella know?"

Dan heard another new name. "Stella?"

"Passante. Nicole had shared a house with her and after Nicole was attacked there, then she came here with me. Stella was at the trial."

"Is Stella a flight attendant?"

"She was. Now she's at the Delta check-in counter at the airport."

"Where does she live?"

"Not far from the airport. Suffield."

"You have not spoken with her either?"

"No. I have to phone her."

"She may not know. Don't call. Let me tell her."

Still dazed, and without hesitation she plucked her cell phone from her sweatpants pocket and input Jeff Karas's number. When his voicemail kicked in, she left a message. "Call me. It's important."

Dan grimaced. "I wish you had allowed me to contact him first. May I have his number, as well as Stella Passante's and her address?"

Alicia wrote the information on a piece of paper and handed it to Dan, then plunged into her chair. "I need to rest. I have to be ready to fly tomorrow." She sniffled and held a tissue. "I'm so devastated. I don't know if I can."

Dan ended the conversation. "I understand, I'll let myself out."

Starting his Accord, he collected his thoughts. *That was one hell of a story. A damned rapist. No wonder Nicole wanted him dead. Convenient for me that Stella Passante lives in Suffield.*

▲

Dan's list of people to speak with now included Jeff Karas and Stella Passante. He set himself at his desk and read the phone numbers he had attained.

Before making any calls, he glanced into his boss's empty office. The detective held his cell and pondered whether to call Stella or Karas first. The pilot boyfriend intrigued him. Dan knew Alicia Greenstein had called him and she left a message. With the man's number on his desk, Dan attempted to phone him and was met with the same result as Alicia, no answer, so he too spouted off a brief voicemail message. His call to Stella resulted in him leaving another voicemail.

Chapter 9

Dan's chat yesterday with Alicia Greenstein had told him a few things, but his interrogation came up short. He was curious to know if Alicia had indeed not gone to work, so he called her. Caller ID must have told her it was him. Dan again heard her shaky voice. "I am so upset. I am taking a few days off."

"I thought you might."

"Stella called me last night and I told her about Nicole. She had no idea."

"I'm going to call her soon. You get some rest."

"I will."

Dan was glad Alicia decided to take a break. He keyed in Stella's number and two rings in she answered her phone. After Dan identified himself, she began, "Detective, I'm sorry. I meant to return your call. I don't know what to say. Alicia said you were at her place and you would get in touch with me. I'm as shocked as she was."

Dan tapped his desk. "I understand you live in Suffield and so do I. Would it be possible for me to visit you on my way home, say four o'clock?"

"I'm off today. Sure."

"Thank you, I'll see you then."

Dan then strode toward the exit. "Where now?" Scotty asked.

"To see our friend, Hancock Sasser."

Sasser, the slick, smart-dressing Cadillac owner and Dan were no strangers to each other. Their relationship swayed like a swing in a playground. The creative, sly lawyer had graduated from Howard University Law School and for the past twenty years he had been on both sides of the law, not to mention taking a hiatus a few years ago. Drugs ruled him at times, but he had finally shaken the habit after spending several months in a Providence rehab.

Sasser's office on Blue Hills was in a one-story building not hard to spot, given the recent renovations that featured a large orange and blue billboard on top of the roof that now included his picture.

As soon as the detective entered Sasser's quarters, he was greeted by the lawyer's secretary, his niece Chantel, a thin, clear-complexioned lady in her mid-thirties with straight black hair. "Mister Shields. I wasn't expecting you."

Dan pointed to the closed door behind her. "Neither is he. I know your uncle is in there. His Cadillac is outside."

"I'll tell him you are here."

"Don't bother. He's always delighted to see me." Dan opened Sasser's door and saw the blue-suited attorney, feet on his desk, speaking into his cell phone.

Sasser's eyes lit up as Dan casually took a seat while the lawyer abruptly ended the call, dropped his feet on the hardwood floor and smiled. "Dan, Dan. You're looking good."

"So are you."

"How you been?"

"Did Chantel redecorate this entire place?"

"Yeah, nice, isn't it?"

"Not bad. You better keep her around."

Dan mocked the diplomas on the back wall. "Boy, they sure don't look real. Are they?"

Sasser frowned. "Uh-oh, Dan. This is no way to start a

conversation. Most of them are."

"I thought so."

"How is your fake badge serving you? Can I see your ID?"

They both chuckled. "Okay," Dan acknowledged, "I hear you did a hell of a job, trying to get Barkley Malone off. Lucky for you there was one not guilty vote."

Sasser gloated. "When you're good, you're good."

Dan wanted to smack him. "Temporary win and you know it."

Sasser leaned forward. "A win is a win."

"Is it when there is a mistrial? You know he'll stand trial again."

"I know, but they'll have a hell of a time finding jurors who don't know anything about Malone."

"You're right. Seriously, do you honestly maintain Malone is innocent?"

Sasser squinted. "You know I can't answer that."

"I know, but let's put it this way. If you could have chosen to prosecute or defend him, which would you have chosen?"

"Clever, Dan. I plead the fifth."

"Okay, so here it is. Are you familiar with the Lady Godiva murder?"

"I heard."

"Do you want to know her name?"

"Do I?"

"Damn right you do. Her name was Nicole Brezinski."

Sasser thought for a second and rocked in his high-back leather chair. "You're kidding, one of the jurors?"

"Not just one of the jurors. Juror number seven. She was the one who voted not guilty!"

"What are you saying?"

"She's dead and someone killed her!"

"I know Malone had nothing to do with it," Sasser asserted.

"Maybe not, but do you want to hear why she voted not guilty?"

"Do I?"

"You bet you do. It was because the Uber driver Malone killed was Emilio Sandovar, a guy who had forcefully sodomized Nicole Brezinski. Nicole was thanking Malone for putting her assailant away. It had nothing to do with your attempt to lead the jury into believing the police bungled the case. Are you still going to defend him at his retrial?"

Unfazed by this news, Sasser was stoic. "Maybe."

Dan scratched his head. "Tell me something. What was the retainer fee?"

"I can't tell you."

"Can you tell me where he got the money from?"

"Doesn't matter to me. I only care if my bank account is satisfied."

Dan huffed. "As of now I have a slew of potential suspects who may have killed Nicole, but which one was vengeful enough to strip her and leave her on a wooden horse?"

Sasser plopped his shiny loafers back on his desktop. "Now, what have I got to do with anything?"

"I wanted you to know what I learned. Malone is not off the hook, and he is in some way responsible for her slaying."

Sasser rose to his feet, put his hands on his hips, raised his voice and angrily growled, "So, you're putting a guilt trip on him and me?"

Dan lifted himself from the chair, did a one-eighty and headed out. "It was nice seeing you, Sass."

Sasser protested. "Where the hell are you going?"

"Back to work. I suggest you do the same."

Changing his demeanor as he sauntered past Chantel toward the exit, he winked at her. "It's always nice to see you, beautiful."

Chapter 10

Dan was outside Stella Passante's yellow clapboarded ranch and halted his car in the wide driveway beside a late-model silver Camry. He moseyed past a large spruce tree in the center of the front lawn and assorted flowers on each side of the landing. He didn't have to ring the doorbell because Stella Passante greeted him. "You're right on time."

"Don't tell my wife. She'd be jealous."

Stella's medium-length dark hair surrounded her round face. The detective thought she was likely to be in her late thirties or early forties. The average-height woman had a dimple on her left cheek and she was well endowed. Stepping into the sitting area, Dan lost his concentration and stared at the unlit fireplace's mantel. There he saw a statue of a woman whose face was obscured by a sheer covering. Stella caught his attention. "Detective Shields."

"I'm sorry, but I was looking at the statue on the mantel."

"Are you familiar with it?"

"No."

"It's *The Veiled Virgin*. A replica of course. It was done in the eighteen hundreds. The woman is the Virgin Mary. You have heard of her?"

"I admit, I am not very religious, but I have."

They occupied chairs opposite each other. Hers was plusher and she sank into it while the detective opened a pad and held a pen before taking a seat. "If you don't mind, I'd like to ask you a few questions."

Suddenly, as if she saw Nicole standing before her, she shivered and became sullen.

"I know this is tough to take and harder to understand. What exactly has Alicia told you?"

"She told me that Nicole was found dead at the carousel. The rest is cloudy."

Dan explained what he knew and began digging into her relationship with Nicole. "I understand you were a flight attendant and are now working in a different capacity at the airport."

"I am at the check-in counter. I stopped flying a while ago."

"I understand Nicole roomed here before she went to Alicia's."

"She did."

"Why were you at the Barkley Malone trial?"

Stella huffed. "I don't know. I just didn't want her to be alone."

"You knew why she wanted to be on that jury, didn't you?"

"Do you mind if I smoke?"

"Go ahead."

She lit a cigarette and blew out a puff.

"You are aware she was raped."

"It occurred here while I was away. Nicole didn't want to stay here afterward and Alicia took her in."

"What can you tell me about Jeff Karas?"

"He's a pilot and dated Nicole."

"I'm aware of their relationship. I am not able to reach him. Tell me more about him."

"There's not much to tell. All I know is that he flew in the Air Force before exiting the service and joining Delta."

Stella's cell was on the table next to her and when the phone rang she answered it and said. "Okay." She faced Dan "I thought I was off today, but I have to work tonight from seven to one."

"I know how it is. I get called in all the time." He continued. "So, you are unable to tell me anything more about Jeff Karas?"

"He's handsome. I need to fix myself something to eat and get ready to go to the airport."

Dan put the pen and pad away. "I understand. May I speak with you again?"

"Sure."

He left her house and drove toward home. *I get the feeling she knows more about Karas. And he better call me soon.*

Chapter 11

Dan's once-frequent jaunts to the holding tank had become once-in-a-while visits. Today was one of those unannounced drop-ins. He delayed marching to his regular perch in the squad room, instead steering himself down to the jail's basement cells. He was greeted by Sergeant Dom Denine, the gatekeeper. "Dan. I haven't seen you or your buddies, Hampton and Rollin, in some time."

"That's a good thing." Dan peeked inside the celled room. "Must have been a slow night. I only see two."

"Yeah. What's up with Hampton?"

"The last time I was with him and Rollin was at the Maple and those two bums swore they retired from stealing cars. Those connivers somehow filed disability claims and our wonderful government bought their lies and sends them checks every month."

Denine grimaced. "And I'm here getting my measly paycheck every other week."

"You know what they say, crime does pay."

"Tell me something. What happened to Haley and what's his name, Travis, who were here a while ago?"

Haley Valente had been arrested along with her baby's father, Travis McCarthy. Drug charges were made against her and dropped after Travis admitted the narcotics found in her car were his. The irony was that Dan's son Mike had dated Haley in high school, and

Mike and Haley started seeing each other again soon after the jail incident.

Dan answered Denine's query. "Travis is out of the picture and Mike is back in the picture. She and baby Joey are staying at her parents' and Mike is still at Arizona State."

"As I remember, Travis did fess up after you talked to him, or should I say threatened him."

"That jackass was fair game and I had to scare the shit out of him in order to have him take the drug charge and absolve Haley."

"And then Mike and Haley ran into him at a bar and Mike beat the crap out of him, if I remember right."

Dan snickered. "Oh yeah. He wound up in the hospital and would have filed charges against Mike if I hadn't stepped in. I not so nicely coerced him into forgetting Mike by promising that Haley would not seek to sever the bandaged guy's visitation rights. The only problem was, I hadn't spoken to her about doing so. He ate it hook, line and sinker and I did get her to settle things in court."

"What's going on with Lady Godiva?"

"As of now, your guess is as good as mine. I gotta get upstairs. See you."

▲

Luke and Mal sauntered into the squad room and headed to Luke's desk. "What's up, guys?" Dan asked. "You two look like you're in a hurry."

Luke held up a disc. "Hell yeah," he said. "We need to take a look at the church security camera footage of Cabrera's shooting."

He fed the disc into his computer and as they waited for the video to start, Dan noticed a three-by-five photo leaning against the computer. "Who is she?" he asked. "She looks familiar."

Luke smiled. "That lady is the best thing in my life. Clarissa,

47

she's great."

Dan winced as he peeked again. "You are kidding, right? Is she the gymnast who won a medal at the Olympics?"

"Damn right, Clarissa Robustelli. Hell of a gymnast. She's a teacher."

"How the hell did you hook up with her?"

"It's almost funny because she's a foot shorter than me. We met at Costco. She had trouble lifting a forty-pack of water into her cart and I helped her. Brawn before brains, I guess. Anyhow, I've been seeing her for almost five months."

"When's the wedding?"

Luke did not reply to the smug remark and pointed to the video. "There. That light-colored vehicle." He zoomed in. "Can't tell what kind. It's hard to make out the shooter, but we can see two people in the car, and it stopped right next to Cabrera's squad car."

Mal gritted his teeth. "Holy shit. The passenger fired shots into the cruiser. The car sped away and unfortunately there are no street cameras."

Dan walked away. "I'm going to run over to see Evan Lincoln."

▲

Dan drove to Lafayette Street, where the unmistakable black and yellow scales of justice emblem was etched into the building he was about to enter. He walked up two steps of the facility housing the state's attorneys and then stopped and waited until a woman in a wheelchair and the man inching her along ended their climb up the handicap ramp. Dan pressed the door button and allowed them to enter ahead of him.

A security guard at the screening machine asked Dan if he had an appointment. The detective opened his wallet and displayed his badge. "I'm here to see Attorney Evan Lincoln."

"Yes sir, Detective Shields."

"I know where he is. Thank you." Walking down the vinyl-floored hallway, he came to the glass door of the attorney's office and opened it.

Lincoln was standing at a cabinet and turned toward his visitor. "Hi, Dan. Have a seat." A ray of sunshine filtered into the room and Lincoln lowered the window shade. "Let me get Sarah Waverly in here."

Dan pulled one of the three chairs in the room closer to the attorney's dark wooden desk as Lincoln went across the hall and brought the young state's attorney back with him. The diminutive woman extended her hand and Dan rose to shake it. "Nice to meet you, Detective Shields."

His first impression of the attorney was that she was all business. Short hair, business pantsuit, and a brief smile accompanying a firm handshake. "Same here."

She then rested a file in front of Lincoln who opened it. "Great. A defense attorney would eat us for lunch," he said to Waverly.

"What case is this?" Dan inquired.

Lincoln flipped the pages of the file. "An assault occurred on Broad Street outside a bar where the victim received a broken jaw, fractured skull and died a few hours later. It was raining and both men were drunk. Another intoxicated male who had been inside the saloon witnessed the beatdown and gave a description of the attacker, naming him. The apparent assailant was subsequently arrested. The problem was that the drunken witness also had a beef with the deceased victim as well as the man he accused as the assailant. Not exactly an unbiased accounting of the incident either. He claimed he saw a gun. None was found. A good defense attorney would drive a truck through this case. No cameras. We have to drop it."

Dan said, "I hear you."

Lincoln closed the file and gritted his teeth in a momentary snit. "This is a great system. This was one sloppy case, but a slam-dunk case like Barkley Malone ends in a damned mistrial, a total farce with one not guilty vote." He snarled, "A sham, and don't get me started on so-called expert witnesses. Liars as I call them, puppets getting paid to testify. And you know money speaks. Another complete mockery of the legal system."

Waverly admonished her fellow attorney, "Your anger is showing."

Lincoln paused before continuing. "The courtroom is a damned circus at times. It's objection after objection. Play by the rules, regardless of whether the accused was a serial killer or a traffic violator. And as evidenced in the Malone trial, the jury system is very flawed. And then there are defense lawyers like Sasser who attempt to shoot holes through the evidence. His tactics worked, resulting in Malone not being convicted."

Dan chimed in. "Maybe, maybe not. Hey, the perception of police these days is we're all crooks and set up every case. Videos obtained from so called observers can be deceiving and don't portray the truth, but right away the public assumes either police brutality or misconduct."

Lincoln sat back. "I'm sorry, Dan. Let's hear what you have."

"I was at the residence of Nicole Brezinski. I should say Alicia Greenstein. It's her condo. Nicole Brezinski roomed there. Alicia is also a flight attendant with Delta. This will surprise you both. Sasser had nothing to do with convincing the jury. Nicole Brezinski intended to get Malone off the whole time."

Lincoln sat back with scorn on his face. "What?"

"Emilio Sandovar, the murdered Uber driver is the reason she voted not guilty."

Waverly gasped. "I don't understand."

"You will now. Emilio Sandovar picked up Nicole at the airport one night and sodomized her when he took her home. At that time she lived with Stella Passante."

"What?" Lincoln bellowed. "So she wanted the killer of the guy who violated her to go free?"

"Yes."

"Wait," said Waverly. "Did she not understand she wasn't exactly freeing him?"

"Who knows?" Dan replied. "I talked with Stella Passante who actually sat in on the trial. She wanted to be there to quietly support Nicole."

Lincoln responded. "Wait. She must have been the woman who left the courtroom right after the polling. She rushed out with a smile on her face."

Waverly agreed. "I saw her first." The young attorney then nodded dejectedly, "Rape. You know most female abuse goes unreported." She made a fist. "Those violent acts madden me to no end."

"Here's another shocker," said Dan. "Alicia Greenstein had no idea Nicole was dead because Alicia was out of town. She is really shaken up."

"After the trial we attempted to speak with Nicole, but she was nowhere to be seen," said Waverly. "However, I was later able to speak with her and convince her to come in and talk with us. And when we voir dired her, she seemed perfectly normal and right for being a jurist."

Lincoln clasped his hands. "A lot of good it did to speak with her afterward. She clammed up and it was like trying to pull her teeth. Silent as a church mouse, stuck to her guns and would not tell us anything. You couldn't have shoved a toothpick through her tight lips. I surmise she came here only to appease us, and not to talk."

"Been there," Dan said. "My investigation is complicated as hell. I have a wide-open field as to who may have killed Nicole, including the eleven jurors who voted guilty. Technically it is not a homicide yet."

"And three alternate jurors," Waverly added.

"The bitch is, we have no proof she was murdered," Dan contended. "Everything about the death screams murder to me and I aim to get the truth. I can't leave anyone who attended the trial and heard the jury poll off my list of potential suspects. And there is the Sandovar family to deal with. They're the ones who stand out. Who had a better motive?"

"I agree," said Lincoln. "They were furious when the trial was declared a mistrial, shouting at Malone, and Alejandro Sandovar had to be restrained."

"And there is a pilot named Jeff Karas who was Nicole's boyfriend. It's a boatload of people. What can you tell me about the Sandovars?"

"Alejandro is a postal worker," Lincoln recalled. "Merriel is a housewife, and Elijah is a college student."

"Elijah?" Dan asked.

"Emilio's brother. He was there for a short time before leaving the trial." Dan swept his hand through his hair. "Can you find out what went on inside the deliberation room?"

"We sure intend to." Lincoln smiled at Waverly. "She has already requested the foreman, excuse me, these days it's foreperson, Elliot McIntire to come here."

"I need the names and addresses of all the jurors, the alternates and the victim's parents," said Dan.

"Easy enough," Lincoln assured him as he shifted to his computer and pressed a few keys. "Got it." He printed out the data and placed four pieces of paper in Dan's hand.

"Thanks."

"One more thing," Lincoln advised, "We are filing for a retrial on the grounds the evidence presented did not support the jury's decision or non-decision. The problem is we have to question a whole new set of prospective jurors and with the court backlog, Malone may not stand trial again until next year. Who the hell knows? I may not hang in long enough to be there. You know, this state is one of a handful where we state's attorneys are appointed by the criminal justice system. In other states, prosecutors are elected. My time may have come. The good news is Malone will remain in custody until then. He deserves to end up in prison for the rest of his life."

Dan nodded on his way out the door. "I agree."

Chapter 12

The next morning, Syms was nowhere to be seen. Dan, Scotty, Bev, Luke, and Mal were gathered around Dan's cubicle. "Where is he?" Luke asked.

Dan stared at the captain's empty office. "He could be anywhere. Off the wall, lunatic, whatever. The way he's been acting, he's a basket case, but I sense he hasn't crashed yet. He'll be here."

Luke and Mal returned to their workspaces and Bev tapped Scotty. "It's time to see if Kendal Westley is around."

"Where to?" Dan asked them.

"Brackett, three thirty-three," Scotty said.

Dan waved his hands as Scotty and Bev started to walk away from him. "Hold it, Bev. Scotty and I have been in that neighborhood before. Let me hit the head and I'll go with him. You stay put."

"I can handle it," Bev protested.

Scotty intervened. "No, Dan is right. We'll go."

Standing her ground, the irritated Bev railed, "Hold it, don't pull that crap with me!"

Dan didn't expect her outburst and sternly said, "It isn't often I pull rank but I am not debating this. Hold tight. I'll be back in a couple of minutes."

Bev huffed scornfully. "Pretty damned sexist, if you ask me," she snidely voiced to Scotty.

"Back off." He advised her. "Maybe so, but it can be hostile down there."

Still perturbed, Bev assertively commented, "It can be plenty hostile here, too. I am a detective. Did you guys forget that?"

Dan returned. "Let's go," he said to Scotty.

Bev peered at Dan and smirked as she said to Scotty, "Remind me to shoot him when you return."

Syms came into view out of nowhere and sneered at Bev's caustic remark. "What's going on?"

"Nothing," Dan said. "We're heading out. Where were you?"

"Captain's meeting," Syms answered, heading toward his office. "Every month, same old stories."

Dan had no doubt that Bev, a seasoned detective, was suited to handle this task, but he also knew he and Scotty were heading into a prime danger zone. Nearly half the deaths resulting from gunfire occurred in this section of town.

As Dan's car rounded Westland onto Brackett Street, a black van passed his Accord and Dan saw the bearded, long-haired driver stare at the detective's vehicle. The Honda sedan maneuvered around potholes and stopped when they arrived at Westley's residence. "Here we go. This should be fun." Dan drew his partner's attention to the throng of what he estimated to be more than a dozen people who were gathered outside a drug store. "Most likely a bunch of smokers and addicts. Some pharmacy."

Scotty sneered. "Pharmacy? You mean drugstore and not the prescription kind."

The detectives walked on a cracked sidewalk leading to the brick two-story apartment building where Westley resided.

"Hey!" shouted a paunchy, pony-tailed male whose leashed pit bull accompanied him. "What you want?"

Dan ignored the thug who wore a short-sleeved black shirt that didn't hide tattoos on both arms. He had torn jeans on and sported a silver nose ring. The unsavory guy smugly said, "Hey, what you boys want?" His voice drew four of his friends, two with bandanas wrapped around their heads, one with dreadlocks, and another tall muscular, scary looking dude who had a long scar on his face to the scene.

Dan knew every eye in sight was on him and Scotty and they kept walking. The intimidating man loudly commanded, "Hold up!"

Dan pivoted toward the menacing crew. "Any of you gentlemen know Kendal Westley?"

"Why you askin'?" the apparent leader with the dog by his side inquired.

Scotty pointed to the driveway. "White Chevy Impala. Is that his?"

"Ain't know," came a reply.

Swiveling his head to scan the area, Dan observed a man who was sitting on a porch directly across the street from them. The guy rocked, rose from the chair, and went inside.

"We have a few questions for mister Westley," Dan assertively advised his nosy inquisitor.

"'Bout what?"

"The Impala is a nice car."

"Don't be shittin' us. What you want?"

Dan was sure there was a gun tucked underneath the shady guy's shirt, and he and Scotty kept their distance from the pit bull. Undaunted, Dan shoved his badge close to the hostile sleazeball's beady eyes and addressed the onlookers. "Let's not play games. Any of you gentleman seen Kendal today, yesterday?"

The dog barked and the angered punk bobbed his head. "You ain't scarin' no one." Holding his dog back, the thug turned his head to the other interested guys. "We ain't know this dude? Right?"

They nodded as if they didn't.

Sarcastically, Dan asked, "Mind if I go up those rickety-looking stairs and ring the doorbell?"

"Go 'head."

Scotty rang the bell of Kendal Westley's listed residence. There was no answer. "Figures. I wouldn't respond either."

A low-rider vehicle with a raised frame and oversized tires drove slowly up to the assembled brood, idled and the driver yelled, "Waas happenin'?"

The dog owner shouted, "Ain't nothin. See you round. Just cops. They'll be gone soon."

Dan decided to try the apartment next door. The bell made no sound, so he knocked on the door. Seconds later, a man wearing shorts and a white tee came down the stairs and opened the door. "What do you want?" he asked sternly. "I seen you talkin' with them. I wouldn't mess with those boys."

Dan stood in front of the overweight, sparsely haired, easily sixty-something tenant. "We're interested in knowing anything you can tell us about Kendal Westley."

"What for?"

"Was Kendal Westley here earlier today?"

"How the hell do I know? I was at Wal-Mart."

"What's your name?"

"I buried my name a long time ago, around here they call me Pops."

The man did not deny ever hearing the name Kendal Westley. His demeanor told Dan and Scotty they were in the right place.

"When was the last time you saw him?" Dan asked.

"A couple days ago, maybe three."

"What kind of car does he have?"

"Jeep."

"Is that your Impala in the driveway?"

"What if it is?"

Dan responded. "No reason." The detective sensed he was not going to obtain any useful information and ceased his questioning. "Thanks for your time."

He and Scotty walked around the pit bull as its leash-holding master kept a close watch on the detectives. "Nice seein' ya." He laughed. "Don't worry, Killer don't bite, unless I tell him to."

Dan nudged Scotty. "There was a man in a rocker across the street. He went inside when we showed up. He may know something."

The detectives had reached the middle of the street when Dan heard another caustic question. "Where you goin'?"

Dan turned to eye his nemesis and the intimidating thug pointed. "Ain't your car over there?"

"We have some unfinished business," Dan scoffed as he avoided a hole in the tar.

"I ain't think so. Neither does Killer."

Staring at the bully, Dan smiled. "So, what's your name, my friend?"

"I ain't no friend."

Dan's instincts were proven right as he caught sight of the butt of a gun tucked inside the guy's shirt. Not displaying anything but toughness, the detective pointed to it. "I'd keep that in my pants if I were you. We'll be gone soon."

He and Scotty crossed the street and the man who had gone inside came out onto the porch. "No-good derelict bastards," he ranted. "Shitheads, all of them. They killed my dog and they ain't liked by no one. I'm seventy-six and I seen lotsa shit. You cops ain't gonna get them off the street." The frail man sat in his rocker and put a blanket over his knees.

Dan asked, "What can you tell me about Kendal Westley?"

The slightly hard-of-hearing man winced, "What about him?"

"When did you see him last?"

Bothered by street noise, the man uttered, "What did you say?"

Scotty tapped Dan. "He's got a hearing aid."

Dan repeated his question, louder. "When did you see him last?"

"Couple of days ago maybe. They all run together."

"Was he alone?"

"I don't know. He took off in his Jeep. How about telling those assholes to get me a new dog?"

Scotty nodded. "We'll see what we can do. What's your name?"

"Game? They ain't play games."

Dan motioned to Scotty. "Let's go." Without finding out the man's name, Dan said to him, "Thank you."

The old guy rocked and shouted, "My dog!"

As the detectives approached the Accord, Dan waved to the thugs. "It's been nice. By the way, do the old guy across the street a favor. Get him a dog."

Dan took a relaxing breath as he and Scotty got into the car, Dan said, "Now we know Kendal Westley resides here. How about going to see our buddies at the Maple? I could use a good laugh about now."

▲

As soon as Dan opened the door of the coffee shop, the smell of fresh doughnuts tickling his nose made him say, "I could get real fat hanging out here." To the detectives' left were the dynamic car thieves Hampton and Rollin.

"Hey!" Hampton shouted.

"Don't bother to stand," Dan commanded.

The hefty beer-bellied Rollin laughed. "Like we ever do?"

Doughnut crumbs adorned Hampton's green shirt. "Frosted doughnuts look good on you," Dan quipped.

"That's nothin'." Hampton opened his mouth to reveal a chipped tooth. "Damn apple I had two days ago ruined my smile."

The bearded Rollin poked his buddy. "That's gonna make a heck of a mugshot."

"Hey, we're done with that," Hampton replied.

"We can't stay long," Scotty said.

Hampton shrugged, "You guys ain't retired yet?"

Dan shook his head. "I don't know how you lying idiots get away with it. Bad enough we bail you out time and again and judges somehow like you two. Retired my ass. I know it's only a matter of time before you guys are back at it."

"Hell, man. No need to play around with the law. Checks roll in like clockwork," Hampton proudly proclaimed.

Dan cackled. "I bet they do."

"Shoot." Hampton poked Rollin. "Wanna snatch a car?"

The detectives and Hampton laughed. He smiled at Dan. "I suppose you have another one for me to steal."

The detective who breaks a rule every now and then had, unbeknownst to his superiors, employed the wily character Hampton in the past to help nab two suspects. "I wanted to see how you guys were doing. Denine sure doesn't miss you."

"Hell," Hampton gloated. "Tomorrow is payday. Beats working for a living." He stood. "Like my new duds?"

"What thrift shop are they from?" Dan inquired.

"Funny, Dan. Nordstrom."

"My ass, I don't even shop there."

"And you're not collecting disability."

"And what bullshit doctors made it possible to get fake compensation?"

"Good ones. They don't even have to see us again."

Dan smirked. "What a racket."

Hampton drew him close and whispered, "Seriously. If you need a favor, you know what I mean. We're in. You know a little extra cash is always appreciated."

"I'll keep it that mind. We have to go. Nice to see you, boys. And stay the hell out of the jailhouse."

Halfway back to the police station, Scotty's phone beeped and he answered his wife's call and reported the news to Dan. "Sallie is picking up the kids early. Eli and Bri are both sick. I hope I don't catch whatever they have."

"I know the feeling. I caught the flu from Josh last year."

Chapter 13

The next morning, Scotty hadn't shown up by ten past eight and Syms strutted to Dan. "Scotty called. He caught what the kids have. Has a fever and headache."

"I hope it isn't the flu."

"All I know is he isn't here." Syms moved away and Dan's cell alerted him to a call from Jeff Karas. "Good morning. Thank you for returning my call."

"I got your message."

"Where are you?"

"In Chicago. I have a layover here. I spoke with Alicia and she told me about Nicole's death. I'm stunned."

"How is it you were not aware of her death?"

"I was away."

Dan thought it odd the pilot, her alleged boyfriend had no idea about Nicole's death. The man's voice was calm and did not reflect any tone of bereavement. *I'd be more upset than he sounds.* "I was told that you two dated. You didn't talk with her?" Now, Dan detected a bit of sadness and heard what he detected as fake sniffles … as if Karas were holding back tears.

"She was a beautiful girl. I'm sorry she's gone."

Really? That's the first thing he says about her? "When was the last time you spoke with her or were with her?"

"I've been flying a lot. Hadn't seen her in about two weeks. We were together in Seattle. I did speak with her a couple of days before she died."

"Can I go back to something. Both Alicia and Stella indicated that you and Nicole were more than just dating. Could you clarify your relationship?"

"I wouldn't exactly call it dating, we were merely friends. Well, I'll admit we flew together and stayed at the same hotels on layovers and to be honest we had we shared more than dinner."

"Can you explain why someone would inscribe the word 'whore' on her back?"

There was a pause. "Look. Nicole was very friendly and let's just say I wasn't the only one who had sex with her."

Dan thought that was another odd answer. "So, you are of the opinion that some guy she had sex with may have killed her and made sure everyone knew she slept around by etching whore on her back?"

"I don't know. It's possible, I guess."

"You were aware of the Barkley Malone trial, correct?"

"Yes. And I know why Nicole voted the way she did." He huffed. "Nicole was assaulted by the Uber driver Malone shot."

"So, she told you?"

"She did."

Dan shifted the conversation. "I understand you flew in the Air Force."

"Six years. Flew C-130s. I decided not to re-up and Delta hired me."

"When was the last time you were in Hartford?"

"Bradley? Not too often. Probably several months ago."

"Where are you going next?"

"I'm off for a couple of days and then I'm flying to London. I have to go. I'm meeting an old friend here shortly."

"Thank for chatting. Have a good day."

Dan had finally spoken with the pilot, but parts of the conversation felt way off. Karas should have been more emotional, concerned, but had sounded matter-of-fact about Nicole's death. While he pondered the pilot's elusive answers, Syms sauntered over to Dan. "Dixon called me. There's a guy downstairs named Marcus Garfield who wants to talk to a detective. It has to do with the arson case."

"I'll go and see what he wants. I'll have Bev come with me."

"She knows a little more than you do."

⬥

Dan and Bev walked into Captain Dixon's quarters, and Dixon introduced everyone. Marcus Garfield was five-ten, medium build, with short wavy black hair and a visible gold medallion around his neck. The neatly clad man wore gray dress pants, a blue button-down shirt, and a navy-blue blazer.

Garfield's oversized hand dwarfed Dan's as they shook. "We understand this is about the Tamara Ashford fire," Dan said.

Dixon rose. "Take this conversation into room one." He handed Dan a pad and pen.

Following Dixon's directive, they proceeded into the interrogation room. Dan knew the discussion would be videoed with Dixon watching. The small quarters had been painted a light bluish green, a color researchers claim is calming and relaxing to interviewees.

Dan set a lined yellow notepad on a rectangular gray table as the visitor sat in a chair along the back wall. The detectives took seats across from him and Dan asked the man, "So, what brought you here?"

"I hear two cops were at my apartment."

Dan was confused. "Come again?"

"I heard you were trying to find me."

Dan tilted his head. "Are you referring to Brackett Street?"

"Yeah."

Dan glanced at Bev and then at the man across from him. "What exactly are you telling us?"

"I'm Kendal Westley."

Bev's ears perked up. "You are? What's with Marcus Garfield?"

Sporting a wry grin, he answered. "I mean, that's my name now."

Bev leaned over to Dan. "We need to talk."

Dan, with a fixed gaze on the man, stood. "We'll be right back. Please stay here."

Outside the closed-door room, Bev advised him. "The picture in Kendal Westley's file sure resembles this guy. Hair is different and he is a bit older, but it sure does look to be him."

"I want him to produce an ID. Why the hell the alias?"

The detectives reentered the interrogation room and took their seats. Dan studied the man's demeanor. "Again, exactly why did you come here?"

Shifting his body, he responded, "I told you. You were trying to find me."

"If you are Kendal Westley, then you are right. Do you have an ID?"

"You bet I do." He reached for his wallet and produced a driver's license, shoving it at the detectives.

Dan inspected both sides of the small, laminated card, read the name Marcus Garfield and grinned. "Is this real?"

"Real enough."

"So, it's fake?"

"I didn't say it was. You did."

"So, it is fake, right?"

Garfield laughed. "Right."

"What's with the alias?"

He shrugged. "How the hell else could I find work? Every fucking job I applied for, the answer was no, or I never heard from them. Nobody wants a guy who served time. Shit, they all have access to my record and do background checks." He nodded. "Pretty slick. I took the name from that cartoon cat named Garfield."

Dan admitted, "I know it's tough."

"No shit, and I fabricated a history and have a Facebook page. For the last two months I've been working at Macy's. Got these clothes there too, thirty percent off."

Dan had seen many storytellers in his time, so he again stared at the man across from him and the subject turned away. To Dan, this was a hint of deceitfulness. When Garfield gazed at Dan again, the veteran detective rubbed his hands together. "So, are you turning yourself in for setting the fire that killed Tamara Ashford?"

Struck by Dan's accusing question, Garfield's calmness gave way to hostility. The man bared his teeth and yelled forcefully, "Fuck no! I'm here because the boyfriend or ex-lover is always the first one you suspect and I'm here to clear the air about me." In a calmer tone, he continued, "I may have been with her, but she was sleeping with some other dude. Hey, she sent me to jail. Seems like a motive to kill her to me."

Dan heard what he thought was a fabricated story and raised his voice. "So, instead of beating her again, you set fire to her house?"

This accusation stung Garfield and he angrily rose faster than a jet plane. "I'm not him anymore! I did my time. I wanna beat the shit out of the guy who killed her too."

"Let's get this straight. You've been seen at her house. Were you trying to get back together with her?"

"I still liked her."

"Did you?" Dan paused for a moment. "So, were you getting

back together? Were you begging for her forgiveness? Were you trying to convince her you've changed? Were you trying to bury Kendal Westley's name?"

"Maybe I was."

Dan noticed Garfield's hand. "And how exactly did you get the bruise on your hand? Did you beat her before starting the fire?"

Garfield shouted at the top of his lungs, "Get off it! I haven't done anything. I did go to talk with her but left way before the fire started."

Dan glanced at Garfield's injured hand. "Explain the bruise."

Garfield rubbed his hand. "A shit-ass dog outside my apartment snapped at me and I pulled my hand back and slammed it on a light pole."

Dan surmised if he were telling the truth about the bruise, it may have been Killer the pit bull that caused it.

"So, you went to a doctor?"

"Come on, I didn't break anything."

"Let me understand this again. You wanted to get back together with her but she didn't want to."

Garfield finally sat back down. "Sort of." He became quiet and it appeared that a moment of sadness came over him as he bowed his head.

Bev inquired, "Did you still love her?"

He raised his head and let out a breath. "I told you I did, but I couldn't convince her I had changed."

Bev took over the questioning. "You swear that you never touched her again?"

"No. I swear it."

"Tell me something. I know you were released from prison several months ago. Where did you go?"

"The only place I could. My cousin Vinnie's, and don't get smart, not the movie one."

"Tell me about him."

"What for?"

Dan couldn't remain silent and snarled, "Because she asked you!"

"You wanna know about Vinnie? He has one good leg and one prosthetic leg, and he's the lucky one. His troop carrier hit an IED and it shredded his leg before it was amputated."

"Sorry to hear it," Bev said. "Where does he live?"

"On Harper Street."

"When did you leave there?"

"A couple of months later. I found my apartment on Brackett and it's cheap. Vinnie was all about pot. I can't blame him but I couldn't stay there."

"Where were you when the fire started? According to neighbors, you had been there earlier in the day."

"I told you. Christ, she was alive when I left. I went to work and was there until the mall closed."

Bev asked the man, "Can I get you some water?"

He shrugged. "Yeah."

She left the room and Dan asked him, "How do you like Macy's?"

"Glad as shit they gave me a job. Money isn't great, but it is enough to get me by."

Bev returned with a bottle of water, handing it to Garfield. He twisted off the cap and guzzled half the liquid.

Bev continued, "You told us she had a lover. Who is he? How about giving us a name?"

"I can't."

Dan didn't expect he would. *Here we go again. Street rules. Rat someone out and you might be next.* The senior detective sought a lead. "Getting back to Tamara's lover, how about giving us the name?"

The man's leg began to twitch, shaking the table. "All I can tell you is she may have a few guys hanging around her."

Dan nudged Bev. "Outside."

"What's your opinion?" she asked.

Dan was reluctant. "I don't know. He sounds like a bald-faced liar. You mean to say a guy who twice beats the crap out of his girlfriend and spends time in jail still wants to get back together with her?"

Bev frowned. "It wouldn't be the first time."

"And it wouldn't be the first murder, either."

"Let's check out the Macy's crap. He could be lying. And now he's adding another unknown suspect or two."

"Damn it. We have to let him go but I want to know a few other things first."

Dan opened the interrogation room door and Bev went in ahead of him. The empty bottle of water was in Garfield's hand. Sitting again, Bev continued the interrogation. "Are you on parole?"

Garfield mumbled, "Three years."

"Who is the parole officer?"

"Her name is Catalina, yeah, like the nice vacation spot. Catalina Montero."

"How often do you report to her?"

"Every thirty days."

"Does she know you as Westley or Garfield?"

"Both. Actually, she is impressed."

"And you see her faithfully?"

"So far."

"You better be truthful," Bev said as she looked to Dan.

Dan stood and decided to end the questioning. "Thanks for coming in. You can leave."

"I gotta be at work in an hour."

Dan escorted him to the police station's front door and watched the man walk toward a silver Jeep Wrangler. Garfield drove off and Dan made the short journey back to Bev and Dixon. "He drives a Jeep."

"It's all on video. I guess time will tell if he's a bullshitter or not," Dixon surmised.

Bev agreed, "He sure has a suspect tag on his back."

"Right," Dan said, "I never had a guilty person waltz in here before and not plead innocence."

Chapter 14

Dan smiled as he pulled into his driveway. The painters were gone, and he assumed his wife's car was in the garage, but once he went inside, the note on the refrigerator told him otherwise. *I took Josh to basketball tryouts. Kate is with us.*

Twenty-five minutes later, Phyllis and the children were home, with Josh carrying a pizza box. "Hey, how'd it go?" Dan asked his son.

He plopped the box on the counter and grinned. "I'm in."

Dan hugged him. "Great."

The home phone rang and Dan picked up the receiver to hear a familiar voice. "Hi, Dad."

"Hey, how is everything?"

"No complaints. What's new at home?"

Dan clicked the phone to speaker. "It's Mike."

"Hi," his siblings echoed almost in unison.

"What are you guys up to?"

"I made the basketball team," Josh excitedly said.

"He did good," Kate added, "but I'm almost as good."

"Great."

"What's new?" Phyllis asked the collegian.

"Hi, Mom. I'm fine. Everything is going well."

"When does baseball start?" Dan asked.

"Practice begins after Thanksgiving. Our first game is groundhog's day."

"How many games?"

"Forty. We have a new manager. He seems okay. My roommate didn't care for our first meeting with him."

Phyllis asked, "Why is that?"

"Honestly? I don't know. Rudy can be a jerk sometimes. Good catcher though."

Josh chimed in. "I'm getting number eleven."

"My number?"

"Yeah."

"Cool, buddy. It's the best one."

"Can you get me a new sweatshirt?" Kate asked.

Mike directed his next question to his father. "Can I still use your credit card?"

"Funny, Mike. Actually, I forgot you have it. Go ahead. Watch the costs."

"Okay, Kate. You too, buddy."

"How is Haley?" Phyllis asked.

"I spoke with her last night, She's doing well. You know she's going to nursing school."

"Good for her."

"Her parents are thankful they have Joey."

Dan mused, "I haven't talked to her father in a while. You're beginning to fade out a little."

"I'm walking around the pond and sometimes the signal fades in and out. I'm meeting a couple of friends here. Can't wait to see you all."

Dan chimed in. "You're holding up dinner anyway. Pizza is getting cold."

Phyllis ended the call. "We'll talk soon."

"Sounds good. Love you all."

After dinner Dan settled into his den chair and clicked his remote to the news. Scrolling across the bottom of the screen was the teaser *Lady Godiva identified. Details later.*

He jumped up as Phyllis entered the room. "What's wrong?" she asked.

"Nothing, damn it. The media. Lady Godiva. They released Nicole Brezinski's name."

She pointed to his chair. "There's nothing you can do about it. You knew the news would be out soon."

"You're right. Those dogs better not hound the station tomorrow."

"You act like they have never done it before."

"I know. This case has me up a tree. There are so many people to rule in or out of suspicion." He continued watching and listened as reporters talked about the nude body and the carousel. *Phyllis is right, we'll see what happens tomorrow.*

Chapter 15

Dan set a copy of the *Hartford Courant* next to a bowlful of Wheaties. Reading the headlines, he let his spoon sink into the bowl. "Oh crap."

"What's the matter?"

He showed Phyllis the headline. *Lady Godiva identified as Nicole Brezinski.* "One good thing is, apparently they have not uncovered the connection to juror seven in the Malone trial." He pushed aside the barely eaten cereal, folded the newspaper, and pushed his chair back. "I have to go." *I can see it now. The damned media will be at our throats today.*

▲

As soon as he entered the squad room, he was assaulted by the raspy voice of his boss. "In here. Now!"

Not having a chance to say good morning to Bev, Luke, or Mal, he obeyed the captain's command and entered the office with the newspaper in hand. Syms closed the door. "Sit down."

"I don't feel like it," Dan grumbled as he tossed the paper at Syms.

"Already read it. You don't have to tell me a damned thing. Whose phone do you suppose has been ringing off the hook?"

"I can guess."

The desk phone rang again. "Now what?" he shouted at Hardison.

Syms spun his chair around to face his beloved bonsai trees, his back to Dan. The detective heard part of the conversation. "Oh. No. I'm not getting involved!"

Spinning to Dan, Syms bobbed his head, slammed the phone back on its receiver and spat out sarcastically. "The Chief is on the warpath. His phone has been ringing nonstop since he got here. Fucking TV, paper snoopers are on his ass."

The captain's phone rang again. He sighed. "Oh shit. Guess who." He answered again and Dan heard Chief Hardison's loud voice echoing into Syms's receiver. Syms replied angrily, "Bullshit, not me. It's your house. Try another number."

The call abruptly came to an end and the unnerved captain bared his teeth. "Fuck me. I may be your boss, but it's his job to answer the media. He's calling a press conference for this afternoon, and I am not gonna be there, and neither are you." Rotating back toward his pet trees, Syms picked the orange plastic squirt gun off the credenza and sprayed water on his friends. Facing Dan again, he barked, "Get out of here and go to work on Lady Godiva's bare ass."

Walking toward his cubicle, Dan spotted Bev at the Keurig. She removed powdered cream, sweeteners, and coffee pods from a shopping bag and set them near the coffee maker where Luke waited to make a cup of brew. "Thanks, Bev," the tall detective said.

"You *should* thank me and this time don't forget to add to the donation box on my desk."

Luke nodded as Dan joined him. "The boss is pretty steamed, isn't he?"

"That's putting it mildly. Hardison is meeting with the media this afternoon, and I need some coffee."

Mal sauntered over to them. "Me too."

They each grabbed their mugs and filled them. Dan took a drink.

"Hey, Luke. I haven't heard you guys mention Blues lately."

"Have you seen the new prices? We're not exactly regulars anymore. Three bucks for a cup of coffee. This pod crap is good enough."

"I heard you," Bev said coyly. "No wonder I'm buying supplies more often."

Luke neared his cubicle with a cupful of hot liquid in his hand and a long-faced Captain Syms marched toward his detectives and growled, "Into the conference room. Now! Where is Scotty?"

"Still sick," Bev replied.

Luke lifted his cup. "Be right there."

Syms barked at him, "Put your mug down. I said now!"

The detectives followed the grouchy captain and gathered around the long conference room table as Syms slammed the door shut. He paced. "Look at me and look hard." He then loudly began ranting while pointing to his long, drawn face. "This sour puss has been through hell the past few weeks and ever since I left Hardison's office yesterday, I've been like a time bomb. After tangling with him this morning, well, it has put me over the top."

Dan raised both his hands in mock surrender.

"Put those down and shut up." Syms continued pacing. "The press and Lady Godiva are just the tip of the iceberg. This defunding shit is hitting us and every other law enforcement agency hard, and the people who need us most are suffering. I don't need to tell you violent crimes have tripled right here. Bad guys are more brazen, more armed and more disrespectful of us and of innocent citizens. We are fighting a losing battle. A plethora of guns are in the hands of real bad guys. Those assholes are making it perilous to even walk into a grocery store. There is no question we're outgunned and the weapons battle is too far advanced when it should have been addressed twenty years ago. Congress can argue over all the gun laws but they do nothing."

Dan silently gestured to Bev, his palms up.

Syms began to sweat and to Dan, the anger etched into his captain's face appeared to age the man ten years. "You guys know firsthand how overworked and underappreciated we are. We're all targets of anyone who may have a phone camera and wants to stir things up, and if Cabrera's shooting wasn't hard enough, it's put a bullet up my ass." Syms took a deep breath. "And if that's not bad enough, the damn news coverage of a mosquito bite gets blown into a crime of killing defenseless insects. The fact is, we have lost nearly twenty percent of our police force and they are not being replaced. Good people are leery of entering into law enforcement." He was silent and Dan noted the defeatist, dour expression the captain wore.

Syms sat and bowed his head. "Now it is coming down on us like a stack of windblown cards. Yesterday, Hardison for the third time rescinded my requests to hire additional detectives." The frustrated captain pounded the table with an open fist. "With all of our budget cuts and the increased number of homicides, it means we have to treat cases differently around here. It's pretty much all for one and one for all." The weary captain peered at Mal. "We were lucky to snag you right in time. I'm sure the Waterbury force is in the same boat." He then sneered at Dan. "And don't you be pulling any shit. We can't afford to lose anyone around here." The captain slowly got up, opened the door, and as his detectives left the room, he lamented, "And no, I don't feel any better."

No sooner had Syms reached his office door, than he rushed back toward his crew and strode purposefully out through the squad room door. Dan watched and said, "I know something is seriously wrong with him." The sight of the captain's unoccupied chair made the detective furious, but he knew he had to let the dust settle where it would. *He better clear his damned head. I'm glad he told me he was not attending Hardison's Lady Godiva news conference and ordered me not to go.*

Dan's cell alerted him to an incoming from Evan Lincoln. "How's it going?"

"Dan, I heard from Elliot McIntire, the jury foreperson from the Malone trial. He's coming down here around three-thirty."

"I'll be there. Hardison is holding a press conference then. Now I have a great excuse for not attending it. Thanks. I'll see you then."

Chapter 16

Elliot McIntire toted a briefcase containing test papers he had to yet to read and grade. Sure enough, the Mister Rogers look-alike teacher wore a yellow bow tie. Lincoln rose from his desk to welcome him. "You remember Attorney Waverly. And this is Detective Shields. Please sit."

McIntire sat next to Dan as Waverly took the third guest chair in the room.

Lincoln turned to the teacher. "Thank you for coming in. We appreciate your service as foreperson on the Barkley Malone trial."

McIntire acknowledged the thanks. "I was honored to serve."

"We all know the trial ended in a hung jury and you know as well as we do that the one not guilty vote was cast by juror number seven," Lincoln commented.

Dan chimed in. "Mr. McIntire, are you aware of the woman who was found dead at the park carousel? Her name was released last night."

"I don't watch TV much and my paper never showed up this morning."

"Then I guess it is news to you that her name was Nicole Brezinski."

McIntire's eyes opened wide and his mouth dropped open. "Oh my God!"

Dan writhed, "That's an understatement. We don't know who is responsible for her death, and there is a lengthy list of suspects including every juror."

McIntire gasped. "Oh no."

Dan tapped his pen on the arm of his chair. "All we know at this point is she died at the Bushnell Park Carousel and I want to get as much information as possible about what went on in the deliberation room."

"I admit at times it was chaotic and none of us were pleased with her unbreakable stance."

Lincoln inquired, "What do you mean by that, not being pleased? Arguments, confrontations, nasty words? Can you tell us what exactly went on inside the deliberation room?"

The teacher took a breath. "I don't know what to say. It was as if she paid no attention to the evidence, testimony, or anything else and was adamant about not convicting Malone. She seemed stubborn and tuned out at times, filtering out everything that everyone else had to say. We were all unanimous from the outset except for her, but nothing could convince her to conclude the man was a killer."

"How hostile was it in there?" Dan wanted to know.

"Pretty heated at times. We wondered if she could be replaced by an alternate, but how the hell do you get rid of a juror because she was the lone holdout?"

"You don't," Lincoln advised, "unless you can prove she is incompetent or biased. And the latter is an avenue no one, including us, wants to pursue."

Dan asked, "Did anyone appear to be particularly angered?"

"Oh yeah. The bailiff came in and tried to calm us down. Jordan Lymon nearly leapt across the table to strangle her. He had to be restrained."

"Anyone else?"

"Bernard Porter used a lot of four-letter words trying to get her to change her mind, and at one point wished she were on trial."

"Anyone else come across as threatening?"

"We all were in a way. Everyone despised her."

Lincoln asked, "Could you tell us more about Nicole Brezinski's demeanor?"

"She sat smugly in a chair at the end of the table and didn't seem to listen to anything the rest of us had to say. Actually, she peered steadfastly out the window. We took one last vote and you know the results. There was no way she was going to change her decision. We recognized the balloting was done and we had to deliver the news to the judge."

"We are filing for a retrial, so Malone will be tried again," Lincoln advised. "We don't know when it will occur."

"Is he still in jail?"

"Yes. Barkley Malone was neither convicted nor found innocent."

Waverly added, "The retrial request is ready to be filed."

Lincoln rose. "Thank you for sharing your experience, Mr. McIntire."

As the teacher exited the room, Dan knew he had a giant task ahead. "I'll have to consider all the jurors, especially the hostile ones."

▲

It was obvious to Dan that the press conference had ended, but one TV news vehicle was still parked in front of the police station. *Newsmongers don't know when to leave.*

Two uniformed cops walked purposefully out of the station's front door and up to the van. Seconds later the vehicle was gone.

Making it to the squad room, the detective spotted all two

81

hundred-fifty pounds of Chief Hardison who was sitting with Syms and the detective ventured down the hallway to hear the latest news. The chief's shoulders sagged. "It's over. The damn press. They know, in no uncertain terms, the carousel investigation is an ongoing one and they are not to contact us and we will let them know when we deem it appropriate."

Dan said, "I'm glad I was not there." He watched Hardison blow out a breath and exit the room. "I'm leaving. Home sounds good."

Syms acknowledged the comment. "It sure does."

Dan and Syms were alone. "I was with Lincoln and the Malone jury foreman, Elliot McIntire. He told us a mouthful about the mood and the actions of the other eleven jurors inside the deliberation room, including their interactions with Nicole Brezinski. It has been a long day."

Syms eyed the aspirin bottle in front of him. "Get the hell out of here. I'm leaving too."

Chapter 17

The next morning, Scotty was back to work, sniffling and sneezing every now and then. With a box of Kleenex on his desk, his voice deeper than normal, he mumbled, "Luckily I have no fever and can function okay."

Bev swerved to face him. "We'll see. Just keep those tissues with you."

Dan heard the bantering while he was deep in thought and still had no thread he could follow on the Lady Godiva case that would lead him to classify the incident as a homicide. *What the hell happened? Clothing? No one walks into a park carousel naked and ends up dead. And the original Lady Godiva, all she did was ride naked through town.*

Dan had no reason to suspect Elliot McIntire. That left ten other jurors and three alternates that he knew he had to eliminate one by one. Then there were the victim's family members, Alejandro, Merriel, and Elijah Sandovar.

His journey down juror lane began. On the detective's list were list were fifteen names that included the alternates.

Juror 1: Elliot McIntire, 37, teacher. Dan crossed a line through his name.

Juror 2: Emily Griese, 44, investment broker.

Juror 3: Nelson Pittman, 40, Yale graduate, actuary and vice president at Umbrella Insurance Company.

Juror 4: Mary McGregor, 52, Wal-Mart employee.

Juror 5: Jordan Lymon, 29, gym instructor at Clover Leaf. Dan placed an asterisk beside his name. Lymon had reportedly come close to crossing the line by nearly attacking Nicole.

Juror 6: Andrea Salzman, 67, retired.

Juror 7: Nicole Brezinski. He drew a line through her name.

Juror 8: Jamus Barrows, 33, electrician.

Juror 9: Bernard Porter, 44, concierge at the Hilton. Dan placed an asterisk beside his name. An enraged juror who slung expletives at her.

Juror 10: Enrico Feliciano, 37, mechanic.

Juror 11: Antonio Gaetano, 29, Motor Vehicle Department employee.

Juror 12: Patricia Monahan, 22, unemployed, recent UConn graduate.

Alternate 1: Fredrica Rose, 35, waitress.

Alternate 2: Lamont Charles, 50, magic store co-owner.

Alternate 3: Phillip Risley, 46, Amazon warehouse employee.

An initial study of these people did not raise the detective's eyebrows, except for Lymon and Porter. *You never know. They may be suspects and they may not be.* Sitting back and digesting this information, he browsed the list again and circled the name Lamont Charles. *Who better to not leave a clue? A disappearing act. Only a strange thought, or is it?*

He put his pen down as his phone rang. He did not expect to hear Dom Denine's voice, but he did when he answered, "Hey Dom, to what honor do I owe this call?"

"You don't want to know. Are you sitting or standing?"

"No, not Haley?"

"Guess again."

Dan groaned. "Are you serious? Hampton?"

"Bingo, and Rollin."

"What the hell? I'll be right down."

Scotty was curious. "What now?"

Dan rubbed his eyes and then threw his hands up. "You won't believe it. Our good pals are downstairs in lockup."

"You're kidding."

"I wish the hell I was. Denine was surprised too, especially after I had told him those two idiots were retired. You know where I'm headed."

With a sense of doom, Dan strode through the squad room exit and raced downstairs to the jungle so fast the stairs might as well not have been there. He faced Denine. "When did the knuckleheads get here?"

"A couple of hours ago, after they were booked again."

Catching his breath, Dan said, "Okay, open up."

Denine gave the detective access to the tank. His footsteps on the concrete floor got louder as he stomped his way to their cell. The two men were sitting on flimsy beds and were startled as Dan screamed at them. "Hey, get the hell over here!"

Hampton wrapped his hands around the bars. "You scared the daylights out of us."

If Dan's hair could have stood on end, it would have. He was enraged by his friends latest arrest. "What the hell are you here for?"

Hampton took a couple of steps backward and seemed embarrassed, as if he were searching for the right words to spill out. Rollin was silent as Hampton bowed his head. He came forward again and placed his hands on the bars. "It's like this. We kinda stole a Cadillac."

Hampton's response unnerved Dan. "You what? You can't stay away, can you? Not Sasser's!"

Hampton moved closer to Dan. "No. Don't be so agitated."

Dan grimaced. "Oh, that's rich. Talk."

Rubbing his hands together, Hampton gloated. "Nice car. Wasn't my fault. Damn thing hit a pothole, damned city roads, and swerved into a telephone pole."

Dan took a short breath and marveled at Hampton's aloofness. "Really? Did you forget how to drive since you are supposedly retired?"

Brazenly sneering at Dan, Hampton answered, "Amazing how easy a car can upend a utility pole, but we didn't get hurt. Should see the car."

Dan had heard comical tales from Hampton over the years, but this time nothing was humorous. He wasn't sure if the car thieves could avoid prison. "And you're proud of that? Some poor guy's car is damaged."

Hampton wrinkled his face. "Well. Not quite. It's sorta not runnin' anymore."

Dan dropped his head and groaned before looking at Hampton again. "You mean totaled?"

"That's what I said. It don't run no more. Are we going to get billed for the pole?"

Dan sighed. "My God. What the hell got you back on the stealing track?"

"Had to."

Staring with daggers in his eyes at Hampton, Dan asked, "Had to? What the hell are you saying?"

"Well. It's sorta like this. You know those disability checks we get? Those donkeys notified us they're stopping them." He shook his head. "They kinda want their money back."

Dan broke into a small grin. "So, they caught onto your scam?"

"Hey, I wouldn't call it a scam. We did go to the doctor and got hearing aids."

"Right, Witch doctors?"

"Hey, we got hearing aids?"

"Nice."

"Well. We kinda sold them."

"Holy crap. We're done. I knew it. I knew it was a matter of time before your sorry asses would be back here." Dan made a fist. "And I suppose you want Sasser to get you off again?"

"Kinda."

"Damn it. Do you know how many times you've been here?"

"This is my third."

"Did you forget how to count, too?"

"You mean altogether?" Hampton put his finger to his lips. "I meant seven. Three here and four at the old jail."

Exasperated, the detective said, "You sure put me and Sasser in a huge hole this time. The right judge will put you guys away, maybe where you belong."

Hampton winced. "Ouch. So you and him will get us out?"

Dan huffed. "Did I say I would?"

"But you'll try?"

Blowing out a deep breath, the flustered detective said, "Shit. I'll do what I can. I don't know why, but I will. And this will be the last time. Do you understand? After this, you meatheads are poison."

As Dan walked away, Hampton shouted, "We love you too."

Back in the squad room, Dan sank heavily into his chair. The thud made Scotty rise and face Dan. "What the hell happened this time?"

"I have to call Sasser. Those two jugheads are wearing me out."

"Cars again?"

"Hell of a story. Being down there with them gave me a headache. Crime scenes and dead bodies are one thing, but somehow Hampton grates on me worse than murder." Dan broke out a wry grin. "But I like him, and he's helped us in the past."

"Do you suppose Sasser will go to bat for them again?"

Dan's recent visit to Hancock Sasser had been tense and he

couldn't be sure the lawyer would want to hear from him again so soon, but the humbled detective had to contact his sleazy sometime friend. *Sasser has a way with some judges and he's been able to get the idiots off in the past and he may be able to do so again.* Staring at his phone, reluctant to contact the lawyer, he bit the proverbial bullet and did so.

Chantel answered, "Hi, Dan."

"Hey beautiful, can I speak with your uncle?"

"He's busy right now."

"Is he shining his shoes again?"

"Dan, he's busy."

"Can you have him call me as soon as he's done. It's important."

"I'll let him know."

Dan muttered to Scotty, "He'd better call me back and it better be soon because I'm sure arraignment will be tomorrow."

Twenty minutes later, the attorney returned the call. "What's up?"

"What are you so cheerful about?" Dan asked.

"Talking to you."

Dan laughed. "Right. Listen, I have a favor to ask."

Dan heard the attorney's feet land where they usually did. "Uh oh, here we go again. Let me have it."

"It's our friends, Hampton and Rollin. They're in lockup again."

A huge huff came through Dan's phone. "Whose car did they steal this time? And I thought you told me they quit the shenanigans."

"Long story. Bottom line is, I need you to be at their arraignment."

"Tomorrow?"

"Maybe. I don't know. You can find out."

"Shit, Dan. They have a long-ass list of priors." Sasser's irritation was evident as he raised his voice. "You have a short memory? Hampton stole my car. Remember?"

Dan amped up his tone. "You deserved it. I told him to do it to scare you. You got it back without a scratch. Remember?"

"Shit. Here we go again. I'll tell you, we've been lucky so far, but if they get Judge Cooney, she'll set a high bond and they could be locked up for a while until their hearing, unless they come up with bail. And hopefully she'll assign one. What are the charges this time?"

"Let's put it this way. Hampton crashed a stolen car into a utility pole. The car was totaled and I know he'll have to pay for the pole."

"Damn it, Dan. I don't owe you a damned thing. And sometimes I don't even like you. And I sure as hell don't owe them a dime."

"Right. So will you do it?"

"Are you listening to me?"

Dan yelled, "So, will you do it or not?" There was silence and Dan waited, "Talk to me. Yes or no."

A huge sigh came through the phone. "God damn it. I shouldn't."

"Shouldn't, as in you'll be there?"

"This is the last one for me and them."

"Thanks, pal."

"You know you'll owe me lunch again. Barbecue and no excuses."

"Right."

Dan ran his hand across his forehead, but whether Sasser could save Hampton and Rollin from serving time was not a slam dunk.

Chapter 18

Thirsting, Dan headed toward the water cooler to wet his whistle when he saw Luke standing nearby who wore a frowned look of bewilderment. "What's got you puzzled?" Dan asked.

"Cabrera has me and Mal stumped. We may have to get a break, a silent witness."

Dan folded his arms. "Have you asked yourself a question?"

"What do you mean?"

Grabbing a paper cup and filling it, Dan downed the water and asked, "Why was he parked outside the church? You know that area is like a ghost town late at night unless an event's occurring at the XL. And judging from the video of the parking lot across the street, it didn't appear that anything was going on."

"What are you getting at?"

"I'm thinking, maybe he did know his killers. Maybe he was there for a reason. Maybe he was waiting for that vehicle."

Mal sauntered over to them. "I heard you," he said to Dan. "Are you suggesting he was set up?"

"All I'm saying is that he was there for some reason. He wasn't expecting to be killed, but he was."

"That's deep," Luke said with his hands on his hips.

Dan further suggested, "Find out from Dixon if it was unusual for Cabrera to have been parked outside the church."

"We will," Luke assured him.

Dan tossed the empty paper cup into the nearby wastebasket. "I need to talk to Arnstein and find out what he knows. Lady Godiva's cause of death is unknown to me; he should have her autopsy and toxicology results."

"See you later," Luke said.

Dan sat at his desk and called the chief pathologist. Arnstein answered, "Hey, Dan. I was about to call you."

"I guess we think alike. Did you finish Lady Godiva's autopsy?"

"You mean Nicole Brezinski. Yes. I'll have my report finalized later today."

"What can you tell me now?"

"She died of a cardiac arrest."

Dan's jaw dropped. "What are you saying?"

"She had a fatal heart attack. A sudden death. According to toxicology, her BAC was point zero seven. There is no evidence of rape. Here's one other thing, Dan. Nicole Brezinski was pregnant, about four weeks."

Dazed by Arnstein's findings, Dan lamented, "I don't buy it. Her blood alcohol level is just below the intoxication limit, but it doesn't set off any alarms. I'm sure it was murder."

Arnstein agreed, "But she could have had a low alcohol tolerance."

"Maybe. Thanks, but that was not the news I was expecting." Dan hung up and slunk back in his chair. *I've said it before and I say it again. There's no way she stripped herself, somehow got rid of her clothes, climbed up on a wooden horse and had a heart attack. And she sure didn't write whore on her own back. How the hell can a killer induce a heart attack?*

Rising from his chair, he clenched his fists and froze in place where he muttered to himself again. *The Sharpie.* The bewildered detective sat again and phoned Sarkisian.

"Hi, Dan," The forensic expert said. "I suppose you want to know about the Sharpie?"

"Good guess."

"I don't have great news. The pen was full of smudges. Anyone could have used it."

"Is there any way to check if the inscription on her back matched the pen's ink? I just spoke with Arnstein and he hit me with a curveball." Dan rattled off what the pathologist had informed him."

"Wow, those are shockers. Let me call him. I know he can extract DNA from her and if the pen's last contact was her back, it may be possible to link the two samples."

"Give it a try."

"I will."

"Let me know."

"By the way I still have the eyeglasses that were soaked in urine. They aren't any help."

"I sure as hell don't want them."

"I'll get back to you."

Dan stood, thinking. *I'm not sure what a DNA match will prove without knowing who used the pen, but you never know. I need air. What else can go wrong today?* As those words swirled in his mind, he ambled toward the door and a jittery-looking Scotty cornered him. "I need to talk to you."

Dan rolled his eyes. *As if I haven't heard enough discouraging news in the last few minutes.* He asked the antsy detective, "What's wrong?"

"Not here. Let's go to the conference room."

Scotty closed the door behind them and Dan saw the dour look on his comrade's face. "What's this about?"

Scotty was sullen and nervously twitched his leg. "It's Sallie. We have a problem."

Dan's mouth dropped open because the last thing he expected to hear was that those two lovebirds were on the brink of leaving the nest without each other. "Oh no."

Scotty shook his head. "No. It's not that. Jesus!"

Dan blew out a breath. "Phew."

The hot, red-headed girl Scotty had reeled in was still the most beautiful women he'd ever seen. "Remember when Sallie and I began dating?"

"Yeah, you couldn't wait to get her into bed."

"Come on. You know she kept me waiting a long time. And that made me fall deeper in love with her. You also know Sallie was engaged once before. Right?"

"So?"

"That asshole she was with before me went into the Navy and now he's out and he's back here. He called Sallie."

"And you think he's after her?"

Scotty shrugged. "He called her last night. His name is Ed Tarkenton and the guy wants to see her. Horny boat bastard better not have a hard-on for her."

"What did she say?"

"He wants to see her."

"And. Is she going to?"

"She's mulling it. I know she didn't sleep well last night."

"Calm down. You and Sallie have a great relationship and she started her real estate job again. Maybe she does want to see him to set him straight."

Scotty banged the table with his hand. "I can't handle her seeing a guy I know she slept with before."

"Christ. You knew she was no virgin, and I'll tell you something. I wasn't Phyllis's first."

"I'll kill him if he so much as touches her."

"Hold it. Breathe. I never knew you to be so insecure. Go home and talk to her. Tell her how you feel. You know what, when you get home, give her the biggest hug you ever gave her. She's not going anywhere. Trust your wife."

Scotty took a few deep breaths and was silent for a minute. "Thanks, pal."

"Good. Now let's both get the hell out of here."

CHAPTER 19

Dan heard voices and snuck into the den, where Josh and Kate were watching television. "Where's Mom?"

Josh pointed to the stairs. "Mom has a headache."

Dan retreated to the front closet and stowed his gun where he always did before striding up to the bedroom. The lights were off, shades drawn, and Phyllis had a blanket pulled up to her chin and a washcloth covering her eyes. He sat on the edge of the bed. "When did the headache begin?'

"About an hour ago. The ocular migraine is nearly gone. Old age is next."

"Sure, we're both halfway there."

"I took some Maxalt, and those annoying zigzagging flashes of blue, white, yellow lights have gone away. I'll be fine in little while. Your dinner is in the fridge. Spaghetti. I fed the kids early."

"Okay. Thanks."

He got off the bed and fetched his supper. A while later, Phyllis entered the kitchen as Dan twisted pasta around his fork. "How do you feel?"

"I'm better."

He finished eating and stepped to the sink to rinse the plate. As he opened the dishwasher, Phyllis stopped him. "Hold it. You always do it wrong."

"Excuse me?"

She showed him. "You still don't know how to put dishes in." She took the plate and glass and neatly positioned them inside. "Like this. Toward the water, not away from it."

He grunted. "I'm supposed to know there is a proper way? I thought as long as I put dishes in this thing, that was good enough. I guess I never read the manual."

"You don't have to. I've just read it to you."

Changing topics, he commented, "I haven't spoken to Haley's father in a while. I told Sergeant Denine she'd never be in the women's lockup again."

Dan went into the den. "Hey guys, I want to phone Haley's father. How about quieting the TV?"

It was still light outside and Josh grabbed the basketball on the floor and went to the backyard with his sister right behind him.

Phyllis joined her husband, who held the receiver in his hand. He hesitated. "I don't remember Dave Valente's number."

"It's in the address book. I'll get it."

"Thanks, dear."

She was gone for less than a minute and returned with the number on her lips that she recited before stretching herself on the couch as Dan phoned Dave Valente. "Dave, it's been a while since we've spoken."

"It has and I've been meaning to call you. How are you?"

"We're great. Still chasing down bad guys. So, how is Haley?"

Dan heard happiness in Dave's voice. "I'm delighted how much she has changed. She's taking nursing school seriously and I have my daughter back as well as my grandson, Joey."

"How's the custody situation? Is Travis McCarthy taking advantage of his visitations?"

"The court allowed him supervised visits. He was okay for a while, until a child support edict came down. He's gone and I don't know where to. Haley could care less where that drug addict is!"

"We spoke with Mike yesterday. He's doing fine."

"I know your son keeps in touch with Haley. It's almost as if they were back in high school. I'm looking at their senior prom picture now."

"We have one, too. Haley hasn't changed, she's still a beautiful girl."

"Thanks. Mike is as handsome as ever too."

"How's Joey?"

"Keeps us on our toes. A good little boy. What about Josh and Kate?"

"Josh is taking after his brother, almost. He made the school basketball team. Kate is a good gymnast and smart as a whip."

"You know, we need to have you, Phyllis and the kids over for dinner."

"Thanks. We would like to come."

"I'll have Margaret work it out with Phyllis."

"I'm warning you, the kids eat a lot."

"So does our dog."

"Really? You got a dog?"

"Yeah, a beagle. Named him Bagel because that's how Joey pronounces it."

"Can't wait to see them. I'll talk to you again."

"Sure thing. Good to hear from you."

"Likewise."

Phyllis had heard one side of the conversation. "It sounds as if everything is fine with Haley and Joey."

"I hope so. As you heard, we left it to you and Margaret to arrange a dinner date."

"I'll call her."

CHAPTER 20

As soon as Scotty strolled in with gusto in his step and a broad grin on his face, Dan knew his junior comrade had good news to report.

"What's new?" Dan asked.

"Everything is good. Me and Sallie had a talk. She intends to set him straight."

"You gave her a giant hug, right?"

"The biggest."

"I told you."

"You were right. And she thanked me later."

"Go get some coffee."

Dan had his mug in front of him and responded to an incoming call from his beloved pal, Hancock Sasser. The attorney said, "Got some news for you. Hampton and Rollin were arraigned. We got a break because Judge Cooney was sent to the federal courthouse. Eisner filled in. Your lucky-ass friends were each assessed a fifty-thousand-dollar bond. I ain't shelling out any bucks to get them out."

"Are they back in lockup?"

"For now."

"Thanks, Sass. I'll talk to them."

"You bailing them out?"

"Hardly."

"When will their hearings be?"

"Two weeks from today."

"I'm on my way downstairs."

Once again, Dan met Sergeant Denine. "I'm back for guess who?"

"I'll buzz you in."

Dan, as he had done all too often, marched down the hard floor. Closing in on their cell, he called out, "Hey, you two clowns! Are you going to make bail?"

"Yeah, gotta come up with five grand each," Hampton said. "I already called my sister; she'll get us out. Want to laugh? The money will come from the payments we got from Uncle Sam."

Dan shook his head. "And how much do you owe them?"

Hampton turned to Rollin. "You remember?"

"Fourteen."

"Each?" Dan asked.

"Yeah," Rollin replied.

"Great. How are you boys going to pay them back?"

Rollin looked at his buddy and received a blank look. Hampton then said, "Beats me, my sister can't help us swing that one."

Dan shrugged and caustically asked, "When are you going to take life serious?" The detective saw Rollin flinch and he stared at him. "Do you have a sister too?"

"Naw. An ex. She ain't no good."

Dan said, "You guys could be sent to federal prison."

Hampton blurted out. "I hope they have doughnuts."

"Maybe they have ones big enough to squeeze around your neck. Hampton, what the hell am I gonna do with you? Maybe you and

Rollin will each grow a brain in prison." Dan slid his hands to his hips. "And what about the utility pole?"

Hampton grinned. "Ain't got a bill yet? Besides, there's a lot of ripe cars out there."

Dan stepped back. "Hampton. I already told you. If you're nabbed again, it will be the last time and don't expect me or Sasser to be at your beck and call."

Hampton shrugged, "Right, Dan. I'm not losing your number."

"That's it," Dan said as he turned to leave the cellblock. "Fine. See you nutjobs at the Maple, or in prison."

Exiting the detention area, Dan started up the stairs. *I don't trust either one of those clowns. Rollin and Hampton each have a screw loose.*

▲

Thundering footsteps rumbled through the squad room as Syms raced out the exit. Luke scratched his head in wonderment. "Where's he going?"

"To see the chief?" Dan guessed.

Twenty minutes later, Syms stomped back into the squad room without saying a word to anyone and closed the door of his office.

Dan had observed the fiery glow in the captain's eyes and could swear steam was coming from Sym's head. Less than two minutes later. Dan's cell rang, and to his dismay it was Syms who barked, "Get in here. Now!"

"What's going on?"

"You'll see."

Dan scurried past the interview room, conference room and lavatories before coming to a stop at the door of the captain's office. Stunned by a disorderly mess, he demanded, "What the hell is all this?"

Syms dropped his commendation certificate in a box. "What does it look like?"

Dan spied a badge on the cleaned-off desk. "What the hell are you doing?"

Hastily, Syms stuffed a framed picture in the box. "What the hell does it look like I'm doing? I've had enough."

"Stop it. Sit the hell down!" Dan shouted.

Syms shoved a few more mementos into the box, bent over and sealed it. "Not now."

Dan grabbed the captain's arm. "Get hold of yourself and sit your fuming ass down. Enough is enough."

Syms flinched. "Let go of me." The captain plopped himself into his chair.

"Cool off, will you? You've gone cuckoo! Acting like a lunatic."

"I'm cuckoo? This fucking hell house is cuckoo. I've had it. This whole shit system is screwed up. Hoodlums have the upper hand. They outgun us. They don't respect us. We're the hunted. Everything we do is put under a microscope. We get sued now and we go to jail for stopping a criminal. Touch them and it's police brutality. Kill someone and the court slaps their hands and you'll probably end up in jail. Not like the old days. We feared truant officers, obeyed crossing guards and cops on the corner. Shit. My father smacked my black ass so many times, it was almost permanently red."

"So did mine."

Syms continued his tirade. "How the hell does someone like Eric Marmol get off? Remember him? Fucking guy was arrested eight times in two years and goes free. Then he finally kills a guy and is awaiting trial. How many of these assholes are out there when they should have been put away a long time ago? The whole prison system is fucked up. Facilities are closing because there's not enough money to keep them going, and the incarcerated criminals get to exist on our money for years. Screw it, they should all be cremated and free up space for new assholes."

Dan glared at him. "Have you vented enough? All that crap is true, but it doesn't mean we should stop trying to protect the majority of good citizens." Syms took his gun from the top drawer of his desk and Dan asked, "What the hell are you going to do with that?"

"Don't worry, I'm not going to shoot myself. You maybe." He plopped the firearm on the desktop and pointed to the big aspirin bottle on the desk. "It's here because of you. The shit I put up with to save your ass, I shouldn't have, but I put my own behind on the line every time you pulled one of your stunts."

"And I'm thankful. Now come to your senses."

"Dan, you don't get it," Syms grunted. "I *have* come to my senses. It's over."

Dan reached for and grabbed the captain's badge that was near the in-box. "It's not over until Hardison has this."

"Give me that. He'll know when he sees it on his desk in the morning with my farewell note, along with Misters Smith and Wesson."

Dan bristled. "I have a good mind to find the key and lock this door with you inside."

"Nice. And you'll come to the end of the road someday."

"Someday, you said someday. This isn't that day for me or you."

"Yes, it is."

Dan bowed his head. "I thought you were a lot tougher than this. Everyone respects you, even Hardison. If you want to leave here like a mad dog with his tail between his legs, do it!" He took the badge and threw it at Syms. "Here! I remember how riled you were when Hardison was in the hospital, and we didn't know if he would live or die. You were strong then. And even when I was shot, you helped me through it. Where is that man?"

Syms sighed, taking a few deep breaths before settling into his chair. "Those weren't exactly good times, were they?" He sighed again and gripped the aspirin bottle. "Get me some water."

"Don't go anywhere."

"Where the hell do you think I might go?"

Dan brought a cup of water to Syms, who washed down two pain relievers. Neither man spoke for a few minutes when Syms shook his head at his number one friend. "Tell me why I should stay?"

"I already told you. You are strong, have a good heart, and care about getting criminals and killers off the street."

Syms let out a deep breath. "Dan, leave."

"Not until you unpack your bonsais."

Swiveling his chair toward the window, Syms held his position. "Nice view, isn't it?"

"If you're looking for a cloud with a silver lining, I hope you see it."

Syms scrunched his nose and spun around. "If I'm not here in the morning, you'll know why." He rose from his chair and glanced around the room without saying a word.

Dan watched as the captain stood in silence and he asked the sullen Syms, "Where are you?"

"Not here." Syms pointed to the door as he had many times and echoed the same words he always screamed at Dan. "Get out!"

Dan unsatisfyingly sauntered toward his cube and Scotty halted him. "You look as harried as Syms."

"Maybe so. That hyper jackass is still in a snit and he's ready for the insane asylum. I wouldn't cross his path if I were you. He seems to have his mind made up. The hardheaded guy's anger came through loud and clear. We'll know more in the morning."

Chapter 21

The next morning Dan arrived at the police station with a gut-wrenching feeling. He drove slowly into the back lot and saw the space reserved for Captain Syms was vacant. *He didn't*. When the detective walked into the squad room he saw a frowning Bev. "Syms is not here," she said.

"I know, his parking space is empty. It looks like he may have done it, packed it in." Dan peered into the captain's vacant office as he strode to his own cubicle, where he couldn't miss the note waiting for him on the desk. In big black letters, it read, *GET UP TO ME. NOW!*

He recognized the chief's writing and immediately headed upstairs to see the man. "Where are you going?" Bev asked.

"To see Hardison." He shrugged and thundered toward the exit, rushing upstairs and into Hardison's digs.

"Sit the hell down!" the chief ordered.

The detective did as he was commanded. Hardison pointed to his desktop. "See these?"

Sitting on a padded desk protector were Sym's Smith and Wesson and badge. Dan closed his eyes. "Do I have to answer you?"

The chief hotly asked, "Are you next?"

Dan shook his head. "No, I'm not." Sharing his disappointment about the captain's apparent resignation, the detective became concerned about the chief. "You look like you're going to have a heart attack. Him leaving is not your fault."

"No, but me having to deny any request for additional detectives ate at him as much as it does me. The damn mayor is strung out over it as well. City council and state representatives are all wearing shit over defunding and budget restraints. I don't know when they will come to their senses and decide the police are needed." After taking a few deep breaths, Hardison took one bigger one. "God damn it. He was acting like a maniac yesterday when we spoke, but I didn't expect this."

"I can't say I didn't, but I have nothing else to say."

"I do or thought I did. I got back here last night around seven and saw his credentials and his note. Then I phoned him and the jackass didn't answer. I kept calling and he finally picked up. He's inconsolable, adamant and not wanting to discuss it anymore. The dismayed jerk hung up."

"I don't know if something beyond being scared is up his ass," Dan said. "He did tell me that he's afraid his wife will be a widow if he keeps working." Standing and peering out a window just as Syms had done, Dan couldn't help noticing threatening dark clouds moving in. Rain was not far off and the gloominess sparked a sense of doom in his gut. "I hope the sky isn't sending us a bad omen. It sure is overcast."

Hardison sighed. "Dan, as of right now, you are in charge of the detective unit. Go lay it on your comrades."

Dan smirked. "Thanks. I suppose this means a raise?"

The chagrined Hardison waved goodbye. "Go."

Dan went downstairs to break the news to his fellow detectives and afterward, he stared at the empty office down the hall.

Luke was bewildered. "What the heck are these bonsais doing on our desks? We each have one."

Dan had an idea why they were there. *Is Syms sending us a*

message that we should babysit his trees until he decides to change his mind?

It was surreal to Dan. He strolled to the captain's office where the half-full aspirin bottle was where is always was. *Fuck, is he toying with us or is he really gone?* The senior detective rubbed his eyes and noticed one bonsai on the credenza. *You have to be shitting me. The squirt gun is still there. I guess this one is mine.*

Dan sprayed the tree and set the squirter next to the aspirin bottle. Then he marched down the hallway straight into his cubicle, where he again stared outside as rain began to fall. *This is my place; his office is not somewhere I want to be.*

The detective recalled that it ironically was a day much like today when he first came to Hartford. Today's storm dropped several inches of rain and he got soaked when he later raced to his car and he remembered when he began his career on the Hartford police force. It was at the old, now torn-down Morgan Street jail, where the squad room's furniture was antiquated and the lighting was inadequate. He hated the lockup in the basement; it was dark, dingy, and smelled of alcohol and other rotten odors.

As a newbie, he was shown his workplace by Senior Detective Hardison and was greeted by veteran Detective Harold Syms, who took Dan under his wings. They both had more hair then and Syms and Dan began to form a bond.

Scotty interrupted the new boss's short trip back in time. "Let's talk."

"Not again!"

"It will be short."

Dan and Scotty went into an interrogation room and Scotty closed the door.

"Is your worst nightmare still lurking around?"

"He won't be for long. Sallie spoke to him again and put an end to it. He wanted to see her, but Sallie axed the idea and reinforced the fact he and she were over a long time ago and he needs to forget her."

"I knew she would. What the hell were you so worked up about?" Dan opened the door and they left the room when he saw a ray of sunshine beaming through a window. The storm had passed and he fixed his eyes on a rainbow.

Chapter 22

Setting his mind on Lady Godiva, Dan browsed the juror list and zeroed in on the names he had highlighted. Jordan Lymon and Bernard Porter, as well as alternate Lamont Charles. *It would be insane if any of the jurors were so resentful they would murder Nicole, but I can't rule them in or out until after I interview them. And a magic man. He could make anything vanish, even clothes.*

The rain showers had stopped but his car was wet. Dan ventured to the Clover Leaf Gymnasium, a free-standing building in the corner of a small shopping center. Entering the facility, he heard loud music and saw bright lights and different types of workout machines being utilized."

At the front counter, opposite the entrance, was a female employee clad in a pair of yellow shorts printed with the gym's name and a white and yellow top. The youngish, clearly in shape woman was restocking shelves with powdered drink mixes. "Excuse me," Dan said politely.

She acknowledged him with a nod and he said, "Hi. I'm Dan Shields with the Hartford police. No one is in trouble, but I would like to speak with Jordan Lymon."

"He's in the back room with a couple of members." She pointed to an open room where the word 'WEIGHTS' was written above the door.

"Thank you."

Inside the heavy lifter area were indeed three men engaged in working with barbells. The employee dressed in similar clothes as the woman at the front desk was spotting a muscular man. *I'd say there are about two hundred and fifty pounds of discs on the long bar. Not exactly my thing.* After the strong guy completed a few repetitions and then dropped the bar into its slots, the detective neared the spotter and identified himself. Seconds later, Lymon took a break and he and Dan walked to a quieter corner of the room.

The gym instructor, a towel draped over his strong shoulders stood next to Dan. "Mister Lymon, I know you were a juror at the Barkley Malone trial and I also know you were quite upset about the decision. More specifically, I understand you were restrained from attacking Nicole Brezinski."

Lymon swiped his forehead with the towel he had carried with him. "I wasn't the only one. She was an obstinate bitch. Malone was as guilty as O.J. Simpson."

"Are you aware Nicole Brezinski is dead?"

"I am. I suspected someone would be talking to me."

"What made you think that?"

"Come on. You know I was a juror who wasn't exactly thrilled with her."

Dan nodded. "You're right. I know you tried to get at her."

"I was as pissed as anyone, but I never touched her, nor would I."

The detective checked Lymon's demeanor. "Just for the sake of documentation, do you mind telling me where you were on September third, the night her life ended?"

"I remember. Me and Becky were in Boston."

"Is Becky your wife?"

Lymon smiled widely. "Girlfriend. She lives with me. Wait a

minute. I have pictures on my phone." He then showed Dan his proof. "We were in Boston. Here's Quincy Market."

"I recognize it. Great town. Although I'm a Yankees fan, I still like it. Actually went to Fenway once with my kids."

"It's kind of a getaway for us. Ever taken a Duck Tour?"

"No. It's on my agenda." Satisfied with the man's answers and his calm demeanor, Dan didn't detect any vindictiveness or bad vibe. He kept the questioning short, believing Lymon had nothing to do with Nicole's death. "I see you have a busy gym."

"Yeah. I have to get back to work."

"Right, By the way, how much weight is he lifting? Is it more than two-fifty?"

"Hey, I'm good for two-seventy, he's bucking three."

"Thanks. You won't find me here soon."

Dan exited the building, went to his car and crossed Lymon off his list. *One down. The Hilton is next.*

▲

The ten-floor Hilton hotel was located a few blocks from the busy Civic Center. Not too far away were three insurance giants, restaurants, and shopping.

The refurbished lobby had a huge chandelier hanging from the ceiling in the middle of the room. The check-in counter was to his right and a bar was further down the hall to the left of the elevators and restrooms. He spotted a man who was wearing a red and white uniform and speaking with a male and female, apparent guests. He handed them a piece of paper and Dan approached the concierge as the couple walked away. The name affixed to the uniform told the detective who the male was. "Mister Porter."

The concierge acknowledged Dan's presence. "May I help you?"

"I'm Detective Dan Shields, Hartford Police. I'd like to talk with you for a few minutes."

Porter furrowed his brows. "What is this about?"

"The Barkley Malone trial."

"I'm on duty, I can't leave."

"Can you get permission to step away for a few minutes?"

Porter directed the detective to the check-in counter. "Ask the heavyset man over there. He's my manager."

Dan wandered over to the boss and after explaining the reason for his visit, he received permission and informed Porter, "It's okay. How about going to the lounge? It looks pretty empty."

"Okay, but I don't understand. I haven't done anything."

"But you were a juror at the Barkley Malone trial." Dan led Porter to a booth in the far corner. Sitting opposite each other, Dan started lightly. "How long have you been working here?"

"Five years. I was here when it was the Sheraton."

There was no ring on his finger. "Are you married?"

"Not anymore, not for the past three years. My ex has custody of our six-year-old son."

Getting down to the subject at hand, Dan returned to the Barkley Malone trial. "I understand you were extremely vehement during deliberations, quite angry."

Porter bowed his head. "I wasn't the only one, and yes, I sort of blew off steam. Look, I know Nicole Brezinski stuck to her guns and the trial resulted in a hung jury. The carousel isn't far from here. You don't think I had anything to do with her death, do you?"

"I didn't say or imply you did. Tell me where you were that evening?"

"I had my son for the entire weekend and we went to Pizza Hut and the movies, even played miniature golf."

"It sounds like you enjoyed your time with him. What's his name?"

"Benji. He's in first grade and a good kid."

"Is there anything else you can tell me about the trial deliberations? Think about it."

The hotel employee was quiet and appeared to be doing a bit of soul searching. "Well, to me it looked like if anyone thought to inflict harm on her, Jordan Lymon could have."

Dan had already ruled him out, but asked, "In your opinion, would you say he was angry enough to have murdered her?"

"I don't know. He got awfully close to her and had to be pulled back by two of us and the bailiff."

Porter's remark gave Dan a reason to give Lymon a second thought.

He excused Porter and as he left the hotel, he began to question his interview with Jordan Lymon. *Anyone can have photos of Quincy Market on their phone.*

Two down and one to go. The magic store wasn't too far from where Dan was and he was in awe when he entered the shop. There were posters hung all over the store of Houdini, David Copperfield, and other magicians. He saw a straitjacket and a counter full of devices which he had no idea what they did. The gentleman who greeted him was Lamont Charles and he wore a quirky, tall, clown-like red, blue and white hat on his head. "How are you today?" he asked.

"I'm fine. You look happy."

"I'm always happy."

Dan observed the man's strained walk, and the silver-handled cane on which he was leaning. "Are you Lamont Charles?"

"That's me."

"I'm Detective Dan Shields. I understand you were an alternate juror at the Barkley Malone trial."

"I sure was. The guy was guilty. I guess you're here because the young lady who caused the hung jury died at the carousel."

"Yes, I am. I'm checking with all the jurors and alternates to find out if they, you noticed anything out of the ordinary that may lead someone to having her killed."

"The Uber driver's father was a nutcase and had to be forcefully restrained and taken out after the verdict was announced."

"I'm aware of that." *I know this guy had nothing to do with her demise. His walking is impaired and he seems like a decent guy.* Dan took notice of the glass-enclosed cases that were filled with gimmicky devices. "I've never seen so many supplies that are not what they seem to be."

"I wouldn't put it that way. It's how you use them. See those handcuffs? Want to buy a pair? I bet you can't get out of them."

"I suppose you have to know the trick."

"Good thinking."

Dan smirked and displayed the cuffs on his belt loop. "I know you can't get out of these. Would you like to try?"

"No thanks. I'll stick to mine."

Dan saluted the man as he left. "You have a nice day."

▲

There was one detail Dan had to check out. He opened the juror data file on his desk and phoned the gymnasium, again speaking with Jordan Lymon. "I hate to bother you so soon. I am in the process of completing my report and in order finish it, would you mind telling me where you stayed when you and your girlfriend were in Boston?"

"Why are you asking?"

"It's documentation. I won't bother you again."

"We stayed at the Colonnade. Came home the next day."

"What is her name again?"

"Becky."

113

"Thanks. I'll let you get back to your job."

In order to cover all his bases, the detective phoned the Colonnade, and a hotel employee verified that Lymon and Becky had stayed there on the date in question.

Dan held the phone receiver for a moment before placing it back on its stand. *That's that with him.* The detective crossed Lymon's name off the suspect list as well as those of Porter and Charles.

Chapter 23

Dan's house was unusually quiet when he got home. He'd seen his wife's car in the garage and wondered where she and the kids were. There was a note on the refrigerator. "Kids have no school tomorrow. They are at Zach and Alex's house for a sleepover."

"Hon?" he yelled.

There was no answer and he checked the entire downstairs. Then he heard low pitched music coming from upstairs and yelled again. "Are you up there?"

"I am. I have a new outfit I want to show you."

"How much is this one?"

"You'll see. I have no doubt you will like it."

He marched upstairs, entered the bedroom and stopped in his tracks. Gaping at the short pink negligee Phyllis had on, he became transfixed, studying the woman he loved.

"Wake up and go shower," she ordered. "I already did."

"Some outfit. Beautiful." He held her in his arms, feeling her warm body against his as he kissed her and groped her breasts.

"Go." She slid under the covers as Dan made his way to the bathroom and showered. He returned with a towel wrapped around his waist and grinned as he rolled the covers off her and threw the towel on a chair before engaging in hot, steamy intercourse.

Afterwards they snuggled and both wore huge smiles. Phyllis

stroked his hair. "I haven't seen you this relaxed in a while," she said.

He kissed her. "I guess you know what I needed."

She continued to stroke his hair. "We both needed."

"How about sending the kids away overnight more often?"

Phyllis shoved her feet into her slippers and threw on a white bathrobe. "Hungry?"

"You know how to work up an appetite." Dan grabbed a pair of sweats from his closet. "Don't start without me."

Phyllis proceeded to the kitchen where she took the food she had prepared out of the refrigerator and heated it up. Dan sat at the table and they enjoyed a small meal. Afterward, she cleaned up and as she stood at the sink with the water running and her back to him, he put his arms around her robe and rubbed against her backside. It was obvious he was ready for an encore. "How about dessert?"

She giddily turned to him. "What did you have in mind? "Coffee, tea, or me?"

He kissed her and unlaced the robe. "Let's start with you."

Chapter 24

Dan had eliminated three suspects: Lymon, Porter, and Charles. Nicole Brzezinski's death burned like a campfire that would not go out.

Armed with the startling revelation that she had been pregnant and that she had died of a heart attack, Dan turned his attention to Jeff Karas.

The urgency to chat with him amped up. He knew the pilot had a London flight scheduled and hoped it had not departed yet. *Here I go. If he has left, I could be out of luck and may have to wait.*

Surprisingly, the pilot picked up on the first ring, but his voice was competing with background noise. "Where are you?" Dan asked.

"I'm at O'Hare inside the private lounge."

"Can you talk?"

"Hold on." A few seconds later, Karas replied, "This is better. I'm flying out soon to London."

"When we last spoke, you told me a few things about you and Nicole. A couple of facts have come to light and I wondered if you knew about them. First, did you know she was pregnant?"

"Pregnant? No."

"According to the pathologist she was four to five weeks along. My question is, could you have been the father of the unborn child?"

"Holy smithereens. I guess it's possible, but I know she slept around."

"One other thing. She died of a heart attack. Were you aware of any heart issues?"

"She seemed fine to me."

What a callous response. No emotion, no empathy.

"How often did Nicole fly with you?"

"I don't know."

He knows but won't say. "What about Alicia?"

"She has been with me, and Nicole."

"How often do you fly?"

"Usually, two to three times a week. Thirty-two hours max."

"I have to ask you this. Was Nicole the only flight attendant you slept with?"

"I don't think that is any of your business."

Dan heard the pilot's phone beep. "Detective, I have to go. I'm being paged to go to my aircraft."

"Do me a favor. Call me back when you can."

"I will."

I'm sure he knew she was pregnant with his baby and he still displayed no emotion. There is definitely more to his relationship with her as well as with the other flight attendants.

Dan wrestled with whether to call Alicia Greenstein or Stella Passante next. He punched in Alicia's number, but his call went unanswered. *Great, she isn't answering and her voicemail is full. One down.* He moved on, phoned Stella and she answered.

"Detective, I'm at work."

"May we talk?"

"Not really, the only reason I picked up is because I am on break for another five minutes and recognized your call."

"When is a better time for me to get in touch with you? I have new information about Nicole I'd like to share in person. Is tonight okay?"

"Well, I guess. I'll be home after four-thirty but have to leave a while later."

"Fine, I'll stop by then."

▲

Dan was a mile and a half from home and drove down Mountain Road. When he arrived at Stella's, he saw her car as well as a red vehicle parked next to it. He didn't have to ring the doorbell since a shapely young woman with medium-length brunette hair opened the door. "Come in. I'm Chelsea. Stella told me you were coming." The friendly hostess led Dan into the living room. "I'll get her."

"Thank you. Do you live here?"

"At times."

Stella joined them. "Hi, Detective. I see you've met Chelsea."

"You forgot to tell me about her."

Indeed, he had met another good-looking young woman. Stella wore her uniform and Chelsea had on dark blue jeans and a casual blouse. They all made themselves comfortable and Dan addressed Chelsea, "May I ask your last name?"

"Maresca."

"Thank you. Are you a flight attendant too?"

"I am."

"Were you at the Barkley Malone trial?"

"No, I was working."

"Did you, Alicia and Nicole often fly together?"

"At times. Ariel as well."

Dan heard another new name. Ariel. "Is she also a flight attendant?"

Chelsea replied, "Yes."

"And her last name is?"

"Adams."

Stella crossed her legs. "You said there are new revelations about Nicole?"

"There are. Nicole was about four weeks pregnant. Were you aware of that?"

Both women gasped. "Pregnant?" Stella exclaimed.

"Jeff Karas claims he had no knowledge of that either. And we also know Nicole died of a heart attack. Were either of you aware of any heart issues she had?"

"No. I never would have guessed it," Stella said.

"Me neither," Chelsea added.

"About Karas. He claims he was not her boyfriend, but he has slept with her several times. He also alleges she slept with lot of other guys."

Both women were silent. Chelsea's phone beeped and she read the message. "Oh, I almost forgot. I have a dinner date. Excuse me, I have to change."

Chelsea left the room and Dan noticed a photo on the table next to Stella. "That's a nice picture."

"That's from Jeff's birthday party a while ago. We're all in it."

"So I assume the one with his arms around Nicole is Jeff. Who are the other guys in the background?"

"Party guests."

"Where was the party?"

"A hotel. I forgot the name."

Ten minutes later, Chelsea returned. When she did, her appeal rose to a higher number on Dan's internal attractiveness meter. She wore a tight-fitting pair of black slacks and a white blouse. Her hair was straight and shiny and her lips wore a sultry shade of pink. Dan rose. "I may have parked behind you."

She peeked through the small window to the right of the front door. "We're fine. I can get out."

Stella got up. "Do you mind? I have to change. I'm going to the movies with a friend."

While Stella was away, Dan saw a curious item on the table next to him. A green notebook with dollar signs on the outside. He opened it and gasped as he read it. *Really? Is this what I think it is? Holy shit. Guy's names, dates, and dollar amounts and an S next to some and a C next to others. A few pages back he discovered the letter N in a few places. Hookers?* He quickly closed it and placed it back where it was.

Freshened up, Stella returned and sat again. Dan asked, "Do you suppose I can have a copy of that picture?"

"Actually, I have one in the credenza." She retrieved it and handed it to him.

"Thank you." He placed it in his pocket. "May I use your bathroom? I had too much coffee earlier."

Stella pointed to a door off the living room.

The apparent journal intrigued him. He entered the bathroom and closed the door. The scent of hairspray and perfume surrounded him.

Although he had used the excuse of needing to pee, he did not, but he flushed the toilet. Over the sink was a mirrored medicine cabinet so he opened it. He saw no evidence of drugs, only normal things like aspirin and feminine products, but it was the top shelf that caught his attention. An entire row of condoms, one opened box and ten sealed. *These along with the journal give new meaning to frequent flyer.* Glancing down, he spied an unopened gold foil wrapper on the floor next to the wastebasket, which contained an empty Trojan box. He picked up the dropped packet and tucked it into his pocket. *So, they work for Delta and make extra money turning tricks. I saw no indication that Alicia or Ariel are involved, but they don't live here. Could they be? And what about Karas?"*

Dan went back to the living room and continued questioning

Stella. "Tell me more about Karas and his birthday party. Was there a cake and dancing?"

"We had a good time."

"Were you all staying there?"

"Why does that matter?"

"It doesn't. I'm glad it was successful. Karas told me there were stays at other hotels due to layovers where he and flight attendants spent a few nights. It was during one of those times when he and Nicole first hooked up."

Stella retrieved a cigarette from a pack on the coffee table, lit it and took a puff.

He looked directly into her eyes. "Your pilot friend also admitted to having sex with other flight attendants too. Did he mean you as well?"

Stella was noticeably uncomfortable with Dan's question and she shifted her body while gazing at the statue of the veiled Virgin Mary on the mantel.

Dan watched her as she stared at the statue and she uttered, "Isn't it crazy how she never had sex but became pregnant?"

"I know you can tell her what she was missing. You did sleep with the pilot, didn't you?"

Stella blushed. "The answer is yes. He may be a lot younger. There is no law about sleeping with a younger guy is there?"

Dan digested her reaction while Stella crossed her legs again. He focused on her antsy squirming as she glanced at her phone. "I have to be at my friend's house soon. May I see you out?"

Dan held the photo she had given him and tossed the trojan packet at her. "I surmise Chelsea dropped this. I picked it up from the bathroom floor. I hope you enjoy the movie. I can see myself out."

Dan left her place with a new perspective that led him to an unexpected conclusion as to who and what the pilot and flight attendants were involved in.

He drove toward home. *Sounds like Jeff Karas is screwing them all. And it sure appeared Chelsea was on her way to fulfill a service call, and Stella is likely to be on her way to do the same.*

Chapter 25

Scotty and Bev were no closer to solving the arson murder of Tamara Ashford than before. As the recently promoted Dan carried a mug of coffee into his cubicle, and then took a drink, Scotty tapped him on the shoulder. "Marcus Garfield, as we know him, is employed by Macy's and his story about working the night of the fire checks out. However, mysteriously two days ago, he left early and now no one seems to have seen him since. No phone calls either."

"I knew he couldn't be trusted."

Bev joined them. "And his parole officer, Catalina Montero, says she has no problem with the alias as long as he reports regularly and stays out of trouble, which he has done so far. We're going now to see if we can find him, starting with his residence." Bev didn't wait for Dan to object and adamantly snarled, "And this time you're staying here. Be careful. Don't spill the coffee."

The assertive Bev and Scotty walked toward the exit while Dan absorbed her assertation. Then he said, "Wait." Dan pointed to the plants Syms left behind. "Have you guys watered the bonsais?"

Bev replied, "Yes. This may be a homicide unit, but I don't intend these trees to become victims."

Dan took another sip of his coffee and nodded. "As Syms would say, get out of here."

Luke frowned. "You do sound like him."

As Scotty and Bev left, Mal unzipped his jacket and hung it over the back of his chair. "I was downstairs with Dixon. He says they lost contact with Cabrera about an hour before he was killed. Dixon can't answer why the black-and-white was in front of the church. He has seen the videos and we know the assassin's car is hard to make. It's likely stolen."

Dan asked, "Anyone inspect the cruiser? I know it was bloody as hell, but was anything unusual in it?"

"Shit, I'm sure it's been cleaned up by now," Luke said. "We'll see if we can check it out."

Dan's phone was in his hand so he decided to call Alicia Greenstein and was relieved when she answered. "Hi, Alicia. How are you doing?"

"I'm okay."

"I tried to call you, but I couldn't leave a message. I'm curious about something you omitted telling me when I visited you. I was at Stella Passante's and spoke with her and Chelsea. You never mentioned her."

"I forgot."

"You and Stella somehow also forgot to mention your other friend, Ariel Adams." Dan picked up his almost-empty mug. "Alicia, I spoke with Karas but have not been able to see him. He did say he was in Chicago and is on his way to London. Do you know when you will be with him again?"

"Not really, it depends on our schedules."

The bothered detective had something else on his mind that he had to probe. The sex club. He decided to confront Alicia, prefacing his query with a request. "Please be honest with me. This may be an embarrassing question. Stella admitted sleeping with Karas and we know Nicole did. I suspect they aren't the only ones."

Alicia's tone became a tad hostile. "What are you getting at?"

"Alicia, I am asking you to be honest with me. When I was at

Stella's, Chelsea received a phone call and soon after she dolled herself up and left to go on what she said was a date. I have a feeling I know where she was going. I saw a green notebook, a journal that was on an end table and read it. There were notations that included men's names and other things such as dates, dollar amounts and initials beside their names. I think you know what I am talking about. Stella had to leave a while later and I don't buy her story about going to a movie. I also used her bathroom. Inside the medicine cabinet were more condoms than I could count."

Alicia sheepishly asked, "Um, what exactly are you insinuating?"

"Tell me you don't have a similar journal."

She was silent.

"Let's be honest, Alicia. I know Stella and Nicole are not the only flight attendants Jeff Karas has been intimate with. I also have a picture from a party he had and all you girls were there. It was taken at a hotel and I have a feeling some of the men were paying customers. Am I right?"

She kept mum so Dan paused. "Before you speak, know that I am sure you ladies made a few bucks at the birthday party. Alicia, again, please be honest with me."

"And if we did?"

"Please understand, I am trying to find out who is responsible for Nicole's death. I know you are not and I am not interested in busting any of you for solicitation."

Dead air was something Dan was used to, especially when he hit a nerve. Alicia didn't speak right away, then muttered, "You can believe what you want."

"Fair enough. Is he arranging hookups?" A deathly silence filled the line. "Alicia, answer me."

Suddenly, she cut off the conversation, "Detective, I have to leave. It was nice talking with you."

Although Alicia had ended the call abruptly, Dan had confirmed in his own mind, that Karas and all the women were involved in second jobs. *What I don't know and need to find out is whether the flight attendants are willfully engaged or were they somehow lured into selling their bodies? The money must be awfully good.*

Dan's head swirled with conflict. He still couldn't definitively say Nicole's death was murder, but he now knew the notation on her back was truthful and he had to continue his investigation.

He made another phone call, hoping to speak with Syms. Ring after ring, the call to the captain's cell went unanswered. The detective went to plan B and tried Sym's home phone but was met with the same results. *Pick it up, pick up the phone, you sad clown.*

Having failed to reach his ex-boss, Dan made his way upstairs to see Hardison, stumbling on one of the steps as his head was elsewhere. Dan limped into the chief's quarters. "What happened to you?" Hardison asked as the detective rubbed his shin.

"Nothing. I slipped on the stairs. I tried to call Syms, but his phones are not being answered."

"I know. You realize the last thing he needs right now is for us to bother him. I am sure he really needs the space. Leave him be. Maybe time off is all he really needs."

"You might be right. I'll back off."

"Yeah. I have a strong feeling he will be back. Leave him be. He may even contact you or me at some point."

Bags underneath the chief's eyes displayed frustration and tiredness. Dan was sure his own face showed the same signs. "One thing he's right about is the unprecedented stress level in all of us."

"I know," the chief agreed. "We're stuck and have to deal with crime with what we have. I am still on the mayor's ass to obtain money for new hires."

"Right. I'll see you later."

Dan landed back inside his cubicle and contemplated whether or not to make an unannounced visit to Sym's home. It was quiet in the squad room until Scotty and Bev entered. Appearing dejected, Scotty excused himself and went to the men's room. Bev sat next to Dan. "Garfield is gone?"

"What do you mean, disappeared?"

"Yes. The guy upstairs was not exactly friendly. He claims not to have seen Garfield in several days. We knew he hadn't been to work, but now he could be anywhere."

Dan pursed his lips. "Damn it. Dead is a possibility."

Scotty returned. "The asshole with the dog, Killer, was roaming the street. Same shit. He and the other idiots who joined them denied seeing Garfield. I didn't expect an honest answer."

Chapter 26

Karas, the elusive pilot was hard to pin down, although obtaining his flight schedule from Delta might tell the detective a few things, including when Karas would be flying into Bradley.

Dan sensed Alicia Greenstein, with pressured persistence, may reveal what he wanted to know about the service girl operation. *It's one thing to arrest Karas and shut the prostitution down. It's quite another thing to link him to Nicole's death. I'm positive he knew Nicole was carrying his baby. Did she threaten to quit after the child was born, or did he perceive she would not be as useful to his operation as before? Did he get rid of her?*

Karas crawled underneath Dan's skin and he had to be reeled in, but with the pilot dodging him, Dan turned his attention to the sodomization of Nicole. He sought to interview three people who had attended the Barkley Malone trial. The Sandovar's surely had deep resentment for Nicole: Alejandro, Merriel, and Elijah may well have resented her, but the detective's gut told him they had nothing to do with her death. Even so, an interview with the family could conceivably uncover a lead.

Referencing a sticky note with the Sandovar's number on it, he called their home. A woman answered and Dan identified himself before he asked, "Mrs. Sandovar?"

"Yes."

"I'm sorry about your son Emilio. I don't know if you, your husband or your son Elijah may be able to help me. I would like to ask you all a few questions about the Barkley Malone trial. When would be a good time to visit your home?"

"Hold on a second, please."

Dan waited as he heard her appealing to her husband for consent. Then the detective received an answer. "Is later this morning good for you?"

"It is. I have your address, Can you verify it?" He read what he had and Merriel acknowledged it. Then he tore the piece of paper off the pad he'd written the address on and tucked it into his shirt pocket. As he strode toward the exit, he told Scotty and Bev, "I'm heading out to interview the Sandovars."

Luke stopped him. "Dan, guess what? Dixon told us the woman at the funeral, Cabrera's wife, left him nearly a year ago. They were not divorced and she lost contact with him at least six months ago. They had no children. I'm thinking some kind of drug deal may have been going down and it went wrong. Garcia is the head of the gang unit and I want him to level with us."

"What did Dixon say?"

"He said Cabrera had taken some time off to deal with his marriage situation but had no idea that the patrolman and Garcia may have laid out a plan that Dixon did not know about. And the car was examined. Forensics found nothing but glass and blood."

"Stay on it," Dan said. As he was ready to leave, his cell rang and he winced, noting the caller ID. *Sasser, Damn Sasser.* Dan answered, "Hey pal, what's new?"

"Funny you should ask. You know your boys made bail, right?"

"I knew they would. Hampton's sister was going to put up the money. She's apparently the sane one in the family." Dan knew what was coming next but hoped he was wrong.

"So, you owe me lunch and a new barbecue spot opened not far from me called Black Bears."

"Great. Can we go somewhere else?"

"Hell no, man. Barbecue. Ribs to die for."

"For you to enjoy. For me to literally die."

"Come on, you ain't gone vegan or something, have you?"

"No. but you know that smoked food makes me sick."

"Okay, okay. You can pick a place but no vegan crap. I ain't eatin' grass like cows and goats, or fake meat. My doctor says I'm healthy as a horse."

"You do kind of resemble one."

"Funny. How about picking me up later?"

"Not today. I'm on my way to talk with the Sandovars. Remember them?"

"Damn right."

"How's tomorrow?"

"Let me see my calendar." Dan waited a few seconds. "I'm free. Chantel and I will be waiting for you."

"Great, Sass. I can't wait to see Chantel. Bye." He shook his head as he headed to his car. *Sasser, a lunch from hell.*

Chapter 27

Arriving at the Sandovar residence, Merriel greeted Dan at the door of the cream-colored colonial accented with crimson shutters. She was no more than five-two and had her dark hair tied back in a bun. "Come in."

"Thank you."

"My husband is watching TV." She accompanied Dan into the den, where the forty-two-inch television was tuned into *The Price Is Right*. Alejandro snored away in his La-Z-Boy rocker with a dozing dachshund in his lap. She nudged her husband and he opened his eyes.

He flexed his brows and looked up at Dan. "Oh, hi, Detective."

"Hello, Mister Sandovar."

Alejandro grabbed the remote and clicked the off button while the yawning pet leapt to the carpet. "I'm sorry," the waking man said.

"Thank you for allowing me into your home. I'd like to speak with you about the Barkley Malone trial. First off, I'm sorry about the loss of your son."

"Thank you again," Merriel somberly said.

Dan waited a few seconds. "I realize the verdict did not go as you, or frankly, the state's attorneys assumed it would."

Alejandro scowled. "No, it didn't."

Dan's nose caught a familiar scent and he spotted an ashtray filled with cigarette butts on the small table next to Alejandro's chair. An open pack of Newports was there as well as a book of matches. Veins throbbed in Alejandro's neck and anger seemed to fill his entire body. "Who the hell did that bitch think she was? Malone's girlfriend?"

Dan paused to let the stewing man settle down. "No, I can't say she even knew him."

Alejandro gasped and without hesitation, raised his voice. "Good! She deserves to be dead! She let a killer go."

Merriel put her hands on his shoulders. "Calm down. Emilio didn't deserve to die and neither does anyone else."

"She did."

Alejandro was still agitated. Merriel reached for his hand, and he yanked it away. "Stop," she strongly urged him.

Dan waited a few seconds for the father to calm himself, and then he addressed both parents. "When did you first learn her name? Nicole Brezinski?"

Merriel answered, "When we saw the news."

Knowing that Alejandro had to be restrained when the verdict was announced, Dan asked, "Tell me about it?"

"I wanted to kill the bastard," Alejandro said. "They hauled me out before the jury was polled."

Dan, who had a habit of eyeing photos, noticed a row of family pictures that rested on the middle shelf of the bookcase that was against the wall opposite him. "Are those your sons?"

Merriel smiled. "My aunt, uncle, Emilio and Elijah."

"Nice-looking family. Which one is Emilio?"

"Emilio is next to my aunt on the right and Elijah is on the other side of her."

Dan thought, *Those boys could pass for twins, although the ear jewelry sets Elijah apart.*

"Do you mind telling me about Emilio?"

Merriel said, "Uber was part-time. Emilio worked as a veterinary assistant and decided to Uber to supplement his income."

"And Elijah. What about him?"

Alejandro gave Dan a firm and caustic answer, "Leave him alone. He's been through enough."

Appealing to the hostile man's wife, Dan sought her assent. "I merely want to ask Elijah a few questions to complete my documentation."

She glanced at her husband, who was silent and Dan asked, "Where does Elijah work?"

Merriel replied, "He's in his last year at Central, and lives with a roommate on campus. And to make some money, he Ubers like Emilio did."

Dan referred back to the family photos and addressed Merriel, "Would it be alright if I had a photo of the boys? They look so much alike."

"Elijah is a year younger." She opened a photo album from the bookcase, shuffled through a few pages and then slid a recent picture out, handing it to Dan.

"Thank you." He set it in his pocket behind his EpiPen. *They have every right to be upset, but they are not killers and didn't even know Nicole's name until they watched the news. I see no reason to continue and further bring up evil memories.* "Again, thank you for allowing me into your home. If I need to speak with you again, may I?'

"Yes," Merriel answered.

Sounding like his favorite TV detective, Columbo, Dan came to a halt. "Oh, one more thing. Can you give me Elijah's cell number?" Merriel recited it and Dan wrote it on his pad.

"Oh. And another thing. What is his roommate's name?"

Merriel replied, "We've met him a couple of times. Nice boy.

He's from Spain. Joaquin Ruiz. Elijah is envious of his smart roommate's perfect GPA."

"Thank you again. This time I'm really leaving."

In his car, Dan studied the photograph and zeroed in on what he had noticed earlier. *Those boys really could pass for twins.*

Dan attempted to touch base with the college student, but as usual he was unsuccessful and the call went straight to voicemail, so he left a detailed message.

Chapter 28

The next morning, Dan was pleased when Elijah Sandovar returned his call. "Thank you for getting in touch with me."

"I understand you spoke with my mom and dad."

"I did and was informed that you are a senior at Central and have a super-smart roommate."

"Yeah."

"I want to speak with you about the Barkley Malone trial. My preference is to discuss this in person. Are you able to drive to the Hartford police station?"

"Which one?"

"The main facility, downtown."

"I have a late class this afternoon, but I can be there in a little while."

"Great, the visitor lot is in front of the building. Enter through the sliding door and tell whoever is at the reception area that you are here to see me. I'll come get you."

"Okay."

That went well. I can't wait to meet this young man.

Approximately seventy minutes later, Dan was informed that a visitor was waiting in the lobby, so the detective went downstairs to welcome him.

There he was, wearing a school sweatshirt and an orange and

black Orioles cap. The ear adornment dangled from his left lobe. They shook hands. "It doesn't seem likely that we are going to get along," Dan joked. "I have a Yankees mug on my desk."

The young man laughed and they headed upstairs to the next floor. Knowing the squad room was empty, Dan thought interviewing his visitor alone was not a good idea, so the detective escorted Elijah toward Dixon's quarters. They were greeted in the corridor by Train. "Dan, if you're looking for Dixon, good luck. I don't know where he is."

The detective introduced Elijah to the police officer. "We're going to have a chat and I want to use the room here. No one is upstairs."

"Be my guest."

Dan instructed Elijah to go inside and have a seat while the detective turned to Train and said, "Do me a favor and watch the closed circuit."

"You got it."

Dan joined the student and shut the door. Elijah's cap was resting on the table's restraint bar. The detective was again struck by the young man's remarkable resemblance to Emilio. "I mentioned Barkley Malone. By the way, he is not a free man and will stand trial again for slaying your brother."

"I realize he will, but he should have been convicted. If it wasn't for her."

Dan nodded. "Her. I assume you know that Nicole Brezinski, Lady Godiva, was the juror who voted to not convict Malone."

He bobbed his head back. "No. I didn't. What happened?"

"We're trying to figure that out. Can you tell me how you reacted when the mistrial was announced?"

Elijah's head swerved from left to right. "I wasn't there. Mom and Dad were."

"Were you in school?"

"No. I was there when the trial began but I got an anxiety attack and left the room. I never went back. I went home."

"Listen, your parents informed me you drive for Uber, as Emilio did."

"Yeah, I juggle it with my schooling, and sometimes he got calls that he couldn't tend to, so I would sub for him when I could. His vet job kept him busy. I even had to borrow his car a few times because mine isn't that reliable."

Elijah's comments set off thoughts in Dan's mind and he wanted to ease into inquiring more about the Uber job, so he slyly took his next comment sideways, before pursuing the subject. "How do you suppose I would look in an Orioles hat?"

"Like an old Cal Ripken."

Dan chuckled. "I think of myself as more of a Mickey Mantle. Are you thirsty?"

"I'm okay."

The detective began to pursue his perception. "Is the airport a popular destination?"

"Oh, yeah."

"As you know, Malone followed your brother from there to home." Dan bowed his head. "I'm sorry to bring it up again." *He's a dead ringer for Emilio.* "What kind of car did Emilio have?"

"A Subaru Forester."

"So, at times you used it to take fares to or from places?"

"Yeah. Like I said, my car isn't as reliable as his and sometimes he let me use the Subaru."

Dan's suspicions about the use of Emilo's car and Elijah's driving it were about to surface. The detective commented, "Nice hair, I bet a lot of coeds like it?"

Elijah smiled, but did not speak.

"I bet you have a few girlfriends."

Elijah grinned, "A couple."

"I bet Emilio had a few, too."

The grin gave way to a grimace. "Not exactly. Emilio was gay."

Their likeness is really beginning to bother me. Emilio would not have sodomized Nicole Brezinski, but this guy certainly could have.

Staying calm to this point, Dan held steady and stared into his visitor's eyes. "What did you say?"

"Emilio was gay."

Dan allowed himself to yield to his inner demon, leaned forward, and held back what he was almost sure. *Son of a bitch. He raped Nicole, not his dead brother.*

"Did you say you had no idea who Nicole Brezinski was?"

Elijah squirmed. "I didn't."

Dan stared at him. *I'm sure he did know who Nicole Brezinski was. He recognized her at the trial and that's why he exited the courtroom.*

The detective asked, "Why was it again you left the courtroom?"

"I told you, I felt sick. I Had an anxiety attack."

The sleuth went into attack mode by ramping up his voice and staring into Elijah's eyes. "Sick? Or did you become ill when you recognized Nicole Brezinski?" He moved closer to the young man. "You bolted the courtroom because you saw the woman you assaulted. Didn't you?"

Elijah squirmed and shouted, "What are you talking about?"

Dan raised his voice. "You heard me. You picked her up at the airport in Emilio's car and forced your way into her house and sexually assaulted her, didn't you? Not Emilio."

Elijah's face was red as a beet and he shouted, "I don't know what you're talking about." He jumped up and grabbed his cap. "I'm outta here."

Dan stood in front of his prey and pulled out a photo of Nicole's naked body that was atop the carousel horse. "Take a look at this."

The student secured his cap onto his head and glanced at the photo. "Hell no. I had nothing to do with her."

Bocking his target, Dan railed at him. "You would like to have seen her die after the trial, wouldn't you?"

Elijah yanked open the door and bolted from the room. "Hold up!" Dan yelled. "Officer Jackson will see you out."

After completing his chore, Train placed his hands on his hips and cringed as he faced Dan. "That sure changed fast from nicey-nice to leave my ass alone."

"It did, but unless I'm wrong, he's the one who sexually assaulted Nicole Brezinski, not his brother Emilio. And Elijah does have a hell of a motive to want her dead."

"And she thought Emilio was the one who molested her. Wow."

"I'm sure he'll have a rocky night."

CHAPTER 29

Dan stewed over yesterday's agonizing chat with Elijah Sandovar. There was no question in his mind, Emilio's brother was Nicole Brezinski's attacker. Elijah Sandovar was now high on the detective's radar. *Lincoln is going to love this.*

The state's attorney answered his phone. "Good morning, Dan."

"Good morning. Are you busy?"

"I'm always busy."

"I know what you mean. Can I stop in?"

"What have you learned?"

"That's what I want to talk to you about. Do you have court today?"

"No. I'll be here all morning."

"I'll be right there."

⬥

Once inside Lincoln's office, Dan took a seat, placed a notepad on the corner of the attorney's desk and said, "I'm sure you will find this interesting. I've spoken with a few people since I was last here. For starters, a flight attendant named Alicia Greenstein owns a condo and she was Nicole Brezinski's last roommate. Nicole's previous residence was with co-worker Stella Passante in Suffield and here's where it gets interesting. Stella has a new boarder named

Chelsea Maresca, another Delta flight attendant. I conversed with each of them and learned that there is yet another flight attendant named Ariel Adams who completes the foursome. Her I haven't met. Are you with me so far?"

"I am."

"Okay. I also chatted with Jeff Karas, a Delta pilot and the girls claim that he was Nicole's boyfriend, but he doesn't quite agree."

"Where the heck are you going with all this?"

"Sit back. Apparently the inked word on Lady Godiva's back, 'whore,' was not exactly false. It seems that she, Alicia Greenstein, Stella Passante, Chelsea Maresca, and it is likely that Ariel Adams, are all engaged in a prostitution business. As I said, they are all flight attendants with Delta and Karas is more than likely their pimp. I'm sure he's slept with all the women."

"How does this connect with Nicole Brezinski's death?"

"I don't know."

Lincoln leaned forward. "Why do you suppose Nicole Brezinski was singled out and appears to have been killed?"

"You raise a question I have thought about all along. I know she was murdered, but how? The why is a different story. Here's a thought. Arnstein said she was pregnant and even though Karas won't admit it, I believe he was the sperm donor and he claims he didn't know she was with child. He avers that their relationship was casual and I didn't like the pilot's demeanor. To me, he was way too calm and not as upset by her death as one would have thought. It's possible that because of the pregnancy, she was going to be out of service for a while, maybe forever. She may have told him she was done and he didn't like her intent because her body would be useless to him as a money producer. There is no apparent explanation for how she ended up at the carousel, let alone naked. And, like I've said before, I'm sure she didn't walk into that carousel nude."

"What about the Uber driver, Emilio Sandovar?"

"Good question. I'm getting to him. As far as prostitution is concerned, even if I try to bring a charge against Karas and the girls, I have no evidence that he killed Nicole. I also hate to ponder the thought, but maybe her death had nothing to do with him." Reaching into his pocket, Dan positioned the photo he had obtained that included Emilio and Elijah Sandovar on Lincoln's desk. "Elijah is the one with the earring."

"Where did you get this?"

"At the Sandovar residence. Merriel gave it to me. Those boys could double for each other. Emilio is a year older. Elijah is a senior at Central and he too is a part-time Uber driver who occasionally borrowed Emilio's car to pick up fares."

"What are you telling me?"

"I'm telling you, even though Elijah used his brother's car, Emilio's photo and first name were visible to passengers on the app. Nicole thought Emilio was her driver, but it was Elijah and she didn't think anything of the earring. Now comes the interesting part. Emilio was gay. He wouldn't have raped Nicole. Elijah is straight and I am sure he sexually attacked her. I interrogated him and he turned fifty shades of red when I accused him of it, especially after I showed him Nicole's picture, the naked one from the crime scene. It's possible that he killed her. Rape is a definite. I'm dead right on this one. If she had remained alive, she may have realized she made a mistake and it was Emilio's brother who had molested her."

"Hold it. What if you are dead wrong?"

"I know I am not. The other strange thing is that Elijah was at the trial when it began, but he abruptly left the courtroom when he saw Nicole. He never returned and claimed he had an anxiety attack. Bullshit! He recognized her and didn't want her to see him."

Lincoln rolled his eyes. "This is deep."

Dan switched gears. "About Barkley Malone. Has a retrial date been set?"

"It has." Lincoln picked up a file. "I got this yesterday afternoon. The retrial is set for next year, June seventeenth."

"Does Sasser know?"

"He might."

"I had asked that snake if he intended to represent Malone again at the retrial but he didn't commit to it. Then I inferred that he knew his client is guilty and he answered me in a way, saying guilt or innocence is for me and him to have our own opinions about. He laughed and cited the attorney-client privilege."

Lincoln arched his back and nodded. "We all learn that in law school and it's a sacred line we do not cross. And that vow is ironic to me. It's one of the reasons I am tired of this business, and it is a business. You do know money talks and you do know that Black people are not treated on an even level with Whites. I may or may not be around for the retrial. My term is coming to a close and I am leaning toward private practice."

Dan moved his head up and down. "Speaking of doing your own thing, here's a shocker. Syms has thrown in the towel. He left, tossed in his badge and split."

"Are you serious?"

"Yup." Dan threw his hands up. "Me and Hardison both believe Syms will not last long as a civilian. In the meantime, the chief put me in charge. I didn't exactly get a pay raise."

"Join the rest of us."

"Yeah, I'll see you later."

Chapter 30

"**S**asser." *He and I go together like oil and water. Lunch with him is the last thing I need. Not today.*

Dan was about to cancel it. Chantel answered his call. "Dan, good morning. Are we still on for lunch?"

"About that. Something has come up and we have to reschedule. Tell your uncle we'll figure out another time."

"Sorry you can't make it. Me and him will probably go anyway."

"Enjoy. I'll check in later."

Relieved that his unwanted meal with Sasser was put on hold, Dan thought about Karas, who was a thorn in the detective's side and he had to know if he did impregnate Nicole. *I bet Arnstein can find out who the father-to-be was.* Dan buzzed his pathologist friend. "Max, I have a question for you. It has to do with Nicole Brezinski, Lady Godiva."

"Shoot."

"You told me she was pregnant and I'd like to pin down the sperm donor. I'd like to know who it was. I have a feeling I know who it is, but I need confirmation. Delta pilot Jeff Karas is my guess, but he won't admit it. Since she is dead, she can't tell me. Can you get his DNA from the dead fetus?"

"Wow, Dan. One answer is yes, DNA can be gotten from a dead fetus. The other answer, which applies in this case, is no. Nicole

Brezinski was only four to five weeks pregnant. It would have been possible if she were seven or eight weeks pregnant."

Dan slouched in his chair. "You're kidding me. Great. Another detour on this road. I thought for sure you could."

"Maybe sometime down that road it will be possible, but not now."

"Damn."

"Sorry, Dan."

"Thanks anyway, Max."

Dan's head bobbed in frustration. *Nothing is easy.*

Interrupting his inner thought was the voice of Garcia, the department's gang unit leader, who walked toward the detective. "Dan, we need to talk."

"You don't come here often. What's going on?'

"We need to have a chat with Hardison. Dixon is up there now."

"What about?"

"Cabrera."

Luke was sitting alongside Mal and got up to join them. "I knew something wasn't right. What's going on?"

Garcia nudged Dan while speaking to Luke, "You'll know soon." Then Garcia turned to Dan, "We need to see Hardison, now."

Luke and Mal started to follow them, but Garcia held his hands forward. "Hang tight. Not you two. Just me and Dan."

▲

Three chairs were in Hardison's office. Dixon was sitting in one. "Have a seat, guys," Hardison directed Dan and Garcia. He then gave the floor to Garcia. "Why don't you start?"

"First off, we have a lead on Cabrera's shooters. We got a tip from the mother of a member of the upstart gang in town, the Desperados. Her name is Frida Macias. She called and was crying because her son, Matteo, had yanked a purse from her and waved a gun at her when he left. He runs with the name Tango. He likes to dance and has a tall friend who goes by the name Tree. Both boys are on drugs and Tango was recently admitted into the gang. My guess is Cabrera was an initiation killing."

Hardison interrupted him. "Jesus Christ, what the hell are you telling us?"

"I'm saying we were onto the gang and they were getting deeper into drugs, thefts and guns. Cabrera was a mole."

Dixon gazed indignantly at Garcia. "He was what? He was my patrol officer. What do you mean he was a mole?"

"Okay, simmer down," Garcia suggested. "I needed someone like him and I needed to keep it quiet, so I enlisted him to infiltrate the gang and he did."

The veins in Hardison's neck bulged and he glared at Garcia. "You did what? Without me or," he pointed to Dixon, "him involved?"

"I'm telling you, the guy was ripe. He had left his wife and he was in a place where he needed to feel important and the gang infiltration scheme was it. I set him up with drugs and handguns. I knew you both would not approve, so I had to keep it quiet. So did he." Dixon reached over and stopped his hands two inches from Garcia's neck. "You fucking maniac! And when the hell did he do this?"

"Whenever he was not on duty."

Dixon responded, "Damn it, that explains his calling in sick a lot. He said he was seeing a doctor and might have to take a leave for some type of surgery."

Dan restrained the angry captain as Hardison steamed with rage and screamed at his hostile combatants. "Knock it off!"

Garcia distanced himself from Dixon and shook off the attack. "The fact is, we were close to making a deal that would have gotten

Cabrera inside the gang so we could bust them."

"And how would the deal have worked?" Hardison inquired.

"Guns. Cabrera was going to get them a bunch. We know they were intending to become heavily armed and we had to get the thugs off the street before they started causing major harm."

Dixon shouted, "So you played God and got Cabrera killed!

Garcia somberly said, "Somehow they were onto him and knew he was a cop. They knew he would be in the church neighborhood in his black-and-white."

Hardison lashed out at Garcia. "And they executed him!"

The chief stood, his nostrils flared, and he glared at the gang unit leader. With fire in his eyes that could have singed Garcia, he continued his tirade in his loudest voice. "Who the fuck gave you permission to set up a shutdown of the gang? Who the fuck do you think I am? Who the fuck do you think you are? Last time I knew, I was in charge here! I have a good mind to strip you of your badge now!"

Garcia apologized and his face tightened as he stammered, and hoarsely tried to reason with the chief. "I've been the gang unit leader for ten years and I thought it was the right thing to do. I know manpower is down and I know the pressure we're all under. I set it up."

Hardison glared at him. "Get out of here. You can set your ass somewhere else."

Garcia held his ground. "No. Wait. Give me one chance. Tonight we are raiding the clubhouse and Tango and Tree will be there. It's a golden opportunity to bring them in. My guys are all set."

"And what about the gang? What about a possible shootout?"

"We're prepared. The hangout is down a dirt road near the garbage dump. Not much activity in that area. We're going in tonight at ten o'clock."

"How sure are you they will be there?"

"Positive. This is meeting night."

The chief was quiet while pondering what to do. His back was to the others in the room as he looked out the rear window. Then he turned and stood face-to-face with Garcia. "God damn it. You better deliver or I'm telling you, don't bother to show up here tomorrow."

Dixon was furious and his hands were still ready to strangle his counterpart and again he had to be restrained by Dan. "You went behind my back too!" he barked. "Get out of my sight!"

"Enough!" Hardison growled. "Leave, all of you. Go."

▲

Dan had an obligation to inform Luke and Mal of what went down and what was about to take place. Once he did, Luke fumed, holding back expletives. "What the hell? Me and Mal have worked this case and now we should be involved in the takedown of those assholes Tango and Tree."

Mal concurred. "He's right. Garcia likes to handle things himself. He told you where and when he and his crew were moving in."

Luke growled. "We're going."

Dan waved at them. "Hold it. This is not the time to be irrational. Sit tight. It will be over tomorrow."

Luke stomped his foot on the floor. "Oh no. We have a stake in this game and we are going to see those two thugs brought in."

Luke and Mal's attitude reminded Dan of his own past behavior. *These two are as obstinate as I was when I didn't listen and wound up in the hospital with a bullet in my chest.*

"Guys. I know better, stay put and see where the rocks fall. I can't let you risk your lives."

"You can't stop us," Luke argued.

Dan shook his head. "Oh yes I can if I have you put your badges on my desk. Listen, let them handle it, don't be stupid."

Luke shot Mal a glance. "Are you stupid?"

Mal nodded. "No. What the hell are you, crazy?"

"I'm not crazy. I've been here long enough to know that we need to do this. Are you in or not?"

Dan grabbed Luke's arm. "I didn't hear any of this. See you in the morning."

Luke raised his thumb. "We will stay in my truck out of sight until Tango and Tree are in cuffs."

Mal nodded his head in agreement.

"Meet me here around nine in the back lot."

Dan pleaded, "Guys. One last time. Stay away."

Chapter 31

It was nine-thirty and the sparsely lit dump area was quiet as Luke parked his truck inside a fenced enclosure containing several garbage trucks. "It's dark as shit," Luke said as they waited for Garcia.

Mal grabbed the binoculars he brought. "I can see about three football fields down that side road and it looks like there is a light on inside the warehouse."

"Do you hear anything? Music, loud noise?"

"No. And I only can make out what appears to be one motorcycle in front."

Twenty minutes later, Luke said, "Get down, Garcia and his guys are about to pass us."

Garcia and his fully armed officers accompanied an armored vehicle as it motored toward the gang's gathering place. The darkness and the air's stillness gave the night an eerie feeling.

Outside the clubhouse was indeed one Suzuki leaning against the brick façade, its chain dangling. There was nothing indicating any movement inside or outside the building. The raiders inched closer and prepared to exchange gunfire if necessary. The armored vehicle was in position to smash in the warehouse door. As close as they were and with no signs of life inside the building, the armored vehicle stayed put as Garcia and his men rushed inside the dimly lit, abandoned meeting site.

Inside his truck, Luke said, "I don't like this."

"No shit. Garcia is standing outside the place."

Minutes later, the raiders retreated and moved out of the area.

"What a ruse," Luke said. "The gang must have been tipped off that a raid was coming. They're gone. Let's get out of here. You play the lottery?"

"Not too often. Waste of a buck every now and then."

"I feel lucky tonight. There's a Seven-Eleven a few blocks from here. We passed it before."

"I get half if you end up with a winner."

"Most I ever won was fifty bucks."

A white car was parked to the right of a gas pump and Luke pulled into a space in the well-lit area not far from the gas pumps. He entered the store while Mal waited for him outside. Music emanated from the idling vehicle several feet from Luke's truck and the noise bothered Mal. The detective saw a young man who was standing outside the car and paying attention to the phone in his hand. The guy's head bobbed to the car's music and he tossed a cigarette butt to the ground. The inscription on his hat read "TANGO" and Mal hopped out of the truck, immediately drawing his gun. Facing the young man, the detective pointed his weapon at Tango and shouted. "Police! Get your hands up!"

Tango was startled and began running away. Mal yelled, "Stop or I'll shoot!" Tango did not listen and Mal fired his weapon, sending the fleeing man face-first to the ground, his arms spread out and his body twitching.

At the same time, Luke rushed out of the store and reached for his gun. As he did, the tall man who had been inside the store was right behind him and another bang rang out. Luke stumbled forward, bleeding from the gunshot that hit him in the back.

Tree aimed at Mal, who quickly pulled his gun's trigger twice and struck the shooter. The gunman crashed backwards into the storefront window, smashing it. Bloodied glass covered him and the sidewalk.

Mal ran to Luke and called for help as a heavyset store employee rushed out and tried to aid him. Tango and the man Mal assumed was Tree were harmless at this point and Luke was still breathing. As soon as an ambulance arrived, Mal motioned the paramedics to Luke. Three cruisers pulled in and the arriving officers took over the scene.

Luke was gushing blood and the EMTs stabilized him before the ambulance sped off to Woodland's emergency room.

Tree was pronounced dead at the scene and Tango was transported by a second ambulance to Woodland.

The long night ended with Mal driving Luke's truck to Woodland and staying with his partner at the hospital.

▲

Dan's phone rang at one in the morning, and he heard Hardison's harried voice. "Luke's been shot. He's in surgery at Woodland. Mal is there. He's okay. Apparently Garcia's raid went nowhere. Luke and Mal apparently were down there. According to Mal, Luke wanted to buy a lottery ticket after the failed raid was over and he stopped at a Seven-Eleven. There, they ran into Tree and Tango. Mal shot Tango, Tree shot Luke and then Mal shot and killed Tree. Tango is in surgery too. We'll know more later."

Dan leapt out of bed, with the receiver in his hand, waking Phyllis as he did. "What now?" she asked groggily.

Still talking to Hardison, Dan said, "I'm going to the hospital."

"Not now. Mal is there. Wait until later this morning?"

"I can't."

"Dan," Hardison ordered. "Stay put."

153

The call ended and Phyllis, now wide awake, asked, "What's wrong?"

"Luke was shot. He's in surgery at Woodland. Mal is with him. I don't know anything else right now. I'm going downstairs."

"Me too."

"No. I need to be alone."

"I'm coming."

Shaken by the news, Dan whispered, "No, leave me be. It's my fault."

Phyllis rose and stepped out of bed. "What do you mean, it's your fault?"

"Nothing. Go to bed."

Phyllis clasped her hands. "Tell me!"

Dan bowed his head. "Later, go back to sleep. I have to be alone."

Phyllis hugged him. "I love you."

Dan cat-napped on the den couch, woke up groggily at four, and had to shower to wake up properly before heading to the police station.

Chapter 32

When Dan drove into the parking lot at six, he saw Hardison's car in the chief's designated space. The worried detective marched up three flights of stairs and his footsteps seemed to awaken the chief, who sat up suddenly in his chair. His eyes were puffy and the bags under them marked his lack of sleep. Dan sat and Hardison said, "You look beat too."

"Damn right I am. Have you heard anything more about Luke?"

"Not yet, Mal said he would call. No one is jumping for joy this morning and Garcia has a lot to answer for. I talked to him after I alerted you as to what occurred. The gang bust was a total failure. The hangout was abandoned. The only good news was Garcia's crew took guns away from the scene. Garcia knew nothing about Luke's shooting, nor was he aware that Tango and Tree were shot."

"Where is Garcia now?"

"He'll be here. I told him to get his ass down here. He won't be leaving with a job. Luke got shot after the raid, but why the hell were he and Mal anywhere near there?"

Rubbing his forehead, Dan meekly answered, "I should have stopped them. They wanted to be in on capturing Tango and Tree and went down there. I'm as upset as you."

The clock behind Hardison now read six thirty-five and grief-stricken Garcia entered the office and faced Dan. "Why the hell were

Luke and Mal around?"

Standing and shaking his fist at Garcia, Hardison implored him, "Is that all you can say? Luke is fighting for his life."

"I'm sorry."

"Don't bother to sit," Hardison fumed as he anchored himself to his chair. "Sorry, apology or any excuse is unsatisfactory. On one hand we're lucky there was no gang to be found and no violence, at least not at the clubhouse. If you hadn't called this sorry-ass mission, Luke would be here at the station this morning. The good news is that he and Mal ran into Tango and Tree a while later at a Seven-Eleven. Mal shot them both and Tree died at the scene."

"I know."

Hardison swiveled toward Dan. "What's your excuse? Why were Luke and Mal lurking around?"

"I don't have any excuses," Dan meekly said.

"Look at me!" Hardison ordered Garcia. "I'm fed up with your bad judgement and self-righteousness."

"But ..."

At that moment, Dixon entered and sidled up to Hardison and whispered a barrage of information to him.

A few moments later, a gang unit member named Jimmie Seymour stood outside the office.

Garcia asked, "What's going on?"

Dixon replied, "You're about to find out."

Hardison took over. "Get another chair," he ordered Garcia.

The chair was set beside Garcia and the chief addressed Seymour who sat. "I understand you were at the intended raid last night."

"Yes, sir."

Two pairs of footsteps closed in on Hardison's office and Dan espied officers, Jackson and Batterson, who remained standing outside the office.

The chief yielded to Dixon, who held a cell phone that had been retrieved from Tree. He showed Seymour two calls that Tree had made. One was two days ago and one was yesterday. "That is your name and number, isn't it?"

Garcia jumped up. "Excuse me?" He glared at Seymour and with fire in his eyes, he kicked the chair out from underneath the dirty cop. "Are you serious? You tipped them. You fucking no-good piece of shit!"

Seymour said nothing as he fell to the floor. Dixon motioned to Train and ordered the sergeant to handcuff the stooge. "Stand up." Train commanded.

Hardison pointed at Seymour. "You're under arrest and you will be charged with being an accomplice to Cabrera's murder. Read him his rights."

Dixon did so and Seymour was taken away by the officer.

Dan was as stunned as he'd ever been and wiped his hands across his face.

Garcia said, "I don't know what to say. I could kill that bastard."

Hardison eyed the irate Garcia. "And you. There are no excuses for you and your actions. Place your gun and badge on the desk and get your ass out of here. Now!"

"Chief?"

Hardison was in no mood to hear a plea and gritted his teeth. "You heard me," he forcefully repeated. "Get your sorry ass out of here, now!"

Dan was silent as he watched Garcia leave, escorted out by Batterson.

As Dixon left, he said, "Let me know how Luke is."

"I will," Dan said as he stood.

Hardison said, "Where the hell do you think you are going? Don't be so smug. You have a lot to answer for and I'll deal with you later. Right now I want to go see Luke."

"It is early, and he's probably asleep."

"You're right," Instead of heading to the hospital, the chief phoned Mal and pushed the speaker button. "How's Luke?"

Mal said, "He's resting. Tango died an hour ago. I'm staying with Luke. He may not wake up for a while. I've been here all night. The bullet was removed from his back and the doctor mentioned something about his vertebrae, discs."

"You sound exhausted," Dan said. "I'll be down in a little while."

"I'll be here."

"What room?"

"Four-fourteen."

"See you soon."

Chapter 33

An hour and a half later, after Dan told Scotty and Bev what had occurred, he made the unpleasant drive to the hospital, proceeded to the fourth floor and down to Luke's room.

The door was half ajar and Dan entered. Mal's eyes were half-closed as he sat at his partner's bedside. "Hey," Dan said. "I'll take over. Go home."

Mal shook his head. "This is crazy. I'm fine."

"No, you're not. Get some rest. I'll stay with Luke."

Mal reluctantly got off his chair. "I'll drive Luke's truck to the station and get my car. I'll check with you later."

"Bye. Hey, thanks for being here."

Luke, still not conscious, was hooked up to an IV and a monitor with a breathing tube in his nose. Dan touched his hand. *I should have stopped you.*

He sat at Luke's bedside while a nurse came in to check the patient.

Dan viewed the monitor behind Luke and read what the nurse had seen. The patient's blood pressure was 139/77. She completed her check. "His vitals are fine."

As the morning wore on, Dan made a visit to the cafeteria and downed a serving of eggs, toast and coffee. About nine-thirty, while Dan was sitting and observing the sleeping Luke, a short extremely cute, dark-haired woman entered the room. "Clarissa," Dan said.

"Yes." Her eyes were on Luke and they welled up.

"I'm Dan Shields. Luke told me about you and I saw the picture he has on his desk. The nurse said his vital signs are good."

"Is he going to be all right?"

At that moment, a doctor entered the room and examined Luke, then spoke briefly to Dan and Clarissa. "He was shot in the vertebrae between discs four and five. Surgery went well and I expect him to be here a few days. His prognosis is good. He literally dodged a bullet. I don't figure he will have permanent damage, but I'm sure some rehab will be necessary to build up strength and mobility."

Clarissa was curious. "How long?"

"It depends on his progress. He will have exercises to do when he is released and he could have trouble walking, tingling, and muscle weakness. I'd like him to go to rehab for up to thirty days. Overall, he should be fine."

Crying with relief, Clarissa nodded. "Thank you?"

Dan turned to her. "How did you find out?"

"I kept calling his phone and then called Mal. I guess Luke's cell is in the truck."

Forty-five minutes later, Luke's groggy eyes opened slowly. "Where am I?"

"Woodland." Dan revealed.

The bedridden detective's girlfriend touched his hand. "Clarissa," he said.

"Hi. Don't say much."

"I can't with this thing hooked up to me. Ouch," he muttered as he twisted his body.

Dan gave him the news about last night and added, "You were shot in the back, had surgery and here we are."

The patient repositioned himself as best he could. "I don't remember much. Where's Mal? Is he okay?"

"He's fine, a little tired. He was here all night."

Luke eyed Dan, "Wanna pour me some water?"

Clarissa did so and handed it to him. "Drink."

"I could use some breakfast."

Clarissa held his hand and laughed. "Well, that was a fast recovery."

A nurse walked in with medications. "Hello, Mister Hanson, I see you are a bit better. Take these pills." Luke washed them down with the water and the nurse checked him again "You seem ready for breakfast."

"He mentioned he was," Clarissa remarked with a smile.

Dan tapped Luke's hand. "I'll call you later. You're in good hands."

Clarissa stayed until Luke ate and she watched him fall asleep again.

Inside the squad room, Hardison was sitting behind Syms' desk. Dan, Scotty, and Bev were there as well. The chief focused on Dan. "Bev, Scotty, go. Dan, stay and close the door."

"Luke is awake and he's on his way to recovery."

"I know. I spoke with his doctor." The chief glared at his most experienced detective and waved a finger at him. "I put you in charge and you let me down." Hardison's eyebrows lowered. "Hear me now and hear me loud and clear. I put you in charge for a reason. I thought you would make a great leader." He huffed. "A leader. I'm not so sure of my decision now."

"Hold it," Dan interjected.

The harsh voice continued. "Garcia was one bad apple and he abused his power, and apparently had little respect for Dixon, me or anyone else. He's gone. I may disband the gang unit and fold it into

Dixon's responsibility. He's a straight shooter. And you, you knew Luke and Mal intended to accompany Garcia's guys, did you not?"

Dan rued the incident. "I told them not to do it."

"But you did not stop them."

Dan grunted, "Don't you think it has haunted me all night?"

"I'm sure it has but that's what I mean about being a good leader," Hardison scoffed. "I know about you not paying attention to rules, and the shenanigans stop here, right here and now. You understand me? Syms isn't here to cover or make up bullshit stories anymore. I won't buy them. Truthfully, I never did."

Dan was embarrassed by the situation and sheepishly assented. "I understand."

"Good. I'm going upstairs." Hardison glanced at the aspirin bottle Syms had left undisturbed. "By the way, I also know why he had those."

CHAPTER 34

It was early afternoon and Dan was speaking with Mal who had a worried look on his face. "Hey, it's not your fault. Luke will be fine."

"I know, but it could have been me, and it always hits home when a buddy is shot. I once lost a partner in Waterbury. I'll never forget him. I still keep in touch with his family."

Dan asked, "Do you want to talk about it?"

"Not really. I'm glad that Luke will be okay. These things come with the job, don't they? I've been lucky so far." Mal nodded at Dan. "You know it firsthand, don't you?"

"I know the risk comes with being a cop, but no one expects to be shot."

Mal rose. "I'm heading back to the hospital to see Luke."

"Tell him we want him back soon."

Scotty walked toward Dan. "Guess who is downstairs again?"

Not wanting to believe Hampton and Rollin were in custody, he huffed and started walking toward the door. "Those fricking pains in the asses."

"Hold it. It's not them and it's not the jungle."

Dan stopped in his tracks. "What are you telling me?"

"Garfield. Bev went to bring him up here."

"I thought he was gone."

Minutes later, Marcus Garfield, dressed in jeans and a blue pullover and now sporting a short beard, came in with Bev. "Take him into room one," Dan then directed Scotty, "Go to Syms's office and watch the closed circuit. Three's a crowd and I was getting to him last time. Bev calms things down."

"Got it."

Dan entered the room and closed the door. Bev whispered to him. "He hasn't spoken a word. He's kind of stoic."

Garfield was slouched in a chair with his head down as Dan pulled up a chair and held back no punches. "I'm not in the mood for bullshit. By all accounts we had you gone, missing, a fleeing murdering arsonist. Last time you wanted us to believe you didn't come to turn yourself in. Is that what you're doing now?"

Picking up his head, Garfield replied, "Are you serious? Hell no. I'm on the run, but not from you."

Dan barked at him, "Explain yourself."

Sitting up straight, Garfield blurted out, "I'm scared."

Deadpanned, Dan raised his brows. "Right. So am I. Cut the shit!"

Garfield leaned forward. "It's like this."

Dan inched his face a foot away from the story-telling windbag and warned, "I told you. Don't bullshit us again."

The interviewee put his hands on the table, palms up and yawned. "Haven't slept in a few days. I'm being hunted."

Dan bristled at that remark, which set off his short fuse and he angrily retorted, "Hunted? And you haven't slept in days? Boy, that's what I wanted to hear."

"He wants to kill me."

"Who wants to kill you and why?"

"Vinnie."

"Hold it. Your cousin Vinnie who lost a leg in Iraq is after you?"
Swaying his head back and forth, Garfield rubbed his chin.

"Vinnie is my cousin and was my best pal once. Him and Tamara were the only ones who used to visit me in prison." He slumped forward, his head resting between his knees.

Still hot tempered, Dan mused aloud, "Hard to believe. Even after you beat her and she had you put away, she still came to see you."

"Several times."

"Pick your head up and focus on me. She's dead and one-legged Vinnie is after you?"

"Not exactly."

Bev whispered to the highly agitated detective. "Let me continue."

He shook her off. "Not now."

Bev nudged him with her knee and Dan got the subtle message, so he backed off.

"Get on with it," Bev encouraged Garfield.

"Alright." He clasped his hands and a bead of sweat rolled down his forehead. "Vinnie isn't handicapped. Shit, he and Tamara were acing it."

Dan's adherence to Bev's request was short-lived and he rose to his feet. "What the hell are you saying? You made up a story about the leg?"

Bev tapped Dan. "Let's step out for a minute."

Garfield leaned forward as Dan and Bev prepared to exit the room. "Stay here. We'll be right back," she advised the man.

Dan wore the face of an exhausted, pissed-off cop about to lose control. "I know what the hell is eating you," Bev said. "This whole day has you down. Restrain yourself. You might be ready to join Luke at the hospital. Sit quietly for a while and let me rattle his cage."

The frenzied detective took a minute to let his frustrations drain from his body. "I need a drink." He made his way to the water cooler and downed a few cups.

Back inside the room, Bev and a calmer Dan changed seats. She suggested to Garfield, "Sit back. What exactly is going on?"

"Okay, okay. So, my cousin Vinnie was never in Iraq. He's fine except for being a druggie, alcoholic and at times a lunatic. I did settle in with him after being released from jail, but as I told you before, I left and found my own place. I can't go back to work or to Brackett."

"Why?"

"Vinnie is crazy. He set the fire. He thought because him and Tamara were hooking up when I was in jail, that she wanted him. Not so, but she wouldn't take me back either. Vinnie went to see her one last time before he set the fire."

"How do you know he set it?"

"He told me."

Dan shook his head and butted in. "Hold it. You had said that you had no idea who did it. That was an outright lie and now he's after you? You expect us to believe you?"

Garfield cowered. "That's the truth."

"Why would he kill her?"

"He was jealous."

"Of what?"

"She broke it off with him and he thought I was getting back with her, but she shot me down too."

"So, let me get this straight. Your cousin took you in when you were released from jail and after you left his place, he set a fire at her house."

"Yeah."

Dan sat back. "What else do you want us to believe?"

"Bastard called me and I could tell he was high, but dead serious. Shouted all kinds of names including motherfucker, I'm going to kill you."

Bev regained control of the session. "Where are you staying?"

"I'm holed up at a seedy motel on Weston."

"Which one?"

"Eighty-eight."

"We have your cell number and you have ours."

Garfield set his new Samsung on the table. "It's new. I got rid of my old one so he can't call me. Here's my new number."

"What is Vinnie's?"

"I lost it."

Dan interjected, "Did he ever harm anyone before, or does he have an arrest record?"

Garfield nodded up and down. "He's been arrested for DUI's and an assault and battery charge on his ex, but she dropped the charges and left town."

"Is that it?"

"Not really. He killed a guy in Keney Park, took his money and a gold chain and left him for dead. He never got caught."

Dan winced as he remembered an unsolved case. *What did he say? Keney Park?* "Hold it. Are you referring to the jogger who was robbed and murdered? What was his name?" Dan pondered.

"Bowler, Dennis Bowler," Bev said. "That case went cold."

"Yeah. He did it." Garfield said. "He could be anywhere. I'm sure he's armed."

Bev asked, "What is your cousin's full name?"

"Vinnie Tedone. Vinnie, not Vincent."

"And address?"

"Harper Street, not sure of the number, but it's a brown two-family near the end of the street. There is an American flag swinging from the front porch."

Dan had a feeling they were not done. "Is that it? Anything else?"

"Well, I saw Catalina and told her I want to go to Raleigh

because I have a cousin there. She's a nurse and has a husband and three kids."

"What's your cousin's name?"

"Cyndae Jacks."

"Her husband?"

"Jaz. Catalina is working on it."

Bev stood. "Sit tight. I'm going to call Catalina and tell her what is going on."

Dan stayed with the man while Bev went out to Scotty and she used the office phone to call the parole officer. Ten minutes later she returned. "Catalina Montero confirms your request and verified your relatives, but the relocation process will take some time. You realize if you are allowed to move, the Raleigh court may reject the request and you will have no choice but to remain here. How long have you been at the motel?"

"A few days."

"I want you to get out of there. You must have somewhere else to go?"

"Not really. It's not bad there."

"Okay," Dan said. "I want you to call in every day. You got that? Here's my card. We're going to re-open the Bowler file."

"Better do it soon. I gotta go."

Dan stayed with him. "I'll see you out."

The two men went down to the lobby and Dan watched Garfield walk toward his Jeep. Before getting in, he took a pack of cigarettes from his pocket, lit one and then drove off.

Dan reentered the squad room. "The Keney Park homicide. Vinnie Tedone doesn't live far from there."

Bev said to Scotty, "Based upon Garfield's statements, Vinnie Tedone is a person of interest we should bring in and talk to. I want to search the criminal database."

"Do it," Dan said. "Keep in mind, the only things we have as of right now are Marcus Garfield's accusations. Who is Vinnie Tedone? Was or was he not in Iraq? Did he lose a leg? Is he a druggie and alcoholic? Did he commit the murder of Bowler? And is he a murdering arsonist? That's a lot of circumstantial accusations Garfield spilled out. That guy is either playing a hell of a chess game or he is an outright liar. As of now, it's a crapshoot. We can't prove anything."

"We have probable cause to bring in Tedone," Scotty said.

"Do we?" Bev argued.

"I'm not sure," Dan offered. "Pull the case file and we'll have to go from there. The arson case is stalled."

Bev, the computer expert, keyed Tedone's name into the criminal database and got a hit. She scrutinized his record and printed it. Scotty retrieved the data and sat beside her. "He does have priors as Garfield stated for two DUI's and the Harper Street location checks out. There is nothing about a domestic or him being in Iraq or him missing a limb. Nice mug though. I'm going to get to work on the cold case."

CHAPTER 35

Dan journeyed home and had no idea that a surprise was waiting for him. A white Ford compact with Florida plates was parked in one side of his driveway. The curious detective walked by the vehicle, opened his home's front door and listened closely to the voices coming from the den, hearing a familiar female's speech pattern. *No. It can't be.*

Kate and Josh excitedly came running to him almost at the same time and echoed. "Guess who is here?"

Dan raised his brows. "Surprise me."

As soon as he stepped into the den, he laid his eyes on their visitor who was sitting on the couch next to Phyllis and broadly smiled. "Florida agrees with you, welcome home."

Clad in a yellow dress, her silvery hair cropped short, Connie Costanza stood and they embraced. She was now nearly seventy-years-old and sat again. Dan sometimes watched television reruns and couldn't help thinking that Connie reminded him of Hazel, the motherly housekeeper from the old sitcom of the same name. "You're a sight for sore eyes."

"I'm glad you're still alive, and you do look tired."

"How in heck are you and what brings you here? I know it isn't my good looks."

"I came up for my friend Irene's husband's funeral. She was the best employee I ever had, thirteen years. It's the day after tomorrow."

"How long will you be here?"

"I made plans to be here a week. I'm staying with Irene's sister."

Dan was still standing. "I didn't know when we might see you again. We miss you. Is that your new car?"

"It is. I wouldn't have made it up here in the old one. I traded that thing in. I am staying for dinner, any complaints?"

Dan laughed. "Don't eat too much."

Staring at Kate and Josh, Connie said, "These two are growing like weeds. I heard Mike is doing well."

"He is. What are you up to at the Villages?"

"You won't believe it but every Tuesday, I play pickleball."

"You're right. I don't believe it. I suppose you've taken up golf."

"No chance. I do play cards twice a week and I enjoy the lake and sun."

Phyllis went into the kitchen. "Dinner is almost ready. Kids, wash up."

Dan pivoted toward the bathroom. "I have to wash too. What's for supper?"

"Don't ask me," Connie quipped. "I'm not the chef around here anymore."

While they all were dining, Dan winked at Connie. "It's like old times."

She copied him. "It sure is. My friends are playing cards tonight and I'm sitting in. When are you coming down to visit?"

Dan saw his wife eying him and she said, "That's a good idea." She glanced at Josh and Kate. "I think you would like Disneyworld."

Both kids jumped for joy and shouted, "Yes!"

After dinner, it was time for Connie to leave. Dan and Phyllis and the kids walked with her to the door. "Is there a chance we might see you again before you go back?" Phyllis asked.

"Maybe. We'll see."

Dan assured her. "If you need anything let us know."

Connie slowly walked to her car and got in. As she backed into the street and began to drive away, Dan and Phyllis waved to her, as did Josh and Kate.

Phyllis closed the door. "I'm so glad she came by. She seems happy."

Dan smiled. "She deserves to be."

Later, Dan was by himself and the television was on as he snored while clinging to the remote on his lap. Phyllis woke him and he wobbled his way to bed.

Chapter 36

Scotty and Bev reopened the Bowler slaying while Dan set his sights on Lady Godiva. Whether Karas was in London or not, the detective decided to obtain information he was sure would help him: the pilot's flight schedule and phone records. He also sought to pursue the same data for each flight attendant and was sure Delta would have those personnel records.

The detective's computer skills didn't come close to Bev's but he was able to extract Karas's cell phone carrier from LexisNexis. *Now I need data from Verizon as well as Delta. I'm sure neither will release information without a warrant.*

He called Evan Lincoln after writing up the information he sought and requested the attorney's assistance. "Evan, I wrote up warrant requests for Delta and Verizon. Can you look at them and get a judge to sign them?"

"You can do that. Take them to court. get them signed and overnighted."

"I think it will be faster if you do it. How about it?"

Dan heard a moan. "Alright, get the things over here, I'll read them and have them signed. You have an hour."

"Do me a favor and have the data sent to you."

"Be here soon."

▲

Dan completed his chore and ventured to Sasser's office where Chantel welcomed the detective. "Hi, Dan. He told me you were coming."

Dan winked. "Did he say I might shoot him?"

Chantel smiled. "You guys! Go in."

The office door was open and Sasser's feet were propped on his desk. Dan's entered and the attorney yanked them to the floor. "So, what happened to Luke?"

"It's a long story involving Garcia, the gang unit, the Desperados, and Cabrera's shooting." Dan spent the next twenty minutes spilling out the details.

Sasser groaned. "That's heavy stuff. My news is not earth-shattering but I wanted to tell you. Barkley Malone's retrial is scheduled for June seventeenth."

"Lincoln already told me. You know Malone should be in prison."

"Damn it, Dan. I know no such thing. He was acquitted."

Dan sneered at Sasser. "Here we go again. He was not acquitted. It was a mistrial, remember?"

Sasser gave his friend a cold stare. "Will you cut that crap. And don't, excuse me for the pun, cop an attitude."

Dan lamented, "I'm sorry, Sass."

"So, I went to see Malone and talked with him about accepting a plea deal. I want to run it by Lincoln and find out what kind of deal he would make."

"How's life in prison?"

"You sound like a judge. I don't want to risk that outcome. Jury or no jury, I am going to seek twenty-five years with a chance to get out in twenty. It's a fair offer. It's unlikely he will get lucky again and have a juror with an agenda on his side."

"Great system, isn't it? Damned murderers get to spend time letting us support them. Ever worry about the victim's family?"

"You do realize, we are on different sides of the law."

"And what side is the victim's family supposed to be on?"

Shaking his head, Sasser attempted to change the subject. "And where are you taking me and Chantel to lunch?"

"The police station cafeteria, how's that sound?"

Sasser laughed. "Good one. I don't think you want Chantel down there. Do you? Second choice."

"I'll let you know. When are you setting something up with Lincoln?"

"Soon."

"I have to go now."

Sasser stood. "Don't forget to get back to me with a restaurant."

Leaving, the detective didn't reply to him and smiled at Chantel as he passed her. "It's always a pleasure seeing you, young lady."

Dan opened his car door and slid in remembering that he and Hardison had agreed not to call Syms, and thus far the detective had been true to his word. Now, the temptation to break his end of the promise made him disregard that vow. He decided to pay the retired captain a visit. *I bet he can't wait to see my face. Here goes nothing.*

▲

Syms's oversized white ranch had a porcelain figurine of a rabbit on the lawn beside the front steps. A tall oak tree in the center of the front yard provided plenty of shade.

The brazen detective rang the doorbell and seconds later, Ernestine, an apron around her waist, opened the door. "Dan, it's nice to see you."

"Thanks, it's nice to see you too. It smells really good in here."

"Oh. The apron. My banana bread just came out of the oven."

She shouted to her husband, "Harold, we have a visitor."

Syms, wearing jeans with an untucked blue and white polo shirt, grinned. "I should have known it."

"You probably should have. It's good to see you. We all miss your voice."

He and Dan hugged each other before they sat. Syms placed his arm on his wing chair. "You mean to say, my voice is the only thing you miss? How are the bonsais doing?"

"We keep them watered."

"Would you like some banana bread?" Ernestine asked them.

Dan laughed. "Oh no." He checked his pocket, felt his EpiPen and held it up. "I know you're trying to get rid of me. I may have this, but I don't want to be surprised by nuts."

She replied, "The only nut around here is the one sitting in the chair opposite you."

Syms smiled. "Thanks, dear."

"Then, I changed my mind," Dan said.

"I'll be right back with the bread and coffee."

"Hardison temporarily gave me your job."

"Congratulations."

"Don't worry, your office is still intact. The aspirin bottle is waiting for you."

"Hardison told me about Luke and Garcia." He sighed. "The minute I leave crap like this happens."

Aha. Hardison couldn't keep quiet either. "Right. So when are you coming back?"

Syms huffed. "Damn it. I can't. I just can't. Every time I see Ernestine, I worry about what I've put her through over the years."

Ernestine brought in the snacks. Syms sipped his drink and set his cup down.

"Don't get used to the hospitality," Syms said. "I'll be right back." He got up and headed to the bathroom.

Before she left the room, Ernestine shook her head. "Between you and me, he's driving me crazy." She winked at the detective. "Give him a little more time before I boot him out."

Syms sat again and there were moments of silence as they enjoyed their snacks. "Ernestine's a great baker," Dan said.

"Yeah. I think I'm gaining weight. What's with Godiva?"

"You don't want to know. When you come back, I'll fill you in." Snack time was over and Dan chose not to overstay his welcome. "I'm going back to work."

Ernestine reappeared and Dan complimented her. "I loved the banana bread. Thanks. I hope to see you again soon."

She escorted Dan to the door, sans the apron. "Thank you for stopping by. I know he was glad to see you."

Softly, he said, "Give him a good kick."

"I'm working on it. I have sharp heels."

Chapter 37

Dan headed home only to find his arrival was met with a series of chores. The sound of a washing machine in the laundry room opposite the mudroom caught his ear. He encountered his wife, who was folding clothes. Her hair was tied back and she wore jeans and a green blouse he thought she'd thrown out. "How was your day?" he inquired.

"Fine. You have that look again. What's on your mind now?"

"It's nothing. I visited Syms and I wasn't supposed to. He's enjoying his time off. He's not wrong about the extreme stress we are under."

"We all have stress."

"True." Watching Phyllis doing one of her many household tasks, he shook his head. *My days are long, but hers never end.*

She placed a pile of warm, freshly scented folded bath towels in a laundry basket and asked, "How about putting these in the linen closet?"

"Can I unarm myself first?"

"Go."

Dan completed his daily task. "I'm back."

He lifted the basket. "They go in the linen closet," she reminded him.

"I heard you," he replied as he carried the basket toward the stairs. *Where the hell does she think I would put them?*

"Thank you, dear."

Minutes later, he was beside her. "Just in time." A second laundry basket was full of underwear. Without her saying another word, he picked it up.

"Thank you. The kids and I ate early. I'll heat up your dinner."

Dan proceeded back upstairs with the load of underwear and then took himself to the table to have his dinner, a plate of warmed meatloaf, potatoes and carrots and a glass of cold iced tea.

"How is Luke?" his wife asked.

"He's coming along as well as could be."

"I'm happy to hear he is. When you are done, clean up and put everything away, if you don't mind. I'm going to shower and change."

He kept eating and work occupied his thoughts. *Is it more likely Elijah killed Nicole or is it more realistic Karas did it? Or did neither of them do it? Elijah and rape, yes, but how the hell does someone inflict a heart attack unless she was scared to death? And prostitution? What a muddied investigation.*

After eating, he plopped into his lounger and his cell beeped. *Syms?* "Hey, Captain, did you change your mind already?"

"Nah. Stop calling me captain. You left your EpiPen here. You want to get it?"

"Not tonight. I have a couple of spares. Phyllis makes sure I'm supplied. Wanna drop it off tomorrow? You know where?"

"I'd rather mail it."

"Thanks. Hang onto it. I'm covered. You know where I am."

"Okay. Keep me posted on Luke, will you?"

"Yes. Go back to whatever you were doing. I'm going to bed soon."

After the conversation ended, Phyllis joined him after she showered, a towel bundled around her hair, cream on her face and wearing her pink bathrobe. "Who were you talking to?"

"Syms. I left my EpiPen there. We have more, right?"

"We do. I'll set a new one out for you tomorrow. Thanks for putting the towels away. You could have separated the pairs of underwear and put them where they belong, or did you forget who wears what?"

I'm in trouble again. "I forgot. I was hungry."

She laughed. "I don't think a full stomach would have helped."

Dan studied her as she curled up with a book.

"What are you staring at?"

He smiled. "I was just kind of seeing you in that negligee."

"Really. I didn't know Nivea, my toweled hair and robe got you so excited."

"Maybe it was the meatloaf."

She grinned. "Nice try … maybe you'll get lucky again in a few weeks after you figure out who wears what."

"Hey. I helped with the laundry. There's no reward?"

"Of course there is. Clean sheets."

Chapter 38

It was the start of a new day and Dan felt he should share his visit with Syms with the rest of the detectives. As soon as he arrived, Scotty said to him, "Hardison is in the captain's office."

Dan stopped in his tracks. "Again? Great."

"He's waiting for you."

The wondering detective had no choice but to postpone the update and he entered the captain's former quarters. Interestingly, Syms's engraved wooden nameplate still occupied the desktop, but the chief occupied the black chair. "Good morning," he said. "Close the door."

Dan flashed to the recent scolding Hardison had given him. *He knows.*

Hardison tapped the desktop. "Anything new?"

Oh shit. Here we go again. "Not that I'm aware of."

"I mean with Syms."

"Him?"

Hardison sneered at Dan. "Really. You went to visit him yesterday."

Dan nodded. "He told you?"

"He did."

"Well, I know one thing, neither one of us can honor a pledge."

"You didn't think I would keep him in the dark about Luke and

Garcia, did you?" Hardison made an effort to lighten the mood. "You visited him and I phoned him. What did he tell you?"

"Well, Ernestine treated us to freshly baked banana bread. What did you find out?"

"Dan, Dan. I asked you first."

"Honestly, I don't know. He seems determined to not come back. However, Ernestine made no secret about him being a pain in her neck and she said she can't wait to get rid of him."

Hardison smiled. "Yeah, she told me that too. He sounded like he has mixed emotions, but I could tell, it won't be long before he hauls his ass back in here. I could throw the nameplate away, but it belongs here and it is his. Until he's back, maybe against my better judgement, you remain in charge."

"Do you have to remind me?"

"Someone does." Hardison got up and opened the door. "My desk is waiting for me. I suspect yours is too."

"By the way, Lincoln told me Barkley Malone's retrial is scheduled for June seventeenth."

"You're on the ball. I was notified."

Dan followed the chief out and sat with Scotty, Bev, and Mal to fess up about seeing Syms.

"When is he coming back?" Scotty asked.

"Not now. He's still in curmudgeon mode and won't budge from his house. The good news is, Ernestine can't stand him being around all the time and she's not far from telling him he belongs here." Dan turned to Mal. "How's Luke?"

"He's doing good. As far as rehab goes, he'll stay with Clarissa and have home therapy for a while. That's better than being sent to a rehab place."

"It is. That is good news."

Dan knew it was too early to expect results from the warrants that were issued to Delta and Verizon. His investigation was further impacted by his being saddled with acting as the department boss. Nicole, *Lady Godiva*, Karas, Elijah Sandovar, the flight attendants, Garfield, and now Tedone all occupied his crammed mind. His annoyance with Karas made him attempt to get in touch with the pilot again. *Slick-ass guy is hiding more than I know and frankly, more than any of the girls want to tell me.*

After trying again unsuccessfully to reach the man, Dan realized there was no telling where he was. He mulled his next move. *Alicia and Stella can't be itching to hear from me again, but they know they will. It's time to try to pressure one or both of them into telling the real story.*

Alicia Greenstein did not, as Dan anticipated, answer her phone and once again, all the detective could do was leave a message. For all he knew she could be on a flight to Hong Kong. *That's one way to avoid me.* Stella Passante was next and much to his delight, she did answer his call. "Stella, how are you today?"

"Fine, Detective."

"Are you home?"

"Yes. I'm working tonight."

"Stella, I may have been a little rough on you when we last met and I apologize. However, some things have come to light that I have to share with you. Would it be alright if my associate, Bev Dancinger, and I stop over? She's really easy to talk with."

"I suppose. I do have a hair appointment this afternoon."

"We can be there in an hour."

"Sure."

Dan felt accomplished after the call and walked over to Bev. "How about coming along with me to talk with Stella Passante?"

"Why?"

"She's expecting us. I volunteered you to accompany me."

Bev gave Dan an evil stare. "You are acting like a boss. Do you think she'll take me for another hooker?"

Dan laughed.

"What the hell is so funny? Am I that bad?"

His eyes rolled. *Oh boy, wrong response. I can't fight my way out of this one.* Winking at her, he stage-whispered, "You're as sexy as you ever were."

She nodded. "So, that's your answer. Were?"

Dan put a hand to his forehead. "You know, talking to you is like trying to win a battle with Phyllis. It's impossible."

"Tell me more about Stella."

"You know what I've told you so far. Let me show you a couple of pictures. All of these girls are Delta flight attendants, not exactly flying nuns. Stella is the older one. Alicia Greenstein, Nicole Brezinski, Ariel Adams, Stella, Chelsea Maresca, and Jeff Karas."

Chapter 39

An hour later, the two detectives were at Stella Passante's house and Dan introduced Bev to her.

"Come on in."

Entering the sitting area, Bev immediately noticed the Virgin Mary statue. "I'm familiar with that. It's called the *Veiled Virgin*. I believe the original is in Newfoundland. How it got there I don't know. It was done by an Italian sculptor. Where did you get it?"

"In Rome, they have replicas."

"Very nice."

Once seated, Dan deferred to Bev. "I understand that you did fly for Delta and now your job is inside Bradley at the Delta counter."

"I am. I gave up flying a while ago and I am glad I did."

Dan spoke up. "Stella, the last time I was here, I saw some things that were private." He pointed to the green notebook that was on the table next to her. "I browsed that book, so I'd like you to be honest and talk to us. Those names and notations say a lot."

Stella sighed. "You know."

"I guess I do, but I can ignore those writings. I want to know more about Jeff Karas as well as you, Chelsea, and the other girls. By the way, where is Chelsea?"

"Flying to Las Vegas."

"Look, it's obvious to me that working for Delta isn't your only source of income."

Stella crossed her legs and pouted. "Are you going to arrest us?"

Dan peered into her eyes. "As long as you admit it, no. I don't plan to bust any of you ladies. Just tell us about the off-duty activity. How it started and Karas's involvement."

Somberly, she asked, "What do you want to know?"

"It's about Nicole. Was Karas intending to kill her? Tell me the truth about him and Nicole."

She bowed her head. "I don't know where to start."

"Let's start at the beginning. How and when did this adult activity begin?"

Stella took a couple of breaths. "Okay. Jeff is employing us, but for me it's all a bad past. She fidgeted and lit a cigarette. When the smoke from her first puff cleared, she continued, "Before this all happened I was an addict. I was married and had a kid. He's eight now, but because of my problem, the court took him from me and he was adopted when he was two. Those records are sealed. The last I knew. My ex was in jail and we have no contact with each other. For all I care, he can rot in prison. I went to rehab and got off drugs." Stella puffed the cigarette, placed the lit smoke on an ashtray and closed her eyes momentarily. "I had nothing but my body. I lived in a cheap, crummy apartment and couldn't get a job, well, a legitimate one. I started doing what I had to do and began making money."

Her eyes fluttered as she spilled out her sad story. Her trivial smile indicated that she was lifting a weight from her shoulders. She steadied herself and let out a breath. "When I was able to buy some new clothes and get out of the dumpy apartment, a friend took me in. No, she was not a hooker. Carla was older than me and had worked at the airport. She got me an application from Delta and I started working as a flight attendant. It was a great way for me to get away and put the bad times behind me. Unfortunately, Carla passed away. Anyhow, I went through the training program and began my new career. Salary wasn't great, but it was honest It was exciting and I enjoyed it. The reality was twenty-seven grand wasn't great money." She sniffled. "I need to relieve myself." Stella rose and walked toward the bathroom.

Dan whispered to Bev. "Hell of a story so far."

"I can see how she struggled."

Stella returned with a wad of Kleenex in her hand and picked up the still-lit cigarette, finishing it and extinguishing the butt. Then she led the detectives down memory lane while wiping tears away. Her voice splintered. "I had flown with Jeff once before and then we spent a few days in Honolulu." More tears trickled down her face and she cleared her throat. "He knew about my past and after we had dinner together, we walked by the water and he started talking about how puny my salary was and how much more I could make. It brought back my glum days and reminded me of how little money I put my body out for back then. He dangled lucrative cash at me, a grand, and promised a boatload more." Stella paused, as if gathering the courage to continue. "I'm sorry."

Bev said, "Don't be sorry."

Stella continued, "I knew where he was going with his sermon and knew he was right about the money." She welled up again. "He placed a wad of bills in my purse. I didn't know what to say and he held my hand as we walked back to the hotel. I didn't have to do it, but we went to his room and had sex. Then he put an extra two hundred on the nightstand and told me I had earned it." Stella had tears in her eyes and was silent.

Bev said, "This isn't easy. I can see that."

Stella sniffled. "The next night he sent me a customer and I guess you would say I was back in the game." She huffed. "I need some coffee."

"We all do," Bev said.

As Stella went to the kitchen, Dan whispered to Bev, "She is going beyond where I thought she would go. We all need the breather."

Dan and Bev waited until Stella toted in a tray with three cups of coffee on it. "It's instant, I hope you don't mind."

Bev held a cup and drank some coffee. "Not at all."

Dan held off resuming his questions until after Stella swallowed a gulp of caffeine. "How about the other girls? How did he get them involved?"

She took another sip. "Oh. I forgot to mention this. When we were in Hawaii, Chelsea was with us. We all had dined together. Afterward, Jeff and I took that walk while Chelsea said she was meeting her cousin somewhere. She disappeared and I didn't find out until later, she had no cousin. She went to a hotel room to service a customer. The next day she reaffirmed how easy it was to make big bucks."

"So, she was first to engage in prostitution?" Dan asked.

Stella took a deep breath. "She was, but Jeff recruited Francine Devereaux after me. She was from France and as far as we know, she worked a flight to Paris with him and she never returned."

"What do you mean she never came back?"

"All I know is that Jeff told us she submitted a letter of resignation to Delta."

Dan asked, "Are you saying that she may have resisted him?"

"It's possible."

Dan speculated. *My god, another girl. Did she have the courage to reject Karas and was she still alive or was she dead and gone?*

Stella began unraveling another sordid story. "Jeff lined up first-class businessmen. You won't believe how many of them are horny executives who pay good money to get laid. Their wives must have closed legs."

"What's Chelsea's story? And Alicia, and Ariel?"

"Chelsea told me she was addicted to sex and by the time she had graduated high school, nearly the entire football team had been in her pants. She didn't stray too far after connecting with Jeff."

"What's the story with Alicia and Ariel?"

Stella shrugged. "I do know and it isn't pretty. I think you should talk to them."

"Level with me. Do you suppose Karas would have had reason to kill Nicole because she was pregnant and might have wanted out?"

"I don't know."

"Did he ever say he loved her?"

"He loved all of us, if you know what I mean."

"I know this is speculation. Do you sense he wanted Nicole dead?"

"Anything is possible. I do know it was Nicole's birthday the day before the carousel incident and she was like a kid at times."

"I don't suppose you know where Karas was that weekend?"

"If I recall correctly, Alicia mentioned he was in Chicago."

Dan finished his coffee. "I want to talk about one other thing. Nicole was raped, sodomized buy an Uber driver."

"You mean the bastard who Barkley Malone killed."

Dan shrugged. "I'm not sure about that. I have reason to suspect the person who assaulted Nicole was not Emilio Sandovar."

"What?"

"Emilio was gay and his younger brother, Elijah is also an Uber driver. They could pass for twins but are a year or two apart. I have a strong feeling he borrowed Emilio's car and she had seen Emilio's name and photo on the app and assumed the driver, her attacker was him, but I'm sure it was his brother."

"Oh my God."

"I am determined to keep after Elijah and arrest him."

"This is all crazy."

Dan stared directly into her eyes. "I want you to let this sink in.

Again, I am not interested in busting you or any of the other women for prostitution. My aim is to solve Nicole's death and avenge her assault. I intend to speak with Alicia again. I tried to call her before we came here, but she did not answer my call. Do you have any idea where she is?"

"I don't." Stella sighed. "By the way, Nicole did stop hooking for a while and Jeff had a hard time getting her back to doing her job after she was sodomized."

"What do you mean?"

"I mean, he made her continue to have sex. Please don't tell Jeff we had this talk."

"We won't," Dan assured her. Then he signaled to Bev that it was time to go and the detectives departed.

Chapter 40

Stella Passante's revelations made Dan more eager to discover the truth about Nicole Brezinski's death.

He pivoted to an avenue he hadn't yet pursued. *Arnstein stated her BAC was a notch below the DUI intoxication level. Still, it's possible she and someone else frequented one of the bars near Bushnell Park. If she and another person were in one of those establishments before showing up at the carousel, I might get lucky with a lead, hopefully a video. And, can I believe Alicia, who assumed the pilot was in Chicago? Was he?*

Dan wrestled with those thoughts, pulled himself away from his desk and walked toward Bev. "I'm going for a tour of downtown. There are several bars near the park and it's a long shot, but maybe Nicole Brezinski and possibly Jeff Karas or someone else had been in one. My gut tells me the pilot was not in Chicago as I have been led to believe."

"Good luck."

Scotty, his arms crossed stalled Dan's departure. "Hold it. Bev and I have reviewed the Bowler killing and we can't tie anything to Vinnie Tedone. Landry had this case. It was the last one before he died."

Bev joined them. "There is evidence, but nothing validated. Bowler was jogging when he was killed and his head was smashed by a rock that is in custody. There are prints on the rock, but they were not identified. Tedone's prints are on file, so the lack of his identifier most likely eliminates him. Here's another piece of nothing. There are photos of sneaker prints as well as a cast. They are size twelve Nike's and were not traced to anyone."

Scotty added, "The file points to the probability of another jogger being the murderer. Bowler's sister said her brother always had a gold chain around his neck and it was never found. Case closed."

Bev said, "I am calling Tedone to see if we can set up a visit. We'll bring him in for questioning if we have to, but if he is an average shoe size, that further eliminates him."

"Good work. Set it up. I have to go bar hunting."

Dan's Accord waited for him and he drove around Bushnell Park's beer belt. His trek of the bar circuit included holding up traffic at times as he momentarily stopped his car in order to write down the names of the establishments Nicole may have visited.

The Moscow Brew Pub was the closest to the carousel. Down the street was The Mayor's Place. Around the corner, he noted The Hideaway, and across from it was The Owl and Bulldog. Each joint was open when Dan passed by, but it was the night staff the detective wished to drop in on. *I have to do it and this could be a late night.*

He went back to the police station and prepared for a long evening.

⚑

Dan left work early and home waited for him, as did the barhopping. Several yards from his driveway, he recognized the car in it. *If she made chicken pot pie, I'll handcuff her and make her stay.* As soon as he entered the house, his nose detected a familiar welcoming aroma. *Yes.* It was like old times. Connie stood near the oven, ready to remove dinner from it.

"I hope you're moving back," Dan said, giving her a quick hug.

She chided, "You mean you hope the chicken pot pie is moving back."

He hugged her again. "You're right. Don't tell Phyllis, but even with your recipe, it's not the same."

"I heard that," his wife said. "I try."

"Sorry, dear."

"You're stuck with mine. It's not so bad, is it?"

"No. It is good, but the original is the original."

As she had done many times before, Connie plated the meals. "Eat up."

Dan savored the pie. "Can you freeze these and send some up here?"

"I like Phyllis's idea better. You come see me in Florida and we'll have a good time." She smiled at Josh and Kate. "Besides, I haven't been to Disney either."

"I promise," Phyllis said, much to the glee of the kids.

"I guess it's a done deal," Dan said. "We do miss you."

"I'm driving back to Florida in the morning."

Dan smiled at her. "You know I want the best for you. Obviously, you are family."

"Darn you." She picked up a napkin and dabbed at her misty eyes.

An hour after the meal ended, Connie departed.

A good dinner was what he needed before undertaking his journey to the beer belt. Phyllis tried to jog his memory. "Remember the last time you went downtown to a club?"

"Don't remind me. Haley had to drive Mike home after he put Travis McCarthy in the hospital. I'll try not to be late. And for your information, that place is no longer there."

▲

Street parking was always elusive downtown and finding a spot was difficult, but at least at this time of night, eight o'clock, the meters were not on duty. He managed to squeeze his car into a space close to a corner while not infringing on a bus stop. Adding to this night's hustle and bustle was a concert in progress at the XL Center. Uniformed police were highly visible and he observed several people entering his first destination, Moscow Brew Pub. The door was held open for him. *Amazing. I was never too fond of the stuff, but this is a beer joint for sure.* The huge television screen was tuned in to the Buffalo Bills-Patriots game. That, combined with blasting music he didn't recognize, made him momentarily block his ears. Tables were scattered throughout the room and two long counters with backed stools lined the entire right side of the interior. Patrons held beer bottles and he didn't move further into the pub. Dan decided to backtrack. *No way. I seriously doubt Nicole was in here.* He was glad to go back outside and hear normal street noise.

Not far away was The Mayor's Place. Stepping inside, he saw the joint was more than half occupied. This bar was more to his personal liking, with softer music and a less rowdy crowd. He smelled food and saw a large blackboard on the rear wall behind the bar that contained the names of over a dozen alcoholic beverages, some he'd never heard of. He moved forward and spoke with the man behind the bar. The server motioned to the owner, Harry Clemens, and the proprietor came to meet Dan. "What can I do for you?"

Dan explained the reason for his visit and the cooperative Clemens led Dan upstairs into a small room where the detective was shown video surveillance of the evening in question on the club's computer. After viewing the critical hours in question and not spotting any helpful information, Dan thanked him. "I appreciate your cooperation. It's quite hopping downstairs."

"That's normal on game night."

"Thanks again."

Back outside, Dan made his way to The Owl and Bulldog. The vibe he felt when he stepped into this establishment was different than the others and he'd never been inside a karaoke lounge before. Patrons were downing suds and he heard them singing along with songs. Another noisy place. *Not here. I'm moving on.*

The Hideaway was up next. As soon as the detective came to the watering hole, he watched two men who were holding hands as they entered the establishment. Once he went inside, he observed several apparently same-sex couples in the saloon. *I can write this one off too.*

Nearing his car, he looked up at the tall street clock that told him the time was nearing nine-thirty and thought his evening was over until he saw a club he had not been aware of until now. Vesta, an establishment near the corner of Church Street, was a place that turned out to be the lounge inside an upscale downtown hotel, The Charter Oak.

As soon as he opened the lounge's door, he was struck by the sharp contrast with the venues he'd just visited. Vesta was well lit and a step up from the other clubs. Easy-listening music was relaxing to him and several tables in the room were occupied. Other patrons were seated at the bar. Dan walked past the connecting hallway to the hotel and stepped to the bartender, who acknowledged the detective's presence. "How are you this evening?" he asked. "What can I get you?"

Dan opened his wallet, displaying his badge. "I'm a detective. May we talk for a few minutes?"

He and the bartender chatted and Dan was directed to the hotel manager. "Through the glass door. Ask the desk clerk for him."

Dan did so and he spoke with the night manager, who assured

him that security videos of the lounge and lobby were available, but he would have to wait until tomorrow to obtain them. He left, having been promised copies of the requested footage.

As he walked toward his Accord, he yawned and phoned his wife, telling her that he was on his way home, hoping the video would provide the break he needed.

CHAPTER 41

With last evening's barhopping behind him, Dan expected to have the promised videos in his hands at some point in the day, preferably in the morning. But just after he arrived at his desk, the hotel manager called to inform him that the requested surveillance videos would not be ready until tomorrow. *Nothing goes as planned.*

The not-so-computer-savvy detective usually avoided checking his emails, but he did today and found one that had been sent this morning by Alex Sarkisian. Dan clicked on it and read the forensic expert's findings regarding the Sharpie.

Arnstein was able to extract the requested DNA and I was able to match it to DNA taken from the pen. To me it only tells us that the word whore was written with this pen, but it doesn't link the writer to it. Like I said before, there were smudged prints on the pen.

The elevator door outside the squad room squealed and in walked Luke, pushing a walker. Clarissa was behind him.

Dan rocketed from his chair. "Luke! What a surprise!"

"I saved your seat," Mal said.

Luke smiled at his colleagues. "Thanks." He shot a joyful grin at Clarissa. "She's the reason I'm doing so well."

"You look great," Scotty said happily.

Bev agreed, "I bet you'll be back soon."

Scotty joked, "Do you have your gun?"

Luke laughed and confessed, "Hell, Clarissa hasn't let me bring my Smith and Wesson into her residence. I may have to arrest her."

The diminutive Clarissa nodded and shot out a spunky response, "And if I find one, I'll sic my Rottweiler on him."

"Nah, he won't bother me."

"Then I'll bite you."

They all chuckled and Luke said, "I'm a little sore. The doctor says it could be a couple of months. What's new here?"

"Everything is under control," Dan assured him.

"Syms?"

"The stubborn captain isn't budging yet. I'm chomping at the bit to tackle him and pin him behind his desk."

"I see the bonsai next to my computer."

Clarissa peeked at the small tree and uttered, "I love it." She turned to Luke and flashed a smile. "I should get one or two. They would look nice in my kitchen."

He smirked, "Anything you say."

Bev grimaced and needled Luke, "Oh boy. I know who the boss is."

"As it should be," Clarissa asserted.

Luke moved his walker to his chair and sat in the cold seat before stating, "We need a big TV in here."

"How about a king-sized bed?" Mal quipped.

Luke got off his chair and sought Clarissa's hand. "I hate to stay any longer because I could get used to this place again and sitting here isn't helping." Clarissa positioned the walker and Luke grasped it. "It's great to see you guys. I'll be back soon."

Dan waved at the young couple. "Go home. We have work to do."

As Clarissa and Luke neared the exit, Bev called out, "Thanks for dropping in. It was great to see you both."

The unexpected break was short and as soon as he returned to his cubicle, Dan decided to visit Lincoln.

⏶

The state's attorney was walking toward the steps of his office building with a briefcase in his hand when Dan caught his attention. "Evan."

Lincoln waited as Dan strode toward him. "You should have called. What now?'

"I assume you were in court."

"Where else? Half my life is spent there. I'm between hearings. I have about an hour."

"Good enough."

Once inside his office, Lincoln set the briefcase on his desk and withdrew a couple of manila folders. "Let me sign off on these papers."

Dan sat himself down and waited a few minutes for the attorney to complete his paperwork. "Okay, I'm listening," Lincoln said.

"Last night, I checked out the watering holes nearest the park and came up empty, except for possibly the Charter Oak Hotel and its lounge, the Vesta. They have surveillance for me to look at. I was hoping to get them today, but I have to wait until tomorrow. Nicole Brezinski's death keeps getting more interesting. I still do not have evidence to bring charges against Jeff Karas. I do have probable cause to lasso him on running a prostitution operation, but not on murder. And Elijah Sandovar. I can't go any further with him on an assault charge at this time."

"I agree."

"Then there is Stella Passante and what she told me and Bev. The woman had a rough go of it, including drug addiction, her divorce and resorting to hooking to put money in her pocket. The kicker is she sobered up and quit both drugs and selling her body. That is, until Karas came along."

"How so?"

"She was fortunate to land a flight attendant job at Delta after getting clean. On one of her early trip assignments she met the pilot and started flying with him, sorry for the pun. It was on a layover." Dan smirked. "Another pun, sorry. They had sex and somehow he knew about her past and convinced her she should work for him. He recruited wealthy guys as customers. Lots of money. Chelsea sealed the deal when she confided in Stella and told her about own life. She didn't hide her sexuality and almost bragged about being a girl with hot pants and sleeping with half the high school football team. Jeff sure took advantage of her."

Lincoln gaped at Dan's recitation of Chelsea's behavior. "Really. And I couldn't get laid in high school until graduation."

"Thanks for that info. I know Alicia Greenstein is holding back information and I want to test the waters again with her. Oh, and there is one more interesting thing. Apparently another member of the pilot's harem, a girl named Francine Devereaux, mysteriously left the club. She was from France and supposedly she flew back there with him and was never seen again. According to Stella, Francine had tendered her resignation to Delta via mail. I'm doubtful about her being the one who signed the letter. It sounds very suspicious to me."

"It could be a while until I hear back from Delta," Lincoln advised. "All I know is they are working on it."

"I'm hoping the video from last night's pilgrimage pays off. Let me know as soon as you get some response from Delta and Verizon."

"Sure thing. I have to prepare my next case. Two more this afternoon."

▲

Dan returned to the police station where Scotty and Bev waited for him. Before he got to his cubicle, Scotty said, "We have to talk."

Dan scoffed. "Not again!"

Bev squinted. "What does that mean?"

Scotty said, "Nothing. Listen we got back a while ago from Vinnie Tedone's place. For one thing he sure was not in Vietnam and he has two legs, both of which would swim in size twelve shoes. He may have been a little high, but he couldn't have set the fire. He has an ironclad alibi. He was in Raleigh with Cyndae, Jaz Jacks and their kids. We checked it out."

"That bastard, Garfield." Dan rubbed his forehead, "It should have registered. When I saw him leave here and get into his Jeep, he lit a cigarette with a lighter. Butane. The lighter started the fire."

Scotty said, "He hasn't checked in with us."

"Try him," Dan said.

Scotty did. "Voicemail."

"This day is about to get a lot longer. Check the Eighty-Eight. Him staying there may be another crock. I want a BOLO out on his car. You guys get to Brackett. He just may be there."

Dan scurried to Dixon and requested the Jeep alert while Scotty contacted the motel only to learn that no guest named Garfield, nor anyone by the name Westley ever stayed there. Dan returned to the squad room as Scotty and Bev were on their way out. "The motel was more bull. I hope we can catch him at his apartment."

"Go."

CHAPTER 42

As Scotty's car maneuvered through traffic on Garden, he made it to Westland, turned the corner and came to Brackett Street, where the detectives ran into something they could not have foreseen. Flashing lights. Emergency vehicles blocking the road, and cops and curious bystanders milling around the street. "What the hell is going on?" Scotty wondered.

"Whatever it is, it isn't good," Bev replied. "Stop the car."

The detectives joined the frenzy while onlookers, including the neighborhood tough guy and his leashed dog, Killer.

Scotty called Dan. "We're here, but it's chaos. An ambulance and several black-and-whites are here. Looks like someone is down, by the stairs of the apartment building."

"What's going on?"

"It's pretty noisy. We're about to find out." As they neared an apparent victim, Scotty cuffed his phone, pulled it close and said, "Holy shit, it's Garfield."

"Dead?" A surprised Dan asked.

"As a doornail. We'll fill you in later."

There was an officer next to Bev. "What happened?" she asked.

"Upstairs. The old guy up there shot him. This is where the body landed. The coroner is on the way."

As the detectives headed into the building making their way

upstairs, a uniform and two paramedics were in their way. The medical personnel carried a stretcher down the stairs. On it was the man who fired the gun. Bev and Scotty moved aside and spoke with the officer. "What's the deal?" Scotty asked.

"He's being taken to the hospital. His vitals are low and he is incoherent."

"Did you get his name? We know him as Pops."

"Otis Quimby. Before he kind of drifted into babbling, he told us he shot the victim, Marcus Garfield. Supposedly the guy wanted to borrow the Impala out there. Quimby said no and Garfield grabbed the keys off the counter and rushed toward the door. By the time he got to the top of the stairs, Quimby shot him."

The detectives walked back outside and began asking bystanders what they knew. An hour later, Bev and Scotty sat in his car and he phoned Dan. "Hey, your hunch was right. Garfield did show up at his apartment yesterday. The facts as we know them are that the old guy who lives on the second floor shot Garfield. There didn't appear to be a tussle. Garfield was shot twice in the back and Pops, as we know him, is named Otis Quimby, and he was taken to Woodland for observation."

"What the hell else can happen?"

"I haven't told you the rest. It's muddy, we got a different story from our pal with the dog. The thug's name is, get this, Sly Apache. He even has an ID with that name. According to him, he saw Garfield come home last night in the Impala. He claims Garfield was drunk as a skunk and he drove the car into the side of the house after almost running into Killer. Sly and Garfield had words before Garfield stumbled into his apartment. It doesn't make much sense. If Garfield had driven the Impala the night before, that would mean he already had the keys. He'd have no reason to snatch them from Quimby this morning. My take is that Quimby knew what had happened and Garfield went upstairs to explain, and things went haywire. Quimby must have been infuriated so he shot Garfield. Whether Garfield still had the keys or Quimby planted them is anyone's guess."

"What about the car? The damage?"

"I checked the Impala and the driver's seat position is too far forward for the overweight Quimby to have been the last one driving it. That would support Apache's story that Garfield had driven it last. And there is alcohol inside the car. Apache seems credible."

"Where is the Jeep? I thought you said it was there."

"It is. The Impala is in back of it. The Jeep has a flat tire."

"Anyone else support his story?"

"It was late, but there are a couple of people who heard the crash and argument."

"Quimby may have a murder charge on his plate."

"That may well be. We're on our way back."

Chapter 43

The next day, Dan's first order of business was to collect the promised copy of the surveillance footage from the Vesta and Charter Oak.

When he returned to the squad room with two discs in his hand, he gawked at the man who was sitting inside his cubicle. "What the hell are you doing here?" he asked.

The casually clothed Syms said, "I thought I'd say hello. I saw Hardison."

"Are you back?"

"Not so fast. Nope. And I like being with Ernestine."

Dan rolled his eyes. *Too bad she doesn't share that sentiment.*

"What do you have?" Syms asked.

"Footage from one of the places downtown near the carousel. I went to a few clubs and obtained these from the Vesta lounge and the adjoining hotel, The Charter Oak."

"Are you going to watch them?"

"Are you a captain?"

"Run them. I'll make sure you don't miss anything."

"Does this mean you are back?"

Syms was silent as Dan inserted the first disc into his computer. "This one is from the hotel lobby." The video slowly forwarded from 8:00 p.m. and Dan hit stop when it advanced to 9:15.

"What do you see?" Syms asked.

Zooming in, Dan let out a breath. "It's her, Nicole Brezinski. Red-rimmed glasses and blonde hair. She's walking toward an elevator." The video rolled forward and forty-five minutes later, she came into view and walked through the lobby into the Vesta lounge. "I don't see anyone with her, but she likely just returned from a client's room and she could be meeting Karas in the lounge, but we won't see them on this disc."

Syms picked up the disc from the Vesta and handed it to Dan.

"Thanks. Let's see what this tells us."

Dan and Syms glued their eyes to the computer screen and there they were. Nicole and Karas had entered the lounge at nine and Nicole left and reappeared in the hotel. "We know she went next door and he must have waited for her in the lounge."

Dan kept the film moving and stopped it at ten-thirty, where Nicole and Karas got up and walked toward the front door. Dan said, "Did you see that? They were met by another guy outside and he's walking away with them. Who the hell is he?"

"Your guess is as good as mine. His back is the only thing we can make out."

"We do know where they were going, the carousel. Three of them, and she sure isn't naked."

Syms stood. "I'll let you handle it from here. Good luck."

Dan stowed the discs in his desk drawer and walked over to the Keurig. Bev and Scotty entered the squad room and approached him. "We just saw Syms," Bev said.

"He was here and he seems ready to get to work," Dan replied. "Where were you guys?"

"At Woodland. Quimby was held overnight and we spoke with him. We knew something was off. Part of what we were told was true. Garfield had driven the Impala the night before and he did almost hit the dog, Killer. Quimby and Garfield had bumped heads several times and the old man stuck to his story until I told him we don't believe he is telling us everything."

Bev added, "Then he opened up. He did let Garfield borrow the car and the guy apparently went to a bar. Quimby knew his car had been damaged and when Garfield came upstairs in the morning, they got into a heated argument. Garfield hung onto the keys and walked to the door. When he was at the top of the stairs, Quimby shot him. Officers are with him and he is being booked."

Dan commented, "You never know, do you?"

"No," Scotty said. "What are you up to?"

"I watched a security video from a bar I went to and Syms watched too. You can see that Nicole Brezinski, Karas and an unidentified man were at the Vesta and then they headed towards the carousel."

Bev spoke, "So, there is no question that three people were there."

"That's what the video tells me."

Dan remained at his cubicle and a while later, Hardison walked in. "What brings you down here?" the detective asked.

"Syms."

"He was here," Dan commented as he pointed to his comrades. "They weren't."

"What did he tell you?"

"Nothing positive, but I know he's itching to be back in this nuthouse."

"I believe you are right. It's funny though. His eyes lit up like a pinball machine when I shoved his badge in front of him. He didn't commit, but he sure is acting like he's on the edge of the mountain and convincing himself to jump off."

"Should we stay on his back and try to give him a shove?"

"No. From what I gather, Ernestine is pushing pretty hard."

Dan was curious. "Hey, Chief, how's the mayor dealing with the funding and manpower shortage?"

Hardison smirked. "The mayor won't talk about it. She knows, but she is powerless. We have to suck it up. I'll be upstairs."

Dan took several minutes to absorb what he had seen. The security videos from the hotel may have told a story, but he knew that Alicia Greenstein had more to tell. *What exactly does Karas hold over these pretty flight attendants? Money is always a reason to do things one might not ordinarily do, but was there something else he had on these women? How long did they expect to be selling their bodies? The bigger question is, would they be able to quit if they chose? Did Francine Devereaux pay with her life for rebelling? And did Nicole threaten, argue or demand to get out of the business? Was she going to go to the police and reveal this crime? Is that why Karas killed her? And Francine Devereaux is a real mystery.*

Dan knew one person who could listen to him and maybe cut through the haze in his mind. He made a phone call. In a startled voice, the woman on the other end muttered, "What's wrong?"

"Nothing, hon," he assured his wife. "Listen, how is your schedule?"

"Why?"

"I want to see you."

"We can talk at home."

"No, you need to listen to me at work. This is business. Treat me like a client."

"Did you forget, my clients are young people?"

"I'm coming down to your office. You're the smartest person I know and I need to bounce a few things off you."

"As long as it isn't divorce. I'll be here."

Dan grabbed his car keys. "I'll see you guys tomorrow."

"Where are you off to?" Bev asked.

"To see my wife at her office. I need a good shrink about now."

"We all do," Scotty added.

Bev said, "Look, before you go, I want to run this by you. The Bowler file is cold again and for Garfield to have known about the park killing, he had to learn about it somehow. My feeling is that he saw it on TV or read it in the prison. They do have newspapers. That's where he was when it occurred and I don't think Tedone told him about it."

Dan nodded. "That's a good theory. We'll never know. I gotta go."

Chapter 44

Dan pulled up at the medical center where Phyllis worked. The two-story L-shaped facility was set amongst three other similar buildings. The four structures were designated A, B, C, and D, with a large parking area centrally located.

Inside building A, Dan browsed the directory on the wall and found his wife's name listed with the psychology department, *PsyD. Phyllis Shields 104.*

She was one of five therapists in her practice. Dan entered the outer door and announced his presence to the receptionist, who let Phyllis know he was there. She accompanied him inside her quarters. "Care to lie on the couch or sit in the chair?"

"I'll lie on the couch."

Her desk had a large clock mounted over it on the wall and she sat in her chair with her legs crossed, facing her husband. The child psychologist waited for her not-so-young visitor to speak. She had a pad and pen in her lap and smiled at her husband. "Are you going to talk?"

"You know I don't often discuss work with you."

She sobered him up. "You have a short memory. You do it more than you imagine."

"Maybe so, but this time it's better we talk here. Lady Godiva. Nicole Brezinski. It's so bothersome."

"Why are you so hyped up?"

"It's about the flight attendants. There are five who earn extra money by having sex with clients the pilot sends to them. It's a long story, but they all work for a guy named Jeff Karas and he pays them for their services. I don't know what the money split is."

"You mean he is a pimp?"

"He is. Lady Godiva died at the carousel and she was four to five weeks pregnant. I have always been sure she was murdered, but I can't prove it. I can arrest the pilot on prostitution charges. I can arrest the girls too, but I'm only interested in the death of Nicole. It reeks of murder even though Arnstein ruled she died of cardiac arrest. We haven't found her clothes and the word 'whore' was written on her back with a Sharpie. It's tormenting me."

Phyllis seemed befuddled as to why he came to her clinic and she wiggled her pen. "And you are beginning to torment me."

Dan continued as if he had not heard her. "Here's another thing. I don't think all those young women are having sex because they want to. I know it's the money, but I am sure it's something else that is luring or forcing them to pleasure men."

"And you can't figure out why and you want me to?"

"Not exactly. Tell me something. If it were you, how much money would it take you to become a prostitute?"

Phyllis dropped the pen, shuddered and raised her eyebrows, "Really? Are you alright?"

"Damn, you are sexy."

She sighed. "Okay, if you're trying to sell me, you can have the house, kids, cooking, cleaning, and shopping. Four dollars will do it." She sneered. "You are sick!"

"Maybe. Here's my theory. I think he is somehow blackmailing them. He has something over them. He may be threating to kill them. So far no one will fess up. I do have one flight attendant, Alicia Greenstein, who may be ready to tell me the truth, but I have to be careful."

"I don't understand. You're seeing me and spilling out a sexual tale. Why tell me all this? I'm not a sex therapist."

"Because it's driving me crazy. How many times I keep telling myself the same things. I wanted a fresh opinion, an intelligent, independent female, and you're the only one I know."

Wrestling with the pad she held, but never wrote on, Phyllis opined, "If I am so smart, I would have barred you from coming here. I'm glad to have helped. Are we done now? I'm sure you'll get to the bottom of it soon. I have a client coming in. I'll see you at home." She uncrossed her legs, picked up the pen. and rose. She snickered. "It was my pleasure, or maybe not."

Dan gave her a kiss before whispering in her ear, "Have I told you how sexy you are?"

She whimpered, "Oh God, that was your intention after all. Wow. I may never have sex again after this session."

CHAPTER 45

It was no dream and not a mirage. There he was, Captain Syms, sitting where he belonged. It was a sight for Dan's sore eyes, and he barged in on him. A lemony scent filled the air. "Just cleaned up," Syms cheerfully said. "You're early. What is it, six-ten?"

Dan smiled. "You even shined your badge."

"Hell yeah." Holding his squirt pistol, Syms swiveled to the back credenza. "Don't the bonsais look great?"

"Thank Bev. Without her reminding us, they may not have made it."

He placed the water gun down. "Okay, ex-boss for a while. Fill me in."

Dan settled into a chair and spent more than an hour bringing the captain up to date. As Dan left the office, he said, "Hey, Scotty is here."

"Get out."

Dan latched onto Scotty and turned him toward the figure down the hall. "That's no mannequin in there."

Scotty's mouth opened wide. "And he took his bonsais back."

Mal and Bev sauntered in within a few minutes of each other and Dan made them aware of Sym's presence. "Right now he's getting reacclimated. Let him be." Dan picked up his phone and announced, "I have a girl I have to see."

The detective had Alicia Greenstein at the top of his agenda. *I'll have to pin her down and much to my dismay. I might have to pull the jail card. If she cracks, she cracks. If she doesn't, the deck may be missing a card when I'm done. All I can do now is have a heart-to-heart.*

Dan called her and for a change, he hit paydirt. Alicia answered and he remembered his last visit ended abruptly and hoped she would be agreeable to his dropping in on her. "Good morning. How are you?" he asked.

"I'm fine."

"I'm glad to hear it. I assume you knew I was going to get in touch with you again. Listen, I'm sorry that our last session ended as it did. May I come to visit you again? A few things have come up about Nicole's death and I'd like to go over them with you."

She replied, "I have some shopping to do. I got in last night and have to run a few errands."

He wasn't sure if this was a stall, or avoidance tactic. "I understand. Listen. I really have to speak with you and again, I apologize if our last session got a bit testy. When will be a good time for me to come by?"

She sighed before accepting his apology. "How about this afternoon? One-ish?'

"I'll see you then."

Dan was pleased with her response and called Evan Lincoln. The state's attorney answered his phone. "Dan, what's going on?"

"I'm curious. Have you gotten any response from Delta or Verizon?"

A touch of hostility came through Dan's receiver. "Look, those warrants were served by local sheriffs. I told you those companies take time. We have red tape and so do they. I will tell you, I did receive email responses that said they will get back to me as soon as possible. That's the best we can hope for unless you come up with a solid murder suspect."

"I know. Anyhow, I am going to have another chat with Alicia Greenstein today."

"Good luck. Fill me in later."

▲

Afternoon couldn't come soon enough for Dan, but he did arrive at Alicia Greenstein's on time and there was an unfamiliar blue Miata parked in the driveway. The condo's curtains were drawn and he rang the bell while hearing music.

The door opened and the detective was greeted by a shapely young lady he hadn't met before. "You must be Detective Shields. Alicia will be home soon. I'm Ariel Adams."

"Nice to meet you. I saw you in a picture Stella shared with me. May I come in? "

She ushered him in and closed the door. "Please sit. Alicia went to buy groceries, she'll be back soon."

"I forgot to mention to her, how nice this condo is. Are you staying here?"

"I do sometimes."

Dan fumbled with the notepad he was holding. "I have new information to share with you both. As soon as Alicia gets home, you'll hear it." Before they sat, the alert detective espied a cream-colored notebook on a table next to the landline.

Ariel's eyes fluttered. "It's so sad, first the assault and then her death. But that Uber driver got what he deserved. And he had given me a lift once to the airport. I have to tell you, I know he had his eyes on me as I walked into the terminal. He told me to call him for a ride when I get back." She shuddered. "It could have been me that he assaulted."

Bells went off in Dan's head. "Would you mind if I show you a picture?" Without waiting for a response, he retrieved the photo he'd been given by Merriel Sandovar. "Can you identify the Uber driver who took you to the airport?"

She studied the picture and pointed to one of the brothers. "Him, that's Emilio."

"Are you sure?"

"Yes. He had an earring."

"Did you notice the earring the time he picked you up? I mean, was he wearing it?"

"He definitely wore an earring."

Dan put the photo back into his pocket. *She just identified Elijah.*

Ariel whisked her hand through her long hair. "Dying the way she did, as awful as it was, a heart attack is the last thing I would have imagined happening to Nicole."

Dan heard a vehicle pulling into the driveway. "It sounds like Alicia is back."

Ariel opened the door as Alicia, with a shopping bag in her arms, entered. "Can you grab this? Another one is in the car."

Ariel carried the groceries into the kitchen and Alicia came in with another bag. "Hi, Detective."

"Hi. Take your time."

The women joined Dan after they unloaded groceries. Alicia removed her sunglasses and sat beside Ariel. "I'm sorry if I forgot to tell you she was here."

"No apology necessary." Dan looked into one set of blue eyes and one set of brown eyes. "I'm glad to see you both. I'm not going to sugarcoat anything. It is my belief that Nicole's heart attack was prompted by something, perhaps she was scared, freaked out, or even set up to be killed. Thus far, Karas has been a mystery to me and I am sure you ladies can tell me more about him." He directed his next comment to Alicia. "I remember you told me you thought he was in Chicago the night Nicole died. I have to tell you, he and

Nicole are both on video from a downtown club called Vesta as well as the connected hotel."

Alicia glanced toward Ariel. "He told me so."

"And if I remember right, you thought Nicole was in San Diego."

"I thought so."

Dan studied both women and placed his notepad down next to the cream-colored booklet on the table. "Ladies don't be smug now. Jeff Karas controls a lot of your activities, doesn't he? I mean jobwise, both jobs."

Ariel's face grew pale and she glanced toward Alicia. Neither one spoke.

Dan broke the silence. "Ladies, you know what I am talking about. Being a flight attendant and part-time, to put in nicely, escort. Stella has a journal on her table that I browsed. Do I have to open the one next to the telephone?"

The women looked at each other and Alicia nervously asked, "Are you here to arrest us?"

Dan reassured them, "I said it before, and I mean it. No. I only want information, the truth. Let me put it to you this way. I suspect Jeff Karas is responsible for Nicole's death and you can help me arrest him. Stella gave me enough ammunition to arrest him for, lacking other words, being your pimp."

Alicia sighed. "I hate him."

"Look. Stella told me about her darkest days and how she was lured in by him. I also know of Chelsea's checkered past. What do you know about Francine Devereaux? Apparently she had flown to Paris with Karas and never returned."

Alicia softly mumbled, "I didn't know her well."

"Well enough to say she may have wanted to turn him in?"

Neither woman spoke and Dan appealed to them both. "Now is the time to let it all out."

Ariel appeared to be uneasy. She stood for a minute and then settled again into her chair.

"Okay," Alicia began. "Francine told him to go to hell, and she told me she was going home. I never saw her again, none of us did."

Dan leaned forward and raised his brows. "Did he threaten her?"

Ariel pouted and it was obvious she was holding back tears.

"What is it, Ariel? I hit a nerve, didn't I?"

At the same time, Alicia trembled. "We knew he was serious." She raised her voice. "If he killed her, then he would think nothing of killing us or people in our families."

Dan blew out a breath and leaned forward. "So, he intimidated you and you believed your lives as well as your families' lives were in jeopardy?"

Alicia pouted and blushed. "Okay, I don't know where to start." She held Ariel's hand. "We have similar stories. Jeff and I were in Houston. It was a weekend layover. We had eaten dinner together and he spiked my drink." She became sullen and said, "Then I found myself in his room and I woke up naked, and I knew he raped me. Then came the unthinkable. He kept me locked in the room and threw a thousand dollars in front of me, saying how easy it will be for us to earn a lot more cash." Alicia sighed. She shivered and stopped talking.

Dan touched her hand. "You're doing fine. How were you threatened?"

"Bastards. He has an accomplice, a guy we never met. They both knew where I was from. They knew where my mother lived. I can't go on." She rushed toward the bathroom and Dan heard her throwing up. Ariel followed her.

This is hard, extremely hard. It sounds like he convinced her that her family was not safe.

The women returned and settled back in their seats. Alicia continued, "Where was I?'

"Your mother," Dan reminded her.

She sighed. "His accomplice, a guy we never saw except on Facetime. He was masked and he had a rag doll in one hand and a knife in the other. He stabbed the doll, saying this could be you or worse yet, your mother. Then, unbelievably, he ran a video of my mother. She was standing beside her car waiting for help to change a flat tire. His vulgar words were *she could have a more serious vehicle mishap anytime.* I had no choice. I couldn't let them harm my mother. He also had Chelsea tell me how great the money was and not to fret about satisfying a lot of guys. I was scared and tried to block everything out every time he sent me a horny bastard."

"Is there anything you can tell me about the accomplice? Was he tall, short, have any marks you could see?"

"No, he sat and we couldn't see through his mask. He had a gruff voice, deep."

Ariel nodded. "They did the same to me. I have a younger sister and he had a video of her. She's nineteen and he brazenly threatened to kidnap and traffic her if I didn't obey. I was scared out of my mind and forced myself to put up with feeling like the dirty whore I became."

Dan sat back and watched both young women regain their composure. "Remember when I said that Jeff and Nicole are on video? One other person was there. He met Nicole and Karas at the door and they went to the carousel. He could be the masked man."

Alicia frowned, "They killed her. Heart attack or not, I know they did."

"Do you believe they killed Francine?"

"Honestly," Ariel replied, "I do."

"What about Nicole? What are you not telling me?"

Alicia rose and paced. "She had been beaten and I saw bruises she brushed off as an accident. He kept closer tabs on her and she became his toy until she was sodomized."

"My understanding is that he flew to London this week. Do you know when he'll be back?"

Alicia sighed. "Chelsea told me they would be meeting here in town when he returned. She didn't say where."

Ariel began to cry. "We're all supposed to be here because there is a huge convention in Hartford this weekend. Real estate brokers from all over New England." She wiped her eyes. "He ordered us to work it. Chelsea and Stella are supposed to be there too."

Dan didn't like what he heard. "Look. You don't have to do what he commands."

Alicia declared, "You're right. This time we don't plan to please anyone but ourselves. None of us. It's the first time we will all be in one place together. We have to talk to Stella."

"Why?"

Alicia held Ariel's hands again. "Because we intend to end it."

"How?"

"Stella has an idea and we will find out later."

"Don't confront him alone," Dan warned. "His pal may be with him and you know he is dangerous. Trust me. I can have the entire police force there. Let me talk with Stella."

"Please don't," Alicia pleaded. "She may not tell you the truth. I promise, I'll call you when I find out what the plans are."

Chapter 46

Dan needed a shot of caffeine, so he made himself a cupful and carried it to his desk.

"For a guy who hates that machine, you sure do drink your share of coffee," Bev said.

"The way things are around here, mud would taste good. It's not that bad. It's hot anyway."

"So am I," Scotty said as he cozied up to his comrades. "I saw Dixon in the parking lot. Quimby isn't going to be much help. The guy had been in Woodland and he became delusional, off-the-wall and he's now in a nuthouse. The South Asylum. That's one way to get away with murder."

Dan glanced at his cell phone's caller ID *No. Tell me it's not him.* But he knew it was. "Hampton. Where are you? I know it's not downstairs."

"Nope. Home."

"Not the Maple?"

"Yeah, the Maple. Didn't I say that?"

"Sorry, I misunderstood."

"Yeah. Me and Rollin might not be hangin' here much longer. The Feds. They ain't got no sympathy. Know what I mean? Cross 'em once and they are like elephants and do not forget. Shit, we are dead meat."

"What are you saying?"

"They don't fool around. We ain't got the money to pay them back. Shit, Dan, me and Rollin are gonna go away for a while. And get this, we gotta pay a thousand-dollar fine to boot, plus interest. My sister don't wanna hear it."

Dan shrugged. "Neither do I. How long is a while?"

"A year, maybe nine months."

"Can't they make it longer?"

"Come on, Dan. That ain't the nice guy I know."

"You know, nice guys finish last."

"Dan."

"When are you going away?"

"Don't know yet, but jumpsuits are coming."

"You probably won't be in with hardcore criminals."

"No, just with Madoff-like thieves."

Dan laughed. "Maybe they will teach you how to make money."

"Didn't do him no good."

"Well, there's not a damned thing you guys can do about it now, unless you escape to Brazil. Suck it up. It's not like you didn't deserve it."

"Us? And what about the thieves in Washington? Ain't a prison big enough to hold them all. Ouch!"

"Are you okay?"

"Yeah. Rollin spilled hot coffee on me."

In the background, Dan heard, "And get a bunch of napkins, Dodo."

"You realize you two will be split up."

"Good. I need my privates. You gonna come see us?"

"Hampton, I wouldn't miss seeing you in prison for anything. Let me know where and when."

"You gonna bring Sasser?"

"Oh no, but I will tell him. Paste my number to your cell wall."

"And you know what else?"

"I can't wait to hear this. What?"

"You got any idea how much a telephone pole costs? They wanna charge us three grand."

"How about writing it off as a cost of doing business? You do pay taxes, don't you?"

"Sorta. Never thought of a business account."

"Even if you did, I don't believe jail or knocking down telephone poles is deductible."

"Rollin says hi. Hey, nice talkin.' Send money for toothpaste."

"Keep smiling. Don't lose my number."

"Yeah. Bye."

Dan's laughter drew Scotty's attention. "What's so funny?"

"Our boys are. Hampton. He and Rollin are about to go off to prison for defrauding the government."

"I knew they'd end up there someday."

"Me too." Dan resorted to his phone again. "I hope the Delta and Verizon warrants bear fruit soon. I'm going to touch base with Lincoln."

Upon receiving his call, Lincoln said, "You must have read my mind. I'm stunned myself. The Delta information got here this morning."

"Great. What does it say?"

"I'll email the data to you."

"Thanks."

"By the way, nothing from Verizon yet."

Dan signaled Bev to join him and Scotty as he opened the email from Lincoln. "This is it, the Delta flight schedules and personnel information. I'm not sure I need the schedules."

"Why not?" Scotty asked.

Dan faced his comrades. "Because I had a long talk with Alicia Greenstein and Ariel Adams yesterday. Along with Stella and

Chelsea, they are going to be meeting Karas at a real estate convention in Hartford this weekend. As of now, it appears Stella is coming up with a scheme and will lay it out for them. Alicia said she will call me when Stella informs her of the plan. Right now Francine Devereaux is on my radar. I'm sure she was murdered in Paris. There is no trace of her and she apparently resigned. I want to read her file." Dan perused the data on his computer and located the letter of resignation that Francine Devereaux supposedly mailed in from Paris. The suspicious detective compared the signature on it to the one on her employment application. *Those signatures don't match.* He said to Scotty, "To me, these signatures do not match."

Scotty studied them. "No. They sure don't. She never wrote the resignation letter. It's simply typed and signed."

"I believe it was inked by Karas." Dan found the pilot's signature an employment application. "I'm no handwriting expert, but it sure looks to me like he signed the resignation letter."

Scotty glanced Karas's signature. "I agree."

Dan swiveled his chair around, "I want Hardison to check with the French police. I'm going to clue him in now. How about you telling Syms? Bev, you can browse the rest of this data, maybe you'll find other interesting stuff."

Dan left the squad room and made his way to see the chief. Hardison had his phone to his ear and it was obvious to Dan that he was speaking with the captain. "Hey, your boy is here. Looks to me like he wants the job back. Gotta go." The phone was back on its receiver. "Okay, Detective, I'm listening."

"Good. I have information we need to follow up on. It's a flight attendant named Francine Devereaux. I believe she is dead. She may have been killed in Paris and I'd like you to find out who to contact over there."

"Tell me more."

"I have the information we requested from Delta. It's a long story, but the gist right now is that she was a flight attendant who took a trip Jeff Karas piloted to Paris and she never returned. Supposedly she turned in a letter of resignation, but she didn't. Karas did it and I want to find her. Dead or alive."

"Get me the full details and I'll get on it."

"Sure thing."

Dan returned to find Bev at the computer with Scotty beside her. "I told Syms," Scotty said.

"Thanks."

"Karas is a liar," Bev said. "According to the flight schedules, he was in Hartford two days before Nicole Brezinski died. He flew into Bradley and then back out on the following Monday to Dallas."

"That doesn't surprise me," Dan said, "I have him on video. Do me a favor, print out all of Francine Devereaux's information, including the flight she made with Karas to Paris. Hardison wants all the information."

A few minutes later, Dan carried the paperwork to the chief. *Alicia Greenstein better not forget to call me.*

Chapter 47

Phyllis's car was not in sight when Dan got home and he assumed she had a late appointment until he read the note she left on the kitchen counter. *I went to see Margaret Valente. Kids are at their friend's house. I should be home soon.*

A half-hour later, Phyllis ambled in and tossed her purse on the kitchen counter. Still dressed in the gray pantsuit she wore to work, she kissed Dan. "You're home a little early."

"And you're a bit late. Did you and Margaret decide on our dinner date?"

"We discussed it."

Dan gazed at her unsteady hand and seemingly forced smile. "Are you okay?"

"I'm fine, a bit tired. I have to ger dinner ready. Go relax. The kids will be home soon."

"What's cooking?"

"Pasta. Go change."

"I'll be right back."

When he returned, Kate and Josh were home and Phyllis was preparing dinner. "Can you set the table?" she asked. "I want to get out of my suit."

"Sure." He watched his wife leave the room and sensed something was bothering her. *I've seen that worried look before.*

What is she not telling me?

She re-entered the kitchen and didn't say anything.

Dan said, "Hon, I know something is wrong. Do you want to tell me?"

"Later."

"Why later? Tell me now."

She did not smile. "Trust me. After dinner. How about getting the kids in here?"

"Okay."

When the meal was finished, Kate and Josh left the room. Phyllis advised him, "Dave and Margaret are coming over at seven."

"So why the moodiness?"

"Wait until they get here."

"I don't like it. What's going on?"

There was not a hint of a smile on her face. "The four of us have to talk."

Dan shrugged and insisted, "Tell me what's going on. You look like you saw a ghost."

"They'll be here soon. I'm going to put out some cookies in the den. I told Josh and Kate to watch TV upstairs."

Dan touched her arm. "This is not like you."

She backed away. "Wait until they get here."

Dan made one more attempt to get her to talk. "This does not sound like nothing. Why the games?"

Phyllis was poker-faced. "Would you set out some napkins? I'll make coffee."

Dan did as asked and relegated himself to his lounger until the doorbell rang. He was then joined by his wife, Dave, and Margaret. Cookies were on a tray in front of them. "Coffee?" Phyllis asked.

"Please," Margaret answered.

"Me too," Dave added.

Dan began to sense this conversation was about Mike and Haley.

What the hell is going on? It better not be what I think.

They were all seated when Phyllis returned with the drinks and set herself on the couch. Margaret turned to Phyllis, took a drink and repeated what she had told her for Dave and Dan to hear. "I was in Haley's room two days ago and found a pregnancy test in her wastebasket. I wasn't supposed to see it." She paused "I was shocked when I read it and learned Haley was pregnant."

Dan's mouth opened wide. "Are you saying what I think you are saying?"

"Well, I spoke with Haley and she told me."

Dan huffed. "I knew it."

Dave nodded. "It is what it is, Dan. Mike is the father."

With anger on his face, Dan raised his voice. "And you know that how?" His voice was loud enough for the children upstairs to hear.

"Simmer down," Phyllis urged him.

He pretended to calm himself. "Okay, I didn't mean to imply that Haley was sleeping around, but how do you know that Mike is the father?"

Margaret said, "I had a talk with her and she admitted they slept together when he was home and she hasn't had sex with anyone else."

Dan felt a fever building. "I'll kill him. He swore to me when he was here they had not slept together since they broke up after high school. I wonder how many times they had unprotected sex?"

"Oh my God!" Phyllis exclaimed. "It only takes once."

Dan stewed. "I'll break his neck."

Phyllis glared at him. "You'll do no such thing, We can't do anything about the pregnancy. We have to speak with Mike."

The ruffled detective fidgeted. "Does he know?"

Margaret winced. "Haley says not yet."

Dan thought of the girl Mike had been dating at college. "He better not get Rachel pregnant too.”

“Who?“ Dave asked.

“Damn it. Mike is dating a coed named Rachel and you know they are having sex. It’s college life away from home, no different than in our day.”

Annoyed with his comment, Phyllis jabbed him. “Stop it.”

Dan exhaled. “Okay.” The dismayed father lamented, “I’ll ream his ass out tomorrow.”

Phyllis tapped his arm. “I’ll talk with him. You stay out of it for now.”

Josh came downstairs to get a snack and walked in on the foursome. “Dad, we heard you yell. Are you okay?”

“Yes, it’s nothing. I caught my leg in the footrest. I’m fine. Go back upstairs.” Dan smiled at his likely future in-laws and toned down. “I know there was a real glow, sparkle, between them. There always was. You know we love Haley. I guess we’ll get to know Joey a little better.”

Phyllis refilled the coffee cups. “They will be alright. Haley has to tell him.”

“She intends to soon,” Margaret advised.

Nine o’clock came fast and their guests went home. Dan hugged his wife. “How’s it feel to be a grandmother?”

“Not yet. I’ll get used to it.”

“And I’m going on every date Kate ever has until she is thirty.”

“What about Josh? Never, I suppose. If that isn’t a double standard. And your crack about when we were in college was not true.”

Dan smirked. “You’re not telling me now you were a virgin when we had sex?”

“Shut up. And like you had no experience?”

“I need a good night’s sleep. Hope I don’t have a nightmare.”

Chapter 48

The sight of a pair of feet clad in expensive shoes walking into the squad room signaled to Dan that something had gone wrong in the world of Hancock Sasser. He stood and watched as the dapperly dressed lawyer shuffled himself up to him. "This can't be good," Dan remarked.

Sasser grinned. "Would I be here if I didn't have any news?"

Dan snickered. "Do I have to answer that?"

Sasser saw Syms and he did a double take. "When did he get back?"

"My question is, what are you doing here?"

"I wanna say hi."

"Be quick. Seeing you may make him quit again."

Sasser strode into the captain's office and paid his respects before coming back to sidle up next to Dan.

"So, what are you doing here?" Dan asked.

Sasser set his briefcase on the floor. "It's like this. Me and Malone had a meeting with Lincoln and Waverly this morning. Not good, Dan. Not good."

"I'm listening."

"It's Barkley Malone. We know a retrial is set for June seventeenth and he cannot afford to pay me or anyone else for defending him at that trial, so I presented a plea deal to Lincoln. I went for twenty-five years with a chance for parole at twenty. Lincoln didn't want to hear it. He responded with forty period. No chance of parole. It might as well be life. I told you Malone is a stubborn ox and he rejected Lincoln's offer. After I took him aside and told him he could be sentenced to death if he goes to trial again, he stood his ground and he is willing to take his chances in court even if I abandon him, and I don't plan to represent him again." Sasser paused. "Guess what? Lincoln might not be there either. His term is coming up and he might leave."

"I'm aware he may call the public sector quits. By the way, when are you hanging it up?"

"Same day as you, pal. Wanna do lunch?"

Dan checked the time. Eleven-twenty. *I may as well get it over with.* "Sass, sometimes you're not so bad. Take me someplace good. You can do the driving. I promise, I won't mess up the Cadillac."

"Fair enough. And don't pull any of that EpiPen crap."

Dan threw out a not too serious query. "How about me faking food poisoning?"

Sasser laughed. "That sounds like a lawsuit to me. Now we're talking the same game. I'm beginning to like you."

The attorney drove ten miles to a seafood restaurant in Wethersfield, surprising Dan with his amenable choice. "You really do like me," Dan commented.

"Hey, we can't always choose our friends, besides, Chantel suggested this place."

Soon after enjoying their lunches, a lobster roll for Dan and fish and chips for Sasser, Dan picked up the tab and in his mind, settled a debt for having Sasser again represent Hampton and Rollin. "I believe that we are even," the detective said.

"Yeah, and you got off cheap."

Sasser took Dan back to the police station and departed. As soon as he entered the squad room, Dan went to his desk and contacted

Alicia again because he had to find out what was going on, but he was stymied as the flight attendant told him that she had not spoken with Stella and she would call him tomorrow. The unsatisfied detective had no choice and wondered if he could rely on her.

Chapter 49

It was nearing nine-fifteen and Dan had not heard from Alicia and again worried if he could rely on her. What were the flight attendants, part-time prostitutes, planning? Dan's phone remained silent and he traipsed down the hall to the captain's office. "I haven't heard anything from Alicia. In the meantime, I want to see how the carousel is running and how Gracie Allen is. Are you ready to come with me?"

"Is it open? I thought it runs from ten until dark."

"I checked. It's nine and we should go before it gets busy."

Calmly, Syms came out from behind his desk. "Lead the way."

▲

Bushnell Park was starting to fill with pedestrians who were taking advantage of the late summer-like day. As Dan and Syms walked toward the carousel, the detective alerted his boss to someone he'd seen there before and said, "See the guy with his legs hanging off the bench? He was here when Nicole was killed. Then, he had a bottle in his hand and was passed out on one of those benches."

"Homeless, no doubt," Syms said.

"Obviously. I never talked to him, we will now." They neared the man whose clouded eyes were open as he jumped off the bench and Dan positioned himself in front of the inebriated soul, stopping him from fleeing. "Hold it, we're police, but you're not in trouble. Relax, sit again."

The man staggered and fell back onto the bench and Dan caught the stench of alcoholic breath and body odor. *When was the last time this guy had a shower or a shave? I've smelled worse, for sure.* Dan continued, "You were here the day the woman on the carousel horse was found dead. I saw you then. Did you hear or see anything?" *What a dumb question, he was out of it and may as well have been on Mars.*

The man teetered and remained close-mouthed and Dan spotted a round shiny object on the wretched man's right hand. "Is the ring you have on yours?"

"Is now," he slurred.

"May I see it?"

Dan held the man's unsteady finger as he examined the ring and noticed the image of an airplane etched into one side of it. "Where did you find this?"

His head bobbed. "It's mine."

"I won't pull it off. Honest. May I hold it?"

The man pulled his hand back.

"I just want to see it."

The man placed his unsteady hand in front of him so Dan could examine the ring closely. He held the finger out and showed the jewelry to Syms. "This emblem. It's a US Air Force-issued pilot's ring."

The man's finger flinched. "Hold on," Dan said to him. "I only want to know where you found it."

He clumsily pointed under the bench and slurring, he said, "Right there."

Dan whispered to Syms. "This ring is evidence." The detective opened his wallet. "Listen, I'd like to buy it." He waved twenty dollars at the unsteady man. "This is yours for the ring."

Ten seconds later, Dan had the round object and took a closer look. Sure enough, the initials engraved inside were J.K. "It belongs to him, Jeff Karas." Dan carefully tucked the ring into his pocket. "Now the carousel."

The atmosphere at the kiddie ride today was a far cry from when Dan was last there. This time, the bright lights accompanied carnival-like music that were waiting for the first go-round of the day. Gracie Allen stood at the starter control box outside the red railing and Dan saw a younger woman he had not seen before who was at the counter and standing behind the register. He greeted Gracie. "Hi, can we talk with you?"

Gracie grimaced. "The images of that poor naked girl, I'll never forget."

"Can we go back to that day for a few moments? You had told us you found her and called for help."

"I did, before passing out, and that's all I remember until the paramedics helped me."

"Sometimes it takes a while for the mind to recall things. Is there anything you can remember now you may not have remembered then?"

She squinted, seeming to ponder the question. "I don't think so."

Dan tried again. "By the way, I later found a Sharpie by the popcorn machine. Was it yours?"

"Probably. Me, Wally, Stephanie, we all use one to mark prices and other things."

"That's what I assumed. So, there is nothing new to tell me?"

"No, Wally was good to me. You know, he's from Ohio and his grandfather was influential in relocating the carousel from Canton to here. I'm glad he did."

"Where is Wally now?"

"He hasn't been here in a few days. He said he has the flu. Stephanie is filling in as she occasionally does."

"Tell me more about him."

"I don't really know much. I do know he was discharged from the military because of an injury he suffered. He was in the Air Force and he was something called a fuel specialist. He used to gas up planes and he told me that he knew a lot of pilots."

Dan's eyes closed as a light went off in his head. *Jet fuel? Planes? Air Force. Karas was an Air Force pilot.* Dan put his open hand to his forehead and reopened his eyes. *How did I miss that? Of course. How could Forin have known to come to the carousel to see Gracie? She was dazed and in no condition to use a phone. The news hadn't reported on the death yet, so how did he know, unless he was here? Unless he and Karas were here. Wally Forin, the masked partner. And his voice is deep. Bastard had a key, but apparently shoved in the door to make it look like the place was broken into.* "Do you have his number and address?"

"I'll get them." She did and wrote the information on a piece of paper and handed it to Dan.

"Thank you. Have a nice day."

Dan said to Syms, "Let's go. I'll explain it to you on the way back." Once they were inside his Accord, Dan commented, "Bastard. Wally Forin is supposedly sick. He's the henchman working with Karas in the sex business. He's the tough guy who threatened the girls and he was here with Nicole and Karas the night she died. He was the mystery man who met them at the hotel before coming here. We have two guys we need to find. Karas and Forin. We have Forin's address. I want to see what else we can find out about him."

▲

Again, Bev was Dan's computer go-to. "I need your help."

"Don't you always?"

"We were at the carousel and I want to know as much as we can find out about Wally Forin. He knows Karas and he hasn't been seen in a few days because he supposedly has the flu. We have his address and I plan to pay him a visit. Calling is out. You're good at tracking down information. See what you can find out."

Dan left her alone while he talked with Syms.

It wasn't long before Bev interrupted them. "Here's what I can tell you. He's fifty-one, five-ten, born in Canton, Ohio. He was in the Air Force before being discharged with an injury. He lives in Rocky Hill and has a brother in Akron. He has no arrests and is not married."

"What kind of car does he drive?"

"Nissan." She wrote down the plate number, AB4888YZ.

"We don't need a warrant," Syms said. "This is urgent, but I will alert the Rocky Hill police of the urgency to get to his house." After doing so, he said, "Let's go. They are dispatching an officer to meet us there."

CHAPTER 50

It was ten-twenty a.m. and Dan speedily drove to Forin's residence. A Rocky Hill black-and-white cruiser was parked outside the L-shaped one-story home when he and Syms arrived. The inconspicuous, brown-shingled residence had an empty one-car driveway with no garage. A white fence surrounding the lot had a sign nailed to it that screamed BEWARE LARGE DOG.

A patch of land separated Forin's property from his neighbors' residences. Dan, Syms and patrolwoman Jenn Majors neared the entrance. Dan heard no sounds and saw no signs of life on the premises, and certainly no dog.

Syms tried to open the locked gate of the four-foot fence but the wooden door would not budge. He kicked the gate in and the threesome inched toward the front door.

Majors peered through a slit in the front window's curtain. "Lights are not on."

Dan tried to open the door, but it too was locked, so he removed his gun from his holster. "Here we go again." He aimed the butt end at the glass panel to the left of the door and rammed it through the pane. Glass shattered and he carefully reached in and unlatched the lock before they entered. Dan tried a light switch. "Nothing." He pulled the string of a lamp. "The power is off." Drawing the curtains back provided a little more illumination for them to inspect the residence.

Syms went into the kitchen and opened the refrigerator. "He must have left here quickly, the milk appears to be fresh, as do the bananas on the counter."

In the sparsely furnished living area, Dan commented, "He sure doesn't believe in much furniture." Moving into one of three bedrooms, he saw an unmade bed. "Figures."

Majors rifled through the dresser. "I have something. A notebook."

"Let me see it." Dan leafed through it and read several notations. He was stunned when he spotted Francine Devereaux's name and a photo of her pasted onto one page. The note printed under her picture read: *Feisty as shit. Sassy. Would have gone to police. Had to get rid of her.*

Another scribbling. *Nicole: Wanted out. Jeff got her pregnant. Happy birthday carousel ride. Died before we had chance to kill her.*

There was more. *Stella: Getting old. Hot-headed at times. Could blow anytime. Dangerous.*

Alicia: Scared. Don't trust her. May have to bloody mother.

Ariel: Sometimes obstinate. Talks too much. Could be liability.

Chelse: Shaky. Keeping close watch. Too much sass and backtalk. Loose cannon and could go off. Has to go.

There was one more notation Dan didn't understand. *Blanche Morton.* Beside her name the page was blank. He closed the book. "Chelsea is in deep trouble."

Majors went into the second bedroom as Dan and Syms followed. What they encountered cleared up one question. Observing the bed with women's clothes strewn across it, he knew whose they were. "Those are Nicole's clothes. She was wearing them in the hotel security video."

Syms spotted more women's clothing in a corner of the room. "You don't suppose those belong to Chelsea?"

Majors carefully dangled a bra. "Let me see the other one." She compared them and said, "These came from different women. They are not the same sizes."

Dan was deeply troubled. "Where is Chelsea? She may be dead. I don't like this whole thing. These guys appear to have designs on killing them all," he remarked to Syms. "You saw the notebook. It seems to me Karas and Forin know things are coming to an end and they have no other way out, so killing the harem would eliminate the possibility of anyone ever knowing."

Syms opened the basement door and a rancid smell hit his nose. "I don't like this odor."

Majors lit her flashlight and they inched down the stairs into the dank basement. "No," Dan said as he spied a large freezer in one corner.

He slowly proceeded to it and Syms and Majors joined him. Dan pulled the lid up. "God damn it, Chelsea. He killed her. Naked, same as Nicole." Dan spotted a bloodied baseball bat on the floor. "That bastard mashed her with the bat." He closed the lid.

Majors shuddered. "I'll get a team out here."

Syms said, "Dixon needs to get a BOLO out. Forin could be anywhere. So could Karas."

▲

Once Dan and Syms returned to the police station, they went to Dixon, who got right on the car search. Then Dan said to Dixon, "I need to make sure Alicia, Ariel and Stella are alright too. I want unmarked cars stationed outside their residences."

Dixon agreed and Dan and Syms headed to the squad room. "I have to call Alicia," Dan said. He was relieved to hear her voice. "Alicia, how is it going?"

"We discussed everything with Stella last night and we're all going to be at the convention center hotel dining room around six. Jeff is bringing Chelsea. Me and Ariel will be in the restaurant and will be waiting for Stella and them."

Dan opted not to say anything about Chelsea. *Damn, I have to alert her about Forin.*

"Alicia, I want to let you know, we have a bead on the masked man. His name is Wally Forin, and we have a search out for him now. Do me and you a favor. You and Ariel stay together. I need to call Stella." Dan arched back in his chair, blew out a breath and while still connected with Alicia, he heard a cell ring and Ariel telling Alicia that it was Stella. He said, "Don't hang up. Stella needs to know."

"Alicia replied, "So does Ariel. I'll tell them both."

"Make sure Stella is aware of Forin and tell her to be wary and make sure she has my number."

"I will and we will see you later."

Dan hoped the BOLO would soon pay off and suddenly, like a bolt of lightning another light went off in his head, and he grimaced because he'd just made sense of the last notation in Forin's notebook, *Blanche Morton. Christ, I loved that show. George Burns and Gracie Allen. Blanche Morton was their neighbor. Why would Forin have a reason to kill Gracie Allen?*

Before going back to Syms, Dan called Dixon again. "Get units over to the carousel right now. I think Gracie Allen is in danger. I'll get down there with Syms." He informed the captain and they scurried out of the building.

Dan, along with Syms and four police officers, swarmed the mysteriously darkened and locked carousel. Dan didn't waste any time and kicked in the door. As an officer turned on the lights, Dan heard screaming coming from the back room. As the police officers neared the closed door, it swung open and Dan saw Gracie Allen who was tied to a chair with Forin's gun pointed at her head. "I'll kill her now! Get back!"

"What good will that do you?" Dan barked. "You are surrounded. If she dies, you do too. Drop the gun!"

Crying, Gracie pleaded, "Please don't kill me!"

Then came a loud bang and Gracie screamed as policemen rushed toward the fallen body. "He shot himself," Gracie hysterically yelled.

Forin's body was sprawled on the floor, blood gushing from his head and the gun resting next to him. "Get her out of here," Dan ordered.

An officer untied Gracie and removed her from the room where they sat near the carousel and an ambulance soon arrived. For the second time in recent memory, a paramedic tended to Gracie.

Dan asked, "Where is Stephanie?"

"Wally sent her home when he came in. Then he closed up and attacked me."

Dan turned to Syms. "One down and one to go. I have to talk with Alicia Greenstein again."

He phoned her and asked if she had heard from Karas. "As a matter of fact I did and he said he would meet us as planned. Only one change, he said Chelsea was not going to be there, but he would show up with Stella."

Dan knew why Chelsea would not be there, but he asked, "Did he say why Chelsea would not be there?"

"Her flight last night from Florida got cancelled. The hurricane is delaying a lot of flights."

Obviously, that was not true. "Listen, I had told you that Wally Forin was being tracked down. We got him and he is no danger to you." As of now, me, Bev and several officers are planning to be at the dining area. Everyone will be out of sight except for me and Bev. We'll see you there. If anything changes, call me."

"I will."

Dan moved aside as Gracie was assisted to the ambulance and taken to the hospital to be thoroughly examined.

Chapter 51

It was five-forty and the hotel dining room was beginning to fill up. Dan noticed that Alicia and Ariel were seated at a table near the back of the room. "There they are," he said to Bev. He nodded to the women and he knew they were aware he and Bev were there when Alicia nodded back.

The hostess sat the detectives at a red-draped table in the center of the room at Dan's request. He and Bev acted as if they were a couple. A vase of yellow flowers served as a centerpiece and the waiter filled their glasses with water.

Train and five other police officers lurked around outside the dining room, staying out of sight waiting for their time to aid in the arrest of Jeff Karas.

Bev said, "This is a nice place. I'll have to get my husband to take me here."

The waiter presented menus and read off the special entrees. "Thank you," Dan said. "We need a few minutes to decide."

Bev said, "We can't just sit here and look obvious. Buy me dinner."

"Get something cheap."

"I already have something cheap. You! We may only have time for appetizers."

"I hope so."

The waiter returned and the detectives placed their orders.

Ariel and Alicia waited for Karas, Stella and Chelsea, not knowing only two of them would show up.

Each minute passed slowly and at quarter after six, the detectives, Alicia and Ariel were still alone. Alicia zipped open the white tote she had set on the chair next to her and checked her phone. Then she got up, walked into the ladies' room and phoned Dan. "I'm a bit worried. Where are they? I have to call Stella."

After attempting to contact Stella, Alicia called Dan again. "I don't understand, she didn't answer her phone."

"Go back out to the dining room and stay with Ariel."

Dan informed Bev, "Stella is not answering her phone. I don't like it."

"What do you want to do?'

"Let's go. I'm going to tell the girls we are leaving. We're going to her place." He slowly rose, not wanting to alarm any of the patrons and sidled over to Alicia and Ariel. "We don't know what the problem is. It could be traffic." Dan suspected otherwise. "We're going to see if we can find Stella."

The waiter came over to them. "Is something wrong?"

Alicia answered, "There appears to be. Our friends have been delayed and we must go. I'm sorry we have to leave."

Dan ushered them out of the dining area into the lounge. "By the way, were you all booked to stay here tonight?"

"There should be rooms reserved under Jeff's name."

"I'm going to get you two a room under my name. Stay here."

The detective did so and handed Alicia the card key to room 420. "We're going to Stella's. I'll let you know what is happening." He informed Train who ordered a guard to stay with the women.

Dan returned to Bev. "I booked a room for the ladies under my name. I'll pay the bill and then we're going to Stella's house."

Dan surmised Karas had been tipped off somehow. "Stella may

be in trouble," he uttered. "I have to call Dixon." Dan did so and was advised that the Suffield police had not sent a vehicle to her house, and the police car that had been dispatched to stay outside Alicia's condo left as soon as the girls did."

"Shit," Dan said to Bev. "Let's go." He and Bev arrived twenty-five minutes later at Stella Passante's home where her car was in the driveway and he parked next to it. They approached the home and entered through the unlocked front door. The door not being locked worried Dan, as did the silence. He and Bev scanned the living room and then strode down the hall toward the bedrooms and bathroom. Their journey took a ghastly turn when Dan reached Stella's bedroom. "Bev," he yelled. "In here." They both stood at the doorway. Clad in a casual outfit for a night out, Stella lay on the bed atop a plaid comforter, her limp body tied to the bedpost. The irate detective slammed the door with his fist. "Motherfucker."

There was no blood, only a belt strapped tightly around Stella's neck. Her deep brown eyes were frozen open. *Bastard!*

Bev dialed 911 and then called Dixon while Dan phoned Scotty to let him know what he and Bev had run into.

If there was any good news, it was the fact that Stella Passante had a Ring doorbell and from viewing the recent activity recorded by the camera, it was clear to the detectives that a white Ford sedan had pulled into the driveway at three-forty that afternoon and parked right where Dan's car was now. The camera showed a man getting out of the car, a man the detective recognized. Wearing tan jeans and a pullover, Karas walked casually into the house and a half hour later, he emerged and drove off. The car's Florida license plate cover bore an Avis logo.

Dan called Scotty again. "Hey, she has a Ring doorbell and I was able to identify Karas as well as the car. It is a white Ford rented sedan with an Avis plate on it. Check it out. Stella must have told him about their plans and he killed her."

Karas was on the run and he had to be found. The detectives left Stella's residence before her body had been removed by the medical examiner's staff. Dan and Bev were headed back to the hotel when Scotty called and Dan asked, "What have you found?"

"Karas rented the car this morning at eleven. I notified Avis that we are looking for him and the car."

"Thanks."

Dan called Alicia and held back the latest news. He simply asked, "Are you okay?"

"For now. Me and Ariel are nervous."

"That's understandable. The guard will keep you safe. I don't believe Jeff will come anywhere near the hotel. We are trying to locate him."

"How is Stella?"

Dan was put in an awkward position and deflected her question by posing one of his own. "Where is Ariel?"

"She's in the shower."

"We are coming down there. Stay in your room!"

"What's happened? Stella, is she alright?"

"Bev and I will be right there and I'll explain when we see you."

Dan sped to the convention center hotel. He and Bev rushed inside and ran to the elevator, his feet barely touching the ground with Bev keeping pace. He pushed the lift's button. *Come on, come on.* It seemed like an hour before the doors opened, but it was only ten seconds before he and Bev rode up to the eighth floor.

Striding to the room, he breathed hard as the police officer standing outside rapped on the door and Dan announced their arrival. Alicia let the detectives in. Ariel, robed with a towel around her wet hair asked, "Did you find Stella?"

Dan leaned on the bureau while Alicia sat next to Ariel on one of the twin beds. He clenched his lips. "We did find her."

Bev sat on the opposite bed as Dan bowed his head and said,

"The reason Chelsea was not here is because of the man who threatened you, Wally Forin. He murdered Chelsea and then took his own life." Dan left out the details. "I didn't want to alarm you by telling you earlier."

Both girls let out screams and Bev relayed the additional bad news. "Stella is also no longer with us. Karas killed her a few hours ago."

Bev rose and put her arms around Alicia. "We will get Karas."

The two young women displayed a sense of relief along with sadness as they held each other and faced the detectives. Dan asked, "So, what were you going to do to call him out?"

Alicia opened her purse and revealed a small bottle containing several pills. "These. I was going to slip these knockout drugs into his wine, kind of reversing the tactic he used on us. When the time was right, we were going to get him into one of the rooms he booked."

Ariel took a pair of extra-sharp scissors from her tote. "He may not have died, but he sure wasn't going to have sex again."

Dan cringed. "Let me have those. Holy cow."

The detective checked in with Syms. It was well past eight-thirty. Dan then got in touch with Evan Lincoln. "Evan, I need your help." Dan explained everything that went on as quickly as he could. "I want to get Verizon involved. I know they haven't responded to the warrant yet, but if I give you Jeff Karas's phone number, can you get in touch with them? I want to have his phone tracked and they can tell us when it last pinged. I hope we can pin down his location."

"I'll do that as soon as you hang up and I'll have them relay the information to me. It could be a waiting game."

"That's a game we have to play."

Dan and Bev were ready to leave the hotel. "Ladies, try to rest up. The guard will be here all night."

◮

Dan called Phyllis to let her know this would be a long night and Bev notified her husband as well. Ten minutes after returning to headquarters, Dan's cell rang and Lincoln said, "His phone pinged from a tower near Tweed in New Haven. It appears he may have plans to fly somewhere."

"Great. I'll let Syms know and have Hardison notify the New Haven police. Hopefully, they can nab him at the airport."

It was wait time. "This may be all over soon," he said to Bev and Scotty. "Why don't you both go home?" Referring to himself, Syms, and Hardison, he added, "We'll be here."

Bev and Scotty agreed and they left the building.

It was ten past eleven when Hardison came down to Syms's office. The captain and Dan were both yawning when he entered. "Karas is in custody in New Haven. The airlines and TSA were notified and he was captured without incident when he went through the checkpoint."

Dan stretched to relieve the tension in his body. "I can't wait to get my hands on him."

"Time to call it a night," the chief insisted.

Dan yawned again. "Yup."

Chapter 52

Dan showed up at the police station Saturday morning at eight-thirty and thought he would be alone, but he saw Bev who was inside her cubicle. "What are you doing here?" he asked.

"The same as you, I suppose. I didn't sleep that well and I was about to check in on Alicia and Ariel."

Dan sat beside her. "Put them on speaker."

Bev made the call. "Alicia. Good morning. How is everything?"

"Fine, a guard is outside and me and Ariel are going to the breakfast nook."

"Great. It's over. Karas is in custody. You have no one to fear anymore."

She sighed. "I want to go home."

"You will. Your car is there, is it not?"

"It is."

"Good. Why don't you and Ariel get breakfast and check out?"

Dan said, "Hi. I'm glad you are okay. My credit card is on file."

"Thank you."

Dan said, "I want to speak with the officer who is there." He did and though it wasn't his call, he relieved the officer of his duty.

As soon as the conversation ended, Dan said, "I want to buzz the hospital to find out how Gracie Allen is." He keyed in the hospital number and learned that she was fine and her niece had taken her home. He sat back and felt as if a load had been lifted from his shoulders. He was happy for Alicia and Ariel, but still wondered about what had happened to Francine Devereaux. He rose and walked toward the Keurig before backtracking and placing a ten-dollar bill in the coffee fund box on Bev's desk. "I didn't want any. We're getting low on creamers. Go home. I am."

Bev thanked him and walked with her counterpart out to their cars. "Enjoy the rest of the weekend," he said.

"Say hello to Phyllis."

Chapter 53

On Monday morning, Syms gathered his detectives together. "Hardison spoke with the New Haven police. Karas was arraigned and he pleaded not guilty. The good news is that bail was denied and we'll be able to get him transferred here. He has an attorney named Javier Velasquez. I never heard of him. That's it for now."

Dan said, "You'll be glad to know that me and Bev spoke with Alicia Greenstein. She and Ariel are back at her place and are hopefully relaxing. Gracie Allen is fine too. She is home. Her niece picked her up at the hospital."

Today's news got even better as Clarissa and Luke, who anchored himself with a pair of crutches, wandered into the squad room. Clarissa guided him to his chair. "It's good to see you," Bev said.

"I'm doing fine." The crutches rested against Luke's desk. "I won't need them much longer. The doctor said probably a couple of weeks. He's encouraged with my progress."

"So are we," Mal said.

"Great to hear," Dan added.

Syms joined the group. "You know, I don't think I've met this young lady."

Luke smiled broadly as he introduced Clarissa, and said, "Any of you want to be invited to a wedding?"

"Do I have to get a gift?" Scotty asked.

"Son of a gun," Mal said. "I knew it."

Dan joked, "I have a great place for a honeymoon. Denine would love to host you guys downstairs. So when are you getting hitched?"

Luke tried to ignore the snarly comment and gave Dan a mock smile. "Right now we are engaged."

Clarissa flashed her ring. "We haven't set a date yet."

"We'll be there," Bev said.

Luke grabbed his crutches. "I'm getting hungry. Blue's sounds good."

"He hasn't changed," Mal said.

Clarissa leaned on Luke's arm. "It was nice to see you all."

Once they were gone, Dan retreated to his cubicle and phoned Evan Lincoln. "Thanks for your help. We have Karas in custody."

"I know."

"He will be here soon. I can't wait to talk with him."

"Not so fast. He has a lawyer named Javier Velasquez who was at the arraignment. You know what that means."

"Yeah. A fly in the ointment. I really want to speak with Karas."

"You'll have to work that out with his attorney."

"I suppose so. I'm still itching to nail Elijah Sandovar too."

"I understand. Good luck."

Dan had another idea and he phoned his shady friend. "Hey, Sass. How are you today?"

"Uh-oh. You're too polite to be just saying hello. What's up?"

"You got me. Do you know Javier Velasquez?"

"Yeah, why?"

"Jeff Karas was apprehended in New Haven. He was arraigned and we're working on getting him moved here. In the meantime, his lawyer may well block me from speaking with the guy. So, who is Javier Velasquez?"

"Funny you should mention him. He's a lot younger than us. A hotshot and he owes me a favor."

"What kind of favor?"

"Long story. He has an office here as well as in San Juan. I met him there a couple of years ago when I went there. He likes the beach and that's where I saved his life, a limb anyway. He went in the water and a shark almost ate him alive. I spotted the predator and got Javier out of the water after he'd been bitten on the leg. He's okay, but he owes me."

"Can you cash that favor in now? Do you think he will let me at Karas?"

"That's a tall one, Dan. I can't promise anything."

"Thanks, Sass. Let me know as soon as you speak with him."

"Did I say I would do that?"

Dan shrugged. "You did, didn't you?"

He heard silence before Sasser spoke. "Okay. Keep your fingers crossed."

Later that afternoon, Dan received a call he didn't expect. "Detective Shields, this is Javier Velasquez."

"Attorney Velasquez. Thank you for calling."

"Don't thank me yet. Our friend Hancock Sasser told me about your wanting to speak with Jeff Karas. I want you to understand that I am bending my rules for you, or I should say for you and him."

"Thank you."

"Not yet. There are conditions. I will be with you and my client, and I will instruct him whether to answer or not to answer certain questions. I still owe Mister Karas my support."

"I understand."

"Good."

"Look, I know the process of having him brought to Hartford is in the works. It may take a few days. When he gets here, I'll call you and we can set something up. I knew I owed Hancock Sasser a favor, but I didn't think it would be this."

"Thank you again."

CHAPTER 54

Dan settled back, knowing Jeff Karas was likely to be headed to prison, but there was one more crime he had to resolve. *Assault, rape. Elijah Sandovar. Time to reel him in. If he thinks he's off the hook for assaulting Nicole Brezinski, he is sadly mistaken.*

Thinking about how to reel in Elijah made Dan realize he needed to involve the assistance of Ariel. He inched up behind Bev. "Let's go to work again."

"I'm listening."

"Elijah Sandovar has to be dealt with but there is no evidence to tie him to Nicole Brezinski's rape. I know he did it and he knows he did it. Nicole is dead and she can't help us. He has to be charged with sexual assault and pay for his brutalization of her."

"I agree."

"Well, it's risky and I'm not sure it will work. I'm thinking the only way we can arrest him is to have Ariel help us. She recognized him and he gave her a ride once before, but he doesn't know she fingered him."

"What are you conjuring up?"

"I want you to come with me to see the ladies and help me convince Ariel to assist us. I want her to call Elijah and arrange to be picked up at the airport."

Dan took the first step and scheduled a time for him and Bev to stop in at Alicia's condo to speak with the ladies, but did not divulge the reason for the visit. "We're on," he said to Bev. "They both spoke with their families and explained everything they had endured. Alicia sounded relieved. Come on, they are waiting for us."

▲

It didn't take long for the detectives to arrive and Alicia's wide smile and perkiness was noticeable when she opened the door. Ariel was beside her and her bright eyes displayed her happiness.

Bev marveled at how well they appeared. "You both look wonderful."

"I can be myself again, and we decided to take a leave," Ariel said.

Alicia asked, "Can I offer you anything, drinks or snacks? I made brownies."

"Thank you, but we're all set," Dan replied, and then he had second thoughts. "On the other hand, who in their right mind can refuse brownies, as long as there are no nuts."

"No nuts, just chocolate and fudge."

Bev nodded. "My kids would think I was crazy if I refused."

"I'll be right back. Drinks?"

"A little milk will be fine," Dan said.

Bev agreed.

Dan noticed the journal that he had seen before was gone, and minutes later brownies and glasses of milk were on the living room table and munched on his brownie. "Did you make these?" he asked Alicia.

"We made them."

"This is the best brownie I ever had. So much fudge."

"Thank you," she replied.

Dan turned serious. "We appreciate all the help you have both given us. Ariel, I have to request your assistance one more time. I showed you a photo." He took out the picture Ariel had seen before. "You identified the Uber driver who had dropped you off at the airport. Can you pick him out again?"

She confirmed her earlier answer by pointing to earring-wearing Elijah.

"I thought so. You think you identified Emilio Sandovar. Truthfully, you identified his brother, Elijah. I had questioned him earlier and it seems he had driven his deceased brothers car at times to drive fares. It appears Nicole didn't notice the earring and she thought it was Emilio who had sodomized her. It couldn't have been him. Emilio was gay."

"What?" Ariel exclaimed.

"When I spoke with Elijah, I had accused him of raping her, and I knew by his responses that he did it. Ariel, I want to arrest him and can only do it with your help. You will recognize him and he will recognize you."

"What do you want me to do?"

"I want you to call him for a ride. How about it?"

She hesitated. "He gave me his cell number because he had asked me to call him when I needed another ride."

"Call it. Say you are coming back from Las Vegas and wish to be picked up at the airport around ten tonight."

"Okay. Then what?"

"I want you to wear your uniform and a hidden mic so your conversation can be recorded. I hate to resort to this, but you have to sweet-talk him and get him to admit that he molested Nicole."

"Oh no. I'm done with that."

"I believe you, but I will be nearby to protect you. Nothing will happen, except capturing him."

She let out a heavy sigh. "I feel I have no choice. Okay."

Dan recited Elijah's number and Ariel phoned him as Dan

listened. The detective smiled when the call ended. Ariel said, "He bought it. He's going to pick me up in front of the baggage terminal."

"I will bring you to the airport and then I'll give you a mic and we'll test it before you hide it inside your blouse. It's important for you to wear your uniform and bring your flight bag. I'll be listening from my car and it won't be far behind. Another policeman will be in his car, in back of me."

▲

The arrangement was made, and Elijah Sandovar had a fare to pick up. Ariel was standing outside the airport's lower concourse, the baggage area. Even in the nights darkness, her red scarf stood out and when he arrived he exited his car and opened the back door for his passenger. She slid her flight bag onto the seat next to her and sat on the passenger side with her skirt hung below her knees. The allure of her perfume accentuated her sexiness.

Elijah's earring was in plain view. Getting back behind the steering wheel, he asked, "How was your trip?"

She made sure her mic was well hidden beneath her blouse as Dan listened from his Accord. The assisting policeman's vehicle was within viewing distance of the Uber.

"Fine, Las Vegas is fun. This is a new car."

"No. this one is mine. I had my brother's last time. What is that perfume?"

"You like it?"

"I do. What is it?"

"It's new. It's called Breeze. I'm going to my girlfriend's condo, she's letting me stay there while she's away." Alicia rattled off the address.

The Uber headed toward the condo and Alicia leaned forward so

258

he could smell her perfume, and she winked flirtatiously. "You are cute. I thought so before, and I did notice you staring at me last time as I walked away."

He grinned and glanced at her in his rearview mirror. "What can I say?"

Ariel smiled and asked, "How much does a guy like you make?"

"Money is okay, but it's only part-time. I'm still in college."

She leaned over the passenger seat and playfully said, "I know what you are saying about part-time." Her perfume wafted throughout the car as she sat back, pulled her skirt above her knees and swept her hair back. "Flying is fun but it doesn't pay well. I could use some extra money. Are you up for a good time?"

He adjusted his rearview mirror and she noticed him eyeing her slightly spread apart legs. Elijah mumbled something to himself that she could not make out and his driving became momentarily distracted as his car got dangerously close to the vehicle in front of it and he tensed up. "Are you serious?"

Regaining control of his car as oncoming headlights hit his eyes, Alicia coquettishly said, "So, how about it? I'm a bit low on cash."

He began to sweat and eagerly asked, "How much?"

Ariel calmy said, "Three hundred."

Elijah blew out a breath. "Uh, three is a little pricey."

"Not for me." She rolled her skirt higher and gave him a wider view of her inviting inner thighs. "That's my price."

He stared into his rearview mirror again and Ariel saw his eyes studying her leg separation. She curled her lips and said, "You want to get laid, don't you?"

"How's one-fifty?"

"An insult."

"That's all I have at home. Can I owe you?"

"I think not. Cash only and that's too bad for you. I know you have a hard-on."

"What guy wouldn't?"

Ariel's demeanor changed and she leaned forward. "Oh, I can think of one person who would not be interested. Your deceased brother. I understand he was gay."

"How did you know that?"

"I know because you are the one who picked up my friend Nicole and brutally molested her. Your brother would never have forced her to have anal sex."

"You have no idea. I paid her and she wanted to get kinky."

"No. I knew her and she was not into that stuff. Neither am I. She fought you off, but you forced yourself into her."

Stung by her accusation, Elijah had a difficult time keeping his hands on the wheel as he shouted, "I gave her a free ride and she appreciated it."

Ariel leaned forward and asserted, "No, she didn't. Sodomizing her was not appreciated. She was traumatized."

He sped up and pulled over to the curb as the car's brakes screeched. The vehicle stopped and Elijah snapped, "Get your fucking pussy out of my car!"

Ariel opened the door and she slid out onto the sidewalk, fetching her flight bag as she did.

"Bitch!" he yelled.

Suddenly, Train's vehicle's flashing red, white, and blue lights closed in on his rear bumper while Dan positioned his Accord in front of the Uber. The detective walked to the driver's window and held his badge up to Elijah. "Remember me?"

As traffic passed by, Ariel sneered at Elijah.

The Uber driver's jaw dropped as Dan said, "You're under arrest for sexual assault. Get out." The car was still idling when Elija exited and he objected, "You can't do this. It's her word against mine."

Dan read the driver his rights as Train cuffed the detainee.

"We'll see about that," the detective advised Elijah as Ariel slightly unbuttoned her blouse to reveal a microphone and Dan removed his earpiece and said, "Really? These heard everything you and she said in your car and we have it all on tape."

Train placed the arrested Elijah in the back seat of the police car. "I'll have him booked and arrange for his car to be towed," the officer said. "It's still running. I need to shut it down."

Dan escorted Ariel into his Accord. "I'll get her to Alicia's."

Ariel turned her back to him, removed the mic from her blouse and gave it to Dan who smiled. "Thanks. You did a fantastic job."

"I'm glad it's over."

"For now it is. Ariel, you may be summoned to testify against him. He will remain in jail unless a bond is posted. I'm sure Alicia will be happy that Elijah has been arrested and will be charged with molesting Nicole."

"She will. I guess I had to do this and thank you too for staying after him."

Chapter 55

At home, Dan packed his gun away and heard his wife talking to their son on the phone. "Mike, you have a lot to consider about the future. Your life and our lives are going to change." Phyllis held her hand over the receiver and said softly to Dan, "Don't say anything." She resumed the conversation. "We love you. Dad's not home yet. Can I have him call you later?"

The conversation ended and she let out a huge breath before saying to her husband, "He is really stressed and I thought it best that he talks to you tonight. He's a little afraid of what you will have to say."

"I'm sure he is. I'll give him a call after I eat."

"I told him not to worry but he's a bit irrational. Accept what has happened. Haley and Mike's baby will be a blessing, unexpected, but it's a new life to love."

"You sure are taking it well."

"No. I'm dealing with the reality. You need to embrace our grandchild and treat its father like he was your son because he is, and he needs to feel positive about it."

"You're right. You always are. I'll go easy."

"Not easy. Mike is Mike and he needs your best advice."

"What did he tell you?"

"For one thing, Haley has no plans to quit nursing school and

Mike has leveled with Rachel. She is no longer in the picture. Dan, he loves Haley, and so do we."

"I know. He's a good kid."

Phyllis looked into her husband's eyes. "He lost the kid title a couple of years ago. He's a young man, so treat him like one."

"I hope he loves Haley as much as I love you."

She kissed him. "Time will tell."

Two hours later, Dan was by himself and he phoned his son. "Mike. I'm glad you had a good talk with Mom. She was happy to speak with you."

"I'm okay, but my plans are all upside down."

"Like what?"

"School, baseball, Haley."

"Hey, one day a time. I know you will be a great father. And if you didn't know it, we love Haley too. I understand she is staying in nursing school. Be excited about her continuing."

"I broke up with Rachel."

"Mom told me. How do you feel?"

"Okay I guess. I never loved her, know what I mean?"

"I do."

"I want to see Haley."

"I'm sure you do. The baby won't be here until after graduation. Get your degree. You'll have a family to support and you need your degree."

"I'm concerned about baseball, the draft."

"I understand. Your scholarship is tied to baseball so play your best."

"What if I don't get drafted this time? I should have signed with the Red Sox and not returned to school."

Dan who helped Mike make that decision, said, "I know what you are saying, but we agreed that getting drafted doesn't mean going to the major leagues, and you can't treat school as a back-up, especially if you do not graduate. Don't consume yourself with those thoughts. Take advantage of your scholarship. You earned it. Worry about what happens later."

"It's hard, Dad."

"Now it is, but it could be harder without the education. Son do not forget that Mom and I are here as are Haley's parents. Things will work out."

"I hope you're right."

"Mike, some day you will understand. Honestly, Mom and I are excited about being grandparents."

"Do Josh and Kate know?"

"Not yet. Cheer up. You're still the Mike I know."

"Thanks, Dad."

"Alright. Call us anytime."

Phyllis entered the den and asked, "How did it go?"

"It went well. I let him know we are in his corner and he'll be okay. He wants to see Haley."

Phyllis breathed a sigh of relief and Dan hugged his wife. "Like I told him. Things will work out."

Chapter 56

Dan had to play a waiting game and four days after Karas was arrested in New Haven, a police officer accompanied the remanded, handcuffed Karas and his Armani-suited lawyer, Javier Velasquez into the squad room. The attorney was a handsome young man who looked as if he stepped out of a fashion magazine and Dan noticed his slight limp. Karas was escorted into the room by the guard as Dan as Velasquez exchanged pleasantries. Velasquez smiled. "Keep it clean and we'll be alright."

Inside the interrogation room, Dan sat opposite Karas while the suspect's lawyer took a seat beside his client as Dan delivered his first question. "Mister Karas. Tell me about you and Forin and the prostitution business."

"There is nothing to tell."

Dan stroked his chin and said, "I hear otherwise. Stella Passante and Chelsea Maresca were sad stories, but you and Forin held Alicia Greenstein and Ariel Adams families hostage. Those two flight attendants were coerced into giving up their bodies."

Karas remained emotionless and said, "I don't know anything about that."

Dan leaned forward. "But you did know about Francine Devereaux and her resignation. Is she dead?"

Karas looked at his lawyer and paused before he said, "I flew with her to Paris and she resigned. As far as I know she stayed in Paris and never flew back."

"Do you know why she resigned?"

Smugly, Karas said, "I don't think she liked the job."

Dan didn't like that hostile response and ran with the pilot's answer as he pointedly asked, "Which job are you referring to, the flight attendant one, or the prostitution one?"

Karas glanced at Velasquez and did not answer the question.

Dan waited a few seconds for a response, but knew he'd hit a wall and shifted his questions to the hotel and carousel. "Okay, I understand the young ladies were about to end their participation as part-time hookers and have you hauled in, but why go after Gracie Allen?"

"I can't speak for Forin. I had nothing to do with that."

"What about Chelsea?"

Karas blurted out, "Forin hated her."

"And Stella?"

"She was a bitch."

Dan amped up his tone and said, "So, she told you about the plans she and the other ladies had and you killed her."

Velasquez huffed and shook his head at Dan as the attorney advised Karas, "Don't answer that."

Dan acknowledged the attorney's suggestion and continued, "What is the real story with Nicole? You fathered her unborn child, didn't you?"

"I don't know."

"I think you do. Wally Forin's notes say that you did. What happened at the carousel the night she died?"

"I don't know. I was in Chicago."

Dan shook his head and tapped the table. "That is untrue. I have you, her and Forin on video from the Vesta and Charter Oak before the three of you headed to the carousel."

Karas looked at Velasquez, who kept his eyes on Dan and for the first time, Dan saw remorse written on Karas's face, as if he were transfixed by the memory of Nicole. Karas reminisced, "Nicole was like a kid at times. She told me that she always liked the story of Lady Godiva and she knew Wally worked at the carousel. She thought it would be fun to go in privately and take a ride."

"Then what happened?"

"Velasquez intervened and advised Karas that he did not have to answer the question, but Karas kept talking. "I mentioned Lady Godiva, and well, Nicole was a little tipsy so she took off her clothes and climbed onto that horse. Then she began shaking and passed out. We panicked and left."

Dan shrugged and harshly railed at Karas. "You mean you and Forin rushed out while she was having a heart attack and for some reason cleaned up so you wouldn't leave a trace and vanished with her clothes?"

Karas began to sweat as Dan persisted. "But that didn't matter because you and Forin intended to kill her, isn't that right?" Otherwise, why would the door have been kicked in? Forin had keys. Who wrote the word 'whore' on her back?"

Velasquez interrupted and looked into his client's eyes. "I'm advising you to stop talking."

Karas peered at Dan before again ignoring his attorney and hastily answered, "Wally wrote it on her back. I did love her and okay and yes the baby was mine."

Velasquez stared at his client as Karas turned away from him.

Dan pushed forward and probed the frowning Karas about the pilot's flight to Paris. "You said Francine Devereaux flew with you to Paris and she never returned. She supposedly resigned and sent in a letter of resignation. I checked her signature and someone else forged her signature. Do you have any idea who may have done that?"

"No," he insisted.

Dan stood and knew he was about to step over the line again as he pulled a copy of the resignation letter from his pocket and shoved it in front of Karas. "Do you see the signature on this letter?"

"I do."

"Is that your handwriting?"

Karas glanced at it but kept silent.

Dan raised his voice and went after an incriminating answer, "Where is her body? We know you killed her and sent that phony resignation letter to Delta headquarters!"

The perturbed attorney abruptly rose and shouted, "Stop! Detective, this interview is over."

"Not quite," Dan said as he held up the ring that he had obtained from the homeless man up to Karas. "I believe this is yours. It will show up in court."

When Karas, his lawyer and the guard were gone, Dan returned to his colleagues in the squad room and said to Bev and Scotty, "I knew I could only go so far, but at least I know what took place inside the carousel."

Dan then sidled into the captain's office and said, "It's all in Lincoln's hands now."

Syms twirled his aspirin bottle. "I saw it all, I thought you were going to kill him."

"If I could have, I might have. Karas grates on me, having those girls in fear of their lives as well as their families."

"You had your shot and, like you said, It's out of our hands."

"I have to call Sasser."

As he made his way to his desk, Dan reached into his pocket and removed his cell phone. Once he sat in his chair, he called Sasser. "Hey, friend," he said. "I just got done with Karas and Velasquez. Thank you again for making it happen."

"I guess this means you owe me a favor."

"We'll see."

"Yeah. I got some news too. Remember the plea deal Malone rejected?"

"You mean forty years?"

"Yes."

"Well, he has reconsidered. The trial is off and Malone will spend forty years in the penitentiary."

"So you agree he is guilty?"

He heard Sasser laugh. "You're lucky that I agree to be your friend. See you around."

"Sure. Say hi to Chantel."

CHAPTER 57

Two strangely intertwined cases came to a close and Dan took his cleansed mind home. His family life had taken a new turn when he and Phyllis learned the shocking news of Haley's pregnancy and the fact that their older son Mike was the father.

When he got home his two younger children rushed to greet him and couldn't wait to let it out. "Mike is coming home tomorrow!" Josh said.

Phyllis joined them. "I told him you would pick him up."

Dan was between a grimace and a smile. "I guess I will. When did you find out?"

"Earlier. He called me at work."

"Okay."

"Go get ready for dinner," she instructed the kids.

Dan nudged her. "Do they know?"

"Not yet. Be calm."

"I am calm. Today was a good day."

Later in the evening, Phyllis and Dan were alone. "When should we tell the kids?" he asked.

"Not until Mike gets here. I want him to tell them."

"Alright. I wonder what Haley and her parents feel."

"I spoke with Margaret earlier. They are fine and Haley knows Mike is coming for a couple of days. He and she have a lot to talk about."

"They do and I'm glad they are getting together, rather than playing phone and email games. I thought I would get some relaxation time this weekend, but I guess not."

"How about doing something different while waiting for Mike?"

"Like what?"

"Have you noticed the garage lately?"

"Oh no, what are you getting at?"

"It would be nice if you cleaned it and made places for the kids' bikes."

"Right."

She shoved him. "No. I didn't exactly ask you. You need the exercise."

Dan sighed. "You win. I hate it when you win. You always do!"

"You know the old saying. A happy wife makes a happy home. Thank you."

▲

The next morning, Dan put on a pair of old Levi's and a sweatshirt and started his voluntary chore. By lunchtime he had cleaned out most of the clutter and reorganized his tools and gardening equipment. He also filled a garbage can with useless junk, including two sets of ice skates that hadn't been used in years.

He came inside for lunch and Phyllis had left a note saying she had gone grocery shopping and that Josh and Kate were out bowling with Alex and Zach. *She knew I'd ask for their help. I haven't had peanut butter and jelly in a long time."*

He went back to work after downing his sandwich and completed the job by two. Phyllis returned home and he fetched her to see his progress. He opened the mudroom door and she looked into the garage. She smiled in amazement. "Really, I can't believe

271

you did it."

"Now I am going to clean myself and get ready to pick up Mike."

She kissed him. "That's my guy. Maybe you can take both cars to be washed tomorrow."

He laughed. "You're good. Let's see how good you are later."

She nudged him. "I remember our discussion at my office and what I said when you left."

"I heard you. You know what they say. Time heals all wounds."

She smiled. "But not tonight, dear, we'll have a houseful."

Later that afternoon, Josh and Kate returned home and as the time ticked closer to seven, Dan headed for his car. "Let's go pick up Mike."

Both children followed him to the car and hopped into the back seat.

The Accord was stationed outside the baggage area as they waited for Mike. Fifteen minutes elapsed and then Josh yelled, "There he is!"

Dan exited the car and met Mike as he was walking toward him. He hugged his son. "Good to see you."

"Thanks, Dad." He opened the rear door and leaned in. "Hi, guys."

Dan took Mike's carry-on bag and placed it in the trunk before they departed. Not long after they got home, Mike said, "I'm going to see Haley."

Dan whispered to him, "We have not told your siblings. I think you should do it."

"Fine, can it wait until tomorrow?"

"It can. Say hi to Haley."

⯅

The next morning after breakfast, Mike took his brother and

272

sister into the den and they sat together on the couch as the expecting father told them that they were going to be an uncle and an aunt.

Josh looked up at his brother. "You and Haley are getting married?"

"We will. After I finish school."

Kate said, "I like Haley."

Mike replied, "Want to be our flower girl?"

She smiled as Josh asked, "Can I be best man?"

"You bet."

Time passed quickly and Mike's short journey home was coming to an end. The three adults conversed before Mike had to leave. "You look relieved, more relaxed, like you have come to terms with everything," Phyllis said to him.

"I am. I'm glad I saw Haley. She's great, you know. She's determined to become a nurse and is happy about me graduating. Joey is a good little boy."

Dan placed his arm on Mike's broad shoulders. "You know all we want for you and your brother and sister and Haley is happiness. And Joey too."

"I know and I appreciate it. You guys are the best."

Dan glanced at his watch. "We'd better get going."

Mike went to fetch Josh and Kate so they could ride to Bradley. Phyllis said, "I'm coming too."

Mike's visit had ended and Dan and Phyllis were assured that all was well. Dan held his wife's hand. "You make them and then you have to let them go."

"At least we have a few more years with Josh and Kate."

Chapter 58

A new week began with Hardison cornering Dan. "Follow me," he said. "Scotty, Bev, Mal, come on." They all proceeded to captain Syms' office.

Syms said, Good morning. The chief has news to tell us."

Hardison began. "I heard from the Police Nationale, Commandant Alain Barbier tells me they have spoken with Francine Devereaux's parents who live in Giverny. The story is disturbing. Her father says they lost communication with her about a year ago. She must have changed her phone and she never made them aware of it. They knew she was flying with Delta and after not hearing from her for a while, her father contacted them, only to be told she quit and left no forwarding address. The address she had given Delta was her parents' house."

Dan listened attentively as the chief continued, "Here's the gist. Francine did fly to Paris with Karas prior to her disappearance and Delta says they stayed at a hotel near Orly. The police determined she and Karas had checked in there and the hotel security video has them both leaving at nine on a Saturday night. He returned alone two hours later. The next day Karas checked them both out and was gone. Delta confirmed his flight back to the states."

Dan said, "You don't have to tell me, he killed her."

"I'm getting to that. Since he came back two hours after they left the hotel, that means they could have traveled within an hour's radius of the hotel. They dredged the Seine and pulled her body out two days ago and her parents identified her."

"Did they say how she was killed?"

"There were ligature marks around her neck."

Dan raised his brows. "If she listed her home address as her parents' house, where was her severance check sent? Wouldn't her folks have received it and wondered about it?"

"It turns out that she had advised Delta to send her mail to a postbox in Paris. According to Delta, the check was never cashed."

Dan slammed his fist on the desktop in front of him. "I hope that bastard, Karas spends the rest of his life in prison."

"I'm sure he will." Hardison said. "I wanted to share this information with you. I'll be in my office and I don't want to see any of you again today."

As Hardison walked away, Syms stood and said, "Look who is here." He pointed to the squad room. "It's Luke."

Dan turned to see him and motioned to the big guy. "Get in here," he shouted.

Luke entered the office without the crutches he previously relied on. "What's going on?" he asked.

"Hardison gave us a cheerful talk," Dan said. "You look good."

"I am. I'm walking with little discomfort and my doctor says I can come back here soon."

Bev asked," Where is Clarissa?"

"Working. She says Hi. Actually she is shopping for a wedding dress. We set a date. Her birthday is May fourth, and it is a Sunday next year, so that's when we are getting married."

Dan smiled. "It's not too late to back out. I'm warning you."

Luke laughed. "Right. She's the best thing that has ever happened to me."

"I know she is," Dan said. "You're a lucky guy and we can't

wait until you are sitting at your desk again."

"Thanks. Actually my doctor said I could come back in thirty days, so spiffy up this place."

Syms pointed to the exit. "Nothing has changed. Now, get out of here!"

Dan heard his desk phone ring and rushed to answer it. Evan Lincoln was on the other end. "I was just thinking of coming to see you," Dan said. The he informed Lincon about Francine Devereaux."

"You knew he killed her," Lincoln said. Then he turned to the reason he called. "Look, we have a problem."

"Don't we always?"

"Sit back. This is a big one. Elijah Sandovar's parents posted bail and he's out. A hearing has been set for two weeks from today, but that is not the issue. I've read the arrest report and heard the recording of him and Ariel inside the Uber. Frankly, I don't believe we have a good case against him."

"He admitted to sodomizing her."

"No, he didn't admit anything. I listened to the recording twice and what he said was Nicole reciprocated for a free ride and he admitted to having kinky sex with her. Ariel is the one who said he sodomized and traumatized Nicole and she stated Elijah forced Nicole, but he never did actually admit to anything other than the sex act."

"What are you saying?"

"I'm saying his lawyer will drive a truck through the accusation that Elijah Sandovar assaulted Nicole Brezinski."

"I don't believe it. He is going to get away with raping her."

"He might. I can't pursue it. There is no hard evidence of sexual assault. Nicole Brezinski is dead and she certainly can't testify. And Dan, the entrapment card is in play. His attorney will have your ass on a platter if he hears the recording."

Depressed by Lincoln's findings, Dan rested his head on the back of his chair and shoved his feet straight out in front of him. "I hear you, but I sure don't like it."

"No, sometimes the system lets us down and other times it is lack of evidence. This is one of those times."

"Ariel and Alicia will be disappointed to hear that he's getting away with it."

"So are we. Charges will be dropped."

"Thanks."

"Dan, one more thing. I am leaving at the end of my term. I've spoken with a law firm in Boston and I am accepting their offer."

"Great, another Red Sox fan to hate. Seriously, I'm happy for you. Well see each other before you leave, I'm sure of that."

"True. I'll talk to you soon."

Dan didn't relax as he had to touch base with Alicia and Ariel. He phoned Alicia and said, "It's me again. I hope you and Ariel are adjusting to your new lives."

"We are. Ariel and I have decided to end our flight attendant careers. We are resigning from Delta and she is staying with me."

"That's great. Can you put Ariel on?"

"I'll hit speaker."

"Hi, Detective."

"You sound well. I want you to know you will not have to testify against Elijah Sandovar. Thank you so much for your help. Unfortunately, according to the state's attorney who heard the tape, in his eyes, Elijah did not confess to harming Nicole and we have no case."

"I don't understand."

"The reality is that you did what you were asked to do and you did it to perfection. However, everything you said, however true it was, he never admitted to any of the accusations. Don't feel bad. I couldn't get him to fess up either before I asked for your help.

Charges will be dropped. He will go free. I'm sorry."

"I don't know what to say."

"Focus on your new beginnings. When are you turning in your wings?"

"Later today and then we are booking a cruise to Jamaica."

"Good for you. Any idea what you will do when you get back?"

Alicia spoke. "Oddly, both of our families have been in the baking business and we have ideas of starting our own bakeshop."

"That sounds nice. If the brownies are any indication of your skills, then you should be a big hit. Thank you both again for your help. Have fun on your trip and don't lose my number."

"It's on the refrigerator."

"Okay, you ladies be well."

▲

When Dan ended his day and walked into his house, he was greeted by two deliriously happy children. Phyllis smiled as she put her arms around him. "What are you all so happy about?" he asked.

"Connie called a little earlier and, you know how she said she hadn't been to Disneyworld?"

"I remember, and neither have we."

"Well, not yet. Connie has purchased passes for us and her, so start planning a vacation in Florida."

THE END

I hope you enjoyed my novel. Please take a moment to place a favorable rating on Amazon. I will deeply appreciate your kindness.

Thank you,
Mark L. Dressler

About the Author

Mark L. Dressler is a Connecticut native.

His writing prowess has earned him recognition by the *Hartford Courant* as a most notable author. He has appeared on television with Teresa Dufore at WTNH - Channel 8 in New Haven, as well as Fox - Channel 61 in Hartford with Stan Simpson.

Mark is proud to have been honored by The Boston Children's Hospital for his charitable contributions. A portion of each book sale is donated to that incredible institution.

Sudden Death is his sixth novel, the fourth featuring Hartford Detective Dan Shields.

Mark's books are available in paperback as well as e-book format. You may purchase his collections from any bookseller including Amazon.

Follow Mark on Facebook at:
www.facebook.com/MarkLDressler

Email him at mark.dressler17@gmail.com

THE DAN SHIELDS SERIES
(The detective who breaks all the rules)

DEAD AND GONE (2017)

Dan Shields is drawn into the gang world when a drug bust goes wrong. Police, as well as gang members, are killed, and the money is nowhere to be found. Dan soon confronts the thug who shot and nearly killed the detective six years earlier. The savvy sleuth follows a twisted path leading to an unexpected discovery that stuns the entire police force.

DEAD RIGHT (2019)

Dan Shields and powerful attorney Angelo Biaggio engage in a game of life and death. It was the lawyer's car that had struck and killed a twelve-year-old boy on a city street. Without stopping, the vehicle sped away from the scene. As the detective homes in on the driver, the lives of Dan, and his family are placed in grave danger.

DEAD WRONG (2022)

Dan Shields goes to college and investigates the killings of security guard Christine Kole, and DJ Gordon Gunderson while the student is airing his weekly music show. Dan is confronted by the undergraduate's combatative, aspiring politician father, who leads the detective down a path of truths and lies. Sorting facts from fiction, Dan uncovers a scheme that entails more than he could anticipate.

At the same time, the overworked detective tries to untangle the Halloween evening killings of two men whom, at different locations are dressed in Batman costumes. Dan ponders whether these deadly shootings are related and soon discovers the answer that sends him into dangerous territory.

THE LEX STALL SERIES
(Manhattan's tenacious female detective)

DYING FOR FAME (2020)

Lex Stall draws aim on an edgy suspect who had discovered Fredrike Cambourd's bullet-riddled body in the artist's Manhattan basement studio. The person of interest has an alibi, but it soon crumbles, and she is determined to get to the truth. What Lex discovers is more than she could have imagined.

Note: Dan Shields makes a cameo appearance in this story.

WRITE TO THE END (2024)

Lex Stall seeks to find the kidnappers of author Essex Westbrook's wife, Svetlana. A hefty ransom is demanded as Lex tries to convince the reclusive, alcoholic novelist not to hand over the money. The antsy man does not listen to her and decides to obey the hostage takers, but he and Lex are stunned when an unforeseen event turns the case upside down.